The Return

by

Mike Torreano

Ike McAlister sits with his brother-in-law, Hugh Walnutt, Sheriff of Cottonwood.

As dry wood crackled to coals in Agnes' study, Ike set his whiskey down on the marble table next to him. "By the way, did I mention Stilwell's man got shot the other day at the Como station?" He tried to maintain an offhand tone.

"No, I do not believe you did, Ike."

"Did you hear about it?"

"No one has told me anything about it." Hugh took a drink, and balanced the glass on his upholstered chair's arm.

Ike nodded at that non-answer. "Sorta mysterious how it happened, though. Man's name was Strothers and he'd been ramroddin' there for Stilwell. Guess things weren't going fast enough, so Stilwell came to Como to see for himself. Had just got off the train when Strothers stopped a bullet." He took another sip, mirrored by his brother-in-law.

"Any idea who shot him?"

"Nobody knows, but whoever did it was quite a deadeye. Long distance and caught him right in the ear." Ike drummed his fingers on the armchair.

"Surely, someone must have seen the killer." Hugh took another swallow, followed by Ike.

"That's the thing—no one did. Shooter musta hid in the trees that were some distance away." They both placed empty glasses on the table between them. Ike poured another round and set the whiskey bottle down. He eyed Hugh as he raised the glass to his lips. "Had to have been a rifle, probably a Sharps from that far away."

"That is a likely conclusion, Ike. A Winchester fails to match up with a Sharps at longer distances—or so I have been told."

"You have a Sharps, don't you, Hugh?"

"Why yes, I just happen to." He paused for another drink. "I also have a Winchester, and a Remington. All fine weapons."

"Reckon they'll know more when they dig the bullet out." Ike waited for Hugh to respond. In silence, they let their glasses sit while the orange, glowing embers warmed the room.

Hugh steepled his fingers. "Do I sense a question on your mind, Ike?"

Ike stared at the dying fire and after a long pause said, "Nope."

They lifted their glasses and with a mutual *clink* finished off the whiskies.

Excerpt From

The Return

Mike Torreano

This material is protected by copyright. **No AI training permitted.**

Praise for Mike Torreano

The Reckoning

Set in South Park, Colorado in 1868, this fast-moving narrative is a blend of historical and mystery fiction. It's intriguing, and I got hooked from the first page. Every chapter was gripping. For certain, this narration will make a good script for a classic Western movie.

You can't guess what will happen next or how the story will end. Honestly, right now, this narration tops my list of the amazing books I've read recently.

Official review, Online Book Club

The Renewal

Great book! The descriptions of the land and mountains brought me into the location of the book. From that feeling it was easy to get involved with the characters and immersing yourself in the story. It had cowboys, beautiful ladies, horses, good guys and bad guys. I looked forward to finding out where the story would go every time I picked up the book. Loved it!

R. Robison

A Score to Settle

A Score to Settle is a classic historical western set in the 1870s. There are classic themes here which are well-presented with descriptive narration, gritty characters, and a historically accurate plot. Mike Torreano writes a compelling story with plenty of anguish. Every nuance is brilliantly detailed so the reader can escape into the rough landscape of the wild west. The plot moves at a good pace with tons of action scenes. My heart went out to poor Del time and again. I savored *A Score to Settle* and I look forward to reading more from Mike Torreano.

N.N. Light's Book Heaven Reviews

White Sands Gold

The elements we love in Westerns are all here, but they are tweaked in fresh ways that break stereotypes and surprise us! Though a treasure of hidden gold clearly is central, the addition of a priceless relic to this cache is both inventive and unexpected. 1890 New Mexico Territory comes alive with multidimensional characters who breathe life into this compelling story. Torreano makes Lottie, Yancy, Lou, Twill, Ma Gilbert, and the others who drive the action totally believable. You'll be turning pages to know who gets to the treasure first? What price is exacted in personal loss? What is that relic? The answers make WHITE SANDS GOLD a Western you won't forget!

K. Ewig

Fireflies at Dusk

This book is perfect for the person who loves history or for the person who would like to learn more about the Civil War era with facts that are intertwined in an entertaining way. Few authors have the ability to develop characters like Mike Torreano does. You quickly feel like you personally know each of the characters in this mesmerizing book. It is THE BEST historical fiction I have ever read.

J Scheimer

This is a work of fiction. Names, characters, places, or incidents are either the product of the author's imagination or are used fictitiously, and any resemblance to actual persons, living or dead, business establishments, events, or locales, is entirely coincidental.

The Return

Contact information mtorr4650@comcast.net

Cover art by Allen Greene

Map created by Blake Russelavage

First edition 2025

Paperback ISBN: 978-1-968404-23-9

Published by The Code Publishing, LLC in the United States of America

Dedication

The Return honors the values reflected in The Code of the West. Values like loyalty, hard work, honesty, fair play, respect, and self-responsibility. Traits we could use more of. Timeless values that are still relevant today—they never change, only times and cultures do. I hope you enjoy reading about a time and place where these values still held sway.

Acknowledgements

My author's journey has been filled with so many people willing to help me along the way—fortunately, I have been blessed with skilled fellow wordsmiths who have helped me grow as a writer.

I'd especially like to thank my daughter, Lisa, for her support of and research on *The Return*. She particularly helped me fill in some of the blanks surrounding the coming of the Denver, South Park, and Pacific Railroad, which transformed the South Park region. I was able to weave much of her research into the story to make it historically richer.

My wife, Anne, has always been a most valuable sounding board on my overall story arcs, and *The Return* is no exception. She has a keen eye for what works and what doesn't, and I value her feedback.

I'm also privileged to be part of an outstanding national critique group that helped me smooth the story and deepen my characters. Heartfelt thanks go to Dr. John Andrews (*Novels of the Great War*), Rex Griffin (*Moon of Black Hearts*), and Scott Hibbard (*Beyond the Rio Gila*)—all talented writers in their own right.

My beta readers helped apply an important final polish to the manuscript as well. Many thanks to Violetta (Vy) Armour (*I'll Always Be With You*), Rick Bereit, Ph.D. (*In His Service*), Ray Harlan (*The Confident Speaker*), Gary Scheimer (*Deadly Intrusion*), and Hugh Burns, Ph.D. (poetry in many literary publications).

I tip my hat to all of them and thank them for their willingness to help me keep the Old West alive.

The Colorado Territory Map

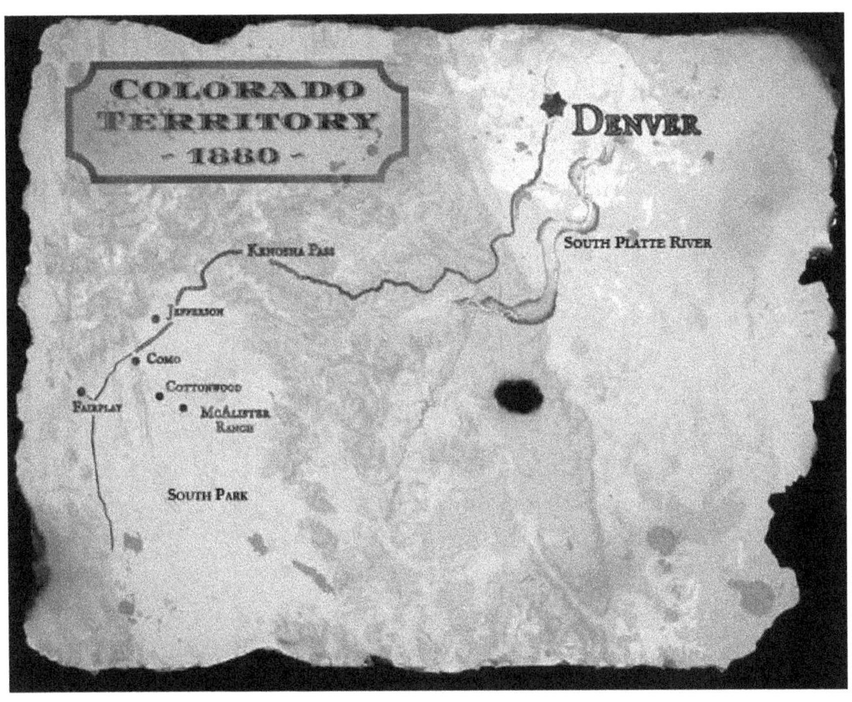

Contents

Chapter One

South Park, Colorado
December 1879

The storm came barreling in as if aimed right at Ike McAlister. A wild whoosh of wind, hell-bent on scouring everything in its path, flung his hat to the heavens. Roiling gray cloud banks hurled snow that needled his face—the only part of him that wasn't bundled up.

The Park's winter grasses were withered stalks even before the gale. Ike's cattle needed this hay he and his men wagoned out from the ranch all the more. The beasts stood still on the open range, rear ends to the storm, with glazed looks in the darkening afternoon. Ike eyed the pull horse—no longer young. If the animal perished in this maelstrom, there wasn't much hope for any of them, as far away from the ranch house as they were. Ike reined in next to Buster and Bert, cupping both hands around his mouth.

"We're gonna have to leave the hay wagon and ride from here on out. Unhitch the horse, Bert."

The rolling hills of this part of the Park basin were native grasslands, so the whipping gusts had their way. Deep pine forests bordered the plateau to the east—farther away to the north. Ike gazed at the western ramparts of the Rockies, where he'd rescued his sister, Sue. Fought with Rain Water, the Ute chief. Seemed like a long time ago now. To the south, the land lay open as far as the horizon and beyond, a bearing the storm erased.

Bert's face reflected all-out worry. "But, Mr. Ike, the wagon's got all the hay. If we leave it here, the cattle won't have nothin' to eat."

"There won't be any hay in it for much longer anyway, not with this blowin'. And eatin's not their concern right now—livin' is. Water is. Need to head 'em into the pines to the east, or they'll never make it. They got their tails to the north wind, and they're stupid enough to just let it push 'em south. There's only more open range that way—no cover, and that'll kill 'em in no time."

The young man pointed a gloved hand toward a long, low row of vertical wooden slats they'd strung together a few years ago. The storm was knocking it askew. "There's closer cover!"

Ike shook his head. "Snow breaks ain't gonna do no good in these winds. This is a hightail-it blizzard." He put a hand to his brow to shield his eyes and scanned the skies. Shook his head. "This ain't no good, no good 'tall. Better we wait things out and round up what cattle's left after this killer finishes its work. Devil storm's tryin' to lure us farther out. No sense bein' fool enough to do that when we can't see anything." He motioned to Buster and gestured back toward the ranch.

Buster yelled, but the storm swallowed his soft voice. With a hand beckoning in return, he jabbed spurs into his horse's flanks and lit out after the herd.

"Damn! Never could talk any sense into that hard-headed old man." Ike cupped his hands around his mouth and yelled. "Can't leave him out here alone, so chase him down, Bert. Front those heifers and turn 'em east. Find the nearest timber and push 'em in deep as you can. Should be less'n a mile away. Gather as many as you can, but don't go chasin' outliers. Ain't worth your lives. Hear?"

"Yessir."

Ike hesitated, facing a hard choice. He wanted to stay with his friends, but if he spent any more time out in this hell, the family dogs would die. "Snow's driftin' too deep to have two short-haired dogs out here anymore. This wind's already stiffenin' 'em up, and the drifts'll suffocate 'em." He squinted at the swirling dull sky and thumped his gloved fist on the saddle. He'd *told* his daughter, Jessie, to keep Rowdy and Penny inside, but they'd scooted after him when he rode out. At first, running excitedly, the dogs now lay motionless on the mounding snow, facing away from the blizzard. He grabbed the wagon horse's reins and wheeled his mount, Dex, to where they were curled, his fingers stiffening around the leathers. Thank the Lord he'd left Ally back at the ranch. His war horse was too old to be out in weather like this.

There were times—many—when Ally strained against the bit but kept her cool in worse weather, worse conditions. Had saved his life more than once. Seemed like a long time ago now. Senseless War.

Swinging his bad leg off, he reached down for Penny first. She was older than Rowdy, and wherever she went, Rowdy followed. He set Penny crosswise on Dex, forward of the saddle, then hefted Rowdy up onto the wagon horse.

He was barely able to swing his bad leg back over the saddle. With his jacket unbuttoned, he pressed Penny in against his flannel shirt, trying to balance Rowdy and aim Dex back to the ranch. Even through his thick coat, he could tell Penny wasn't doing well. Age wasn't working in her favor, either. His hip ached something fierce. Bullet must be working its way somewhere it shouldn't. At least, Doc said that was what it would do. He was used to pain, but this … He narrowed his eyes until they were slits against the raging storm.

To get back to the ranch, he'd have to ride north, right into the teeth of it. That hat would have come in handy right about now.

With a slow swivel, he watched Bert move off after Buster and shook his head. A familiar warmth ran up to his face, even in this maelstrom. He'd kill Buster if he didn't make it back.

He tugged his kerchief over his nose and tucked his chin into his neck, a glove on Penny's short hair. She wasn't moving, and her eyes were nearly closed. Jessie would never speak to him again if she died. He couldn't stand that. Losing cattle was bad enough, but losing his daughter was worse. Rowdy was younger and stronger, and his eyes were still open, but Ike's arm was losing feeling holding Penny tight. Numb and painful at the same time—never would have figured that. He loosed the reins to draw his coat farther over the dog. She didn't look like she had much time. That didn't cover her up but had to help.

He glanced at the wagon horse. The animal had been on the ranch for several years—knew his way around these parts, like Dex did. Maybe a horse's mysterious nose for direction would kick in. Better had, or they'd all die out here. Buster and Bert should be somewhere downrange right about now, hopefully nearing shelter with the cattle. How many would follow them into the trees? Would they even reach the trees?

He said a small prayer for the two men and cursed the choice he'd just had to make.

Whipping snow blinded him. Had to be doing the same with the horses. The animals labored into the blizzard, hooves plodding one in front of the other, forelegs nearly disappearing in the mounting snow. He was freezing—they had to be. How much farther to the ranch house? All depended on how true their path was. Had to be maybe a half mile by now.

Dex faltered. Too much weight. Ike clutched Penny to him and steadied Rowdy on the other horse's saddle as he swung off the gelding. With a free hand, he untied his bedroll and snugged it around Rowdy. Likely wouldn't help much, but the blanket wasn't doing any good hanging off the back of his saddle.

Getting the horses moving again took some doing. Hadn't ever had to before, but Ike laid the whip on their hindquarters. He turned his back to the storm with one hand on Dex, the other clutching Penny close as they trudged. It'd be on foot from here on out—no way he could get his leg back over a horse anyway. His feet knew they were in deep snow. Boots were tough against brambles and stickers, but not much good against numbing cold.

Where land ended and sky began, he couldn't tell. White whirlwinds surrounded him, coming from all directions but mostly straight at him. That had to be north, as that was where he'd seen the darkest clouds gathering when they set out from the ranch. Harsh winds were common this time of year, as if making an unmistakable statement that winter was still here to take the land's measure. But this storm was making double sure no one missed the season's snarl. His breath froze on his bandana as he panted. An image of his father blurred his vision, and the man's words rang in his ears. "Sometimes doin' your best ain't enough. Sometimes you gotta do what's needed." His pa and ma killed all those years ago. Still hurt fresh, though. Quantrill. The bastard. Ike got even with the killers, but that had not healed the hole in his heart.

One foot in front of the other. His blanket sailed off the other horse, leaving Rowdy at the storm's mercy. He tugged the dog off and drew him close, both arms bent in a desperate grip around them. Come on, Penny, hold on.

The wagon horse slowed, then stopped as a ferocious gust hit them. The two horses stood tied bridle-to-bridle together by the leathers. He'd taken to walking between them to shield some of the storm. How much farther could they go? There was no mercy to be found here. His ears pounded, and even his heart felt cold. A stumble, and the wagon horse dropped to the snowy ground. Ike couldn't hear the animal's breathing, but he could see it laboring for breath. Spasms took control of the horse, and its head sank to the snow. The horse's fall yanked Dex into him, and Ike went down. Hadn't taken much to knock him off his feet. He landed hard on his bad hip, arms still wrapped around the dogs.

Even during the War, things were never this bad. But then again, he'd seen too many men burned to death. Wasn't sure which was worse—freezing or burning to death. Probably burning.

The dogs slipped out from his arms, and he shook on the snow next to the frozen horse. Dex leaned toward him at a crazy angle as the reins still tied the two horses together. Had to cut them somehow.

The wagon horse lay still in its final resting place. Most of the head icicled now. A good horse, always ready to work. Never had given him a name. Should have. Now survival depended on Dex, Ally's stand-in. The snow felt almost warm as it enveloped him. He leaned back into the drift, which mounded up over his head in back. Lorraine appeared in a vision. She must be glued to the front windows, watching for him, with Jessie and Sonny at her skirts.

He'd always known he wouldn't die in bed. Other than the fierce wind, lying here dying wasn't so bad. The tempest didn't even sting his frozen cheeks much anymore. Couldn't feel his feet. He was mostly shielded now by the snowbank. The dogs seemed to be beyond suffering as snow began to cover all of them. They looked as stiff as he felt. He closed his eyes, then stirred at something and forced them open, gazing into the distance, trying to focus his eyes and thoughts.

As he lay in the whirlwind, he smiled, wanting to reach out a hand that wouldn't reach. His grin tore at the frozen edges of his mouth. There. Was he really seeing his father?

He struggled to a stand—something he shouldn't have been able to do ever again. And how had he cut the horses's leathers apart? At least the blizzard had numbed his hip. He labored as he stepped through thigh-deep snow, dogs bundled close again. One short step at a time. Dex followed, no longer leading the way. Ike leaned into the gale, eyes frozen nearly shut.

What was that? A faint sound crackled through a break in the blizzard's assault. Another. He turned and aimed toward the sound as it echoed again. Leaden feet carried him in a lurching stumble on numb legs. Was that a gunshot? Couldn't tell over the storm's roar. Keep going.

A huge drift blocked his way forward, and he went down again. Where did that come from? There wasn't anything out here to pile snow this high except—a house or a barn!

No sense trying to push through or over the drift. He had to find a way around it.

Pow! ripped through the maelstrom.

No mistaking it—that was a shot, and close. A stubborn will took over his body. He shuffled sideways until he rounded the edge of the drift and spied a light ahead. A few more steps, and he saw a backlit figure standing in an open doorway.

Lorraine! The ranch house. His children framed their mother in the golden light. She shuffled through the snow to him and grabbed onto his iced jacket. Pulling him toward the door, she led him to the front steps. He stumbled over them and was down on the porch, unable to move. Penny spilled from his grasp onto the snow-drifted deck.

She shouted to the children to stay inside. Ike felt her grasp his collar and tug him toward the light. Jessie bundled Penny in her arms and rushed inside. Ike lay on his back as his wife grunted and inched him along.

The wind howled as if it didn't want to release him from its clutches. He tried pushing on the porch boards with his heels, but his feet were logs. Nothing hurt anymore, not even his face, masked with a layer of ice. He wished he could help her—didn't think he'd ever been as much help to his wife as he would have liked. Ranching was a jealous mistress who'd do you in at the slightest misstep. And he'd made a lot of those.

Jessie pulled Rowdy free from her father's stiff arm and disappeared inside. Lorraine had gotten Ike to the door's threshold but now sank to her knees in exhaustion. She wept as she kept a fist clenched around his collar, then Jessie joined the struggle, and together they yanked and yanked.

When Ike lay fully inside the house, Lorraine cleared snow away from the door and slammed it shut.

Ike whispered through cracked, bleeding lips. "Dex …."

Lorraine shook her head. "Not openin' that door again 'til the damn blizzard's wore itself out."

He exhaled a long breath with a low, "Deeex," and passed out.

***

Lorraine already had the wood stove fired up, and the small ranch house radiated warmth. A snug, small oasis in the killing storm. Several lamps gave off a soft glow in the midst of her desperate struggles.

She opened the door and yanked and yanked a stiff-legged Dex into the house by his mane. Pull by pull, she dragged Ike by the fire, then led Dex to a corner of the front room. The horse thudded to the floor, ice cascading off his hide and tinkling on the wooden floorboards, which cracked like the sound of a rifle shot under the weight. Please don't fall through.

"Sonny! Grab all the blankets and quilts you can find! Jessie, help me get your father's clothes off."

She pried Ike's rigid jacket away and struggled with his shirt buttons but couldn't undo them. Wiping at a tear, she said, "Get me a knife, Jessie!"

"You're not going to cut Papa, are you, Momma?" Wet trails streamed down her young red face.

"The knife—now!"

She sliced the buttons off Ike's shirt and pants and stripped him bare, quickly wrapping a blanket around him. When she cut his boots and socks away and took his gloves off, she lifted a hand to her mouth. "Oh my Lord!"

Stark-white feet that looked frozen solid. Hands that felt like stone. She muffled her tears in the blanket. Her husband lay prone before her—eyes closed, cracked lips caked with blood, and body mottled with blue blotches. No time to waste.

"Jessie, go get those hearth stones and push them under the blankets on the bed. Scoot the dogs under. Bring me that bucket of water. Hurry. You and Sonny get under the covers, too."

What would Doc Early do for Ike now? She dithered between heating the water bucket over the fire or just using blankets to warm him up. Make a decision!

She grabbed the lukewarm bucket and poured water over Ike's feet, then rubbed, then poured and massaged until the bucket was empty. A glance at Dex, who lay still, facing away from her. She kept Ike's hands under an armpit and between her legs as she worked. The cold shivered her, but she kept working on his limbs.

A slap across Ike's pale face didn't even redden his cheek. Her heart pounded as she looked her husband over. Leaning on his chest, she listened for his heartbeat. Couldn't tell anything from his color, but his heart beat fast, steady.

"Jessie! Help me drag your father."

Together, they got Ike to the base of the bed, and between the two of them, worked him up onto the mattress and beneath the covers. Lorraine scooted under as well and wrapped her body alongside her husband's. The bed groaned under all the weight.

"Sonny! Start rubbin' the dogs under the blankets. Rub 'til you can't anymore."

Jessie massaged her father's feet while Lorraine wiped frozen breath off his beard and worked on his stiff hands.

"Come on, Ike! Ike!"

She stared at his closed eyes, hoping for a flicker. Anything.

"At least you ain't shot. That should count for somethin'. Don't you dare up and leave me. That would be just like you. There aren't many times you ever listened to me, but you better be hearin' me now. Open those eyes and come back to us. Ike!"

Her tears dripped.

They rubbed and rubbed. Another slap brought a faint groan. Lorraine grasped his face in both of her hands.

"Ike! Wake up. Wake up. I'm not lettin' go 'til you open those brown eyes."

The shivers started slowly, almost as if they'd been lurking, waiting for him to warm some. They started at his chest, then worked their way toward his hands and feet until his body shook all over. He moaned softly, his head jerking left and right almost too fast to follow. One eye opened to a slit, the other still glued shut. Lorraine moved on top of him, his hands underneath her. She glanced back at Jessie.

"Any color in those feet yet?"

"No, Mama, but I can move his toes some now."

"Don't bust 'em off."

Jessie tented the covers as she sat up, pressed Ike's feet into her midsection, and continued to rub.

"How are the dogs, Sonny?"

"Rowdy's thumpin' his tail some, but Penny don't look so good. Not breathin' much."

"Stroke her back and forth—hard. Curl yourself around her."

She glanced at Dex, who lay still on the other side of the room. She couldn't help him any, and as valuable as he was, husband and dogs came first right now.

Ike's other eye creaked open to a red slit as well. Lorraine couldn't tell if he was looking up at her or somewhere past. His eyes weren't focused on anything, far as she could tell.

"Ike! Can you say something?"

"L-l-like … w-whaaat?"

Lorraine pressed herself against her husband as tears ran onto his bare chest. The shaking grew stronger. She grabbed his hands again and covered them with hers, hard against her ribs.

"Can you feel your fingers?"

"N-no."

"Don't worry, they look fine."

A lie. She kept them hidden from him and peered at Jessie, who'd wrapped herself around frozen feet. Sonny stood by the side of the bed, tears running down his ruddy cheeks. Lorraine didn't have to ask; his face said everything.

Which one, which dog had they lost?

She rose from Ike and held her son tight, then looked under the blankets. Rowdy lifted his head for her, but Penny lay still. She tried to shield Jessie from the sight but couldn't.

"Penny!"

Jessie's dog, as much as a ranch dog could be anyone's. She wailed as she cradled Penny in her arms on the bed. The blankets around Jessie dropped away to reveal the scene. The dog lay limp in Jessie's arms as she rocked with her, mouth open in a silent moan. Sonny stood to the side with a stricken look.

Jessie screamed.

"Mama! Penny's still got a heartbeat."

She opened the dog's mouth wide and kept rocking her, crying and grinning.

"She's okay, Sonny, gonna be fine."

That was to convince herself as much as it was for her five-year-old brother.

Lorraine turned back to Ike and snugged the blankets around him again. She traced her hands down a shaking leg to his feet. Still ice cold. Stark white. Reaching for one of the warm hearthstones, she worked it against the soles of his feet.

"Sonny, go check on Dex and tell me."

Ike would likely live, and his hands seemed to be coming around, but what about his feet?

And where were Buster and Bert?

Chapter Two

The blizzard showed no mercy. Even shouting was swallowed up as whipping winds made it useless for Bert to do more than gesture to Buster in the distance. He relied on the hand signals they used every day on the ranch. Windmilling in the direction he thought was east, he motioned to head the cattle that way. As well as he had grown to know this land, Bert still wasn't sure which way was which now. Ike said to aim for the forest on the east side of the Park, less than a mile or so away. At least there'd be some shelter there. Good idea, but the storm had stolen his bearings—almost as if it aimed to destroy the pitiful herd along with any wranglers in its grasp. Toy with them first, then snatch their lives.

Bert scanned the swirling sky as he tried to snug his collar even tighter, his fingers only able to fumble with his coat's buttons. Gotta keep these beeves moving, or their blood will freeze them dead on their feet. He'd seen it once before—cattle standing lifeless in their tracks, eyes frozen open, mouths agape. But that was only one of many nightmares that stole their way into his head. How was Buster doing? The story he told of that party he tried to guide through the mountains years ago sprang to mind. Said he told them, warned them. They ran into a bitter storm like this one that had saved up fury so it could unleash it all at once.

Bert squinted at the few cattle he could still make out. In any herd, there were lead cows. Steers followed wherever these bell cows led. As he watched, one of them went down like it had been shot, and the rest kept their rears to the wrath, unmoving. Couldn't let them stand still—had to get them moving again. It had been a long time since he used his whip, but he pried it loose from the saddle and uncoiled stiff coils with numb fingers. He drew next to one of the front cows and snapped the snake across her rear end.

Nothing. The animal was as numb as he was. Another lash, harder. The cow looked back this time, red streaks showing on its hide through the hurtling snow. For a third time, Bert laid into the animal with all the force a young man could, and the cow stumbled ahead on stiff legs. Whips to the followers got the herd moving again—but was it the right direction?

As the cattle lurched forward, Bert rode with his hat tilted against the tempest. Not for long, though, as it sailed away like it had wings. He rode at the drag end of the herd, as much as there was a back end. Cattle continued to drop in their tracks as they fanned out aimlessly. Couldn't corral them anymore. Probably weren't all theirs, anyway. Would be lucky to find the forest shelter, much less push any cattle in. Ike knew what he was doing, didn't he? He never learned how to snap his whip like Buster—and Ike. How was the boss faring? He should have been able to make it back to the ranch with those two horses. The dogs didn't look too good, though.

He shielded his eyes against the gusts of stinging snow, checking for drifters and searching for Buster. No sense chasing wanderers in all this—he'd stick with the main herd. Hard to tell horses from cattle in this weather, but … there he was. Age had bent him in the saddle over time, but this was more than a slump. His horse wasn't moving, either. Must have been how he looked during that villainous winter freeze in the mountains years ago. Ever since, Buster complained of cold hands, except in the hottest part of summer. Wouldn't be just his hands now, though.

Time to leave the dogies and join his friend. He hoped they'd keep following him and not trundle south, but they'd do what they would. Cattle weren't the smartest animals, but at least they had a herd instinct. Weaving his mount between the staggering cows, he angled toward Buster. The man looked almost frozen on his mount—tilted forward, hands clasped around the horn, leathers loose to either side of the horse.

"Buster! Buster!" The man couldn't hear a rifle shot on a quiet day anymore, much less his voice during this storm. His eyesight had seen better days, too. The storm's roar sounded like a two-thousand-head stampede, but the ground wasn't shaking, just freezing. He grabbed hold of the old man's reins and pulled the horse along with him. Buster slowly turned toward him, a bandana frozen fast against his cheeks. Bert pointed and rode on. No sense looking back, the storm's rage and the day's failing light already stealing his sight. He leaned into the battering gusts—the ranch only a memory, hidden somewhere behind him in the furious swirl. Made no sense to try to head that way. Their only hope was to find the shelter of the forest. Even then, any protection the trees provided would only slow, not stop, the tempest's sledgehammer fist. He'd have to find some warmth there, or they'd freeze among the pines, same as here on the flat.

Mr. Ike made it home all right, didn't he? He had to. And the dogs, horses? He was partial to Rowdy—always had been, for some reason. Keep moving, keep moving, or tomorrow they'd find them frozen, still in the saddle. If the storm didn't kill them both, their freezing blood would. He knew that much. No telling how much farther the trees were, but it didn't matter. They'd make shelter, or they wouldn't. And if they made it, would Buster be alive? How many times could a body take savage freezes before it gave up?

His fingers curled around his and Buster's reins. He couldn't feel them. Shivers shook his body a while back, but not anymore. Please, Lord, let there be shelter soon. His mind drifted, along with the snow. Had to breathe open-mouthed under the bandana, and his lungs screamed. A gust took most of his breath away and scattered his thoughts. Some cattle followed, but he couldn't tell how many. Mr. Ike and Lorraine needed this herd—it was all they had. Even in this maelstrom, his memory stung at the thought of Lorraine. The awful thing he'd done and how she'd forgiven him. Even made him a place at the ranch—his home for the last seven, eight years. It was clear Mr. Ike hadn't wanted him there, but Lorraine had a way about her. Her husband ran things, but Lorraine wore the apron.

He slowed and pulled Buster's horse up next to him. It took a while, as neither horse moved well anymore. Buster didn't budge as his horse stumbled forward. Lord, let him be alive. The man had taken care of Bert when he first came, smoothed a way between him and Mr. Ike.

Snow blew in waves in front of his eyes, threatening the life of everything that still lived. The forest was almost on him before he saw it faintly ahead. Gray trunks appeared like haughty ghosts between blurry dashes of white, as if waiting to swallow them. Bert tugged at both reins and guided the horses around scratchy pine branches and deep into the woods. The deeper he went, the more cattle could follow. Trees cut the wind but didn't cut the cold. He pulled up where several pines stood bunched together and dismounted. He reached up for Buster and tipped the rigid old man off his mount. Couldn't tell if he was alive.

A hand to his neck said he was. Bert set the old man behind the tree windbreak. He unsaddled the horses, tugged them down, and pushed Buster into the curve they made. Cattle crowded around— no moos, no groans. Too frozen to do more than take shallow breaths. With a swipe of his knife, Bert sliced the life out of one that dropped to the snowy turf like a rock, the dead animal's gaping neck showing no blood. Cutting into the beast, he drew out bloody insides. He knelt next to Buster and placed ragged, lukewarm steaks on his feet, hands, and neck. The man looked like someone had carved him up with all the red that covered him. Bert reached back to the saddles and unrolled his and Buster's thin bedrolls. He hadn't used his in all the chaos, but it would have been small comfort anyway. He wrapped both blankets around the still man and lay down next to him.

Morning couldn't come too soon, if it came at all.

Chapter Three

The day dawned grudgingly, a steel gray the storm robbed of color. A leaden sky backdropped white hills that stretched all the way to the dim horizon. Even the sun seemed reluctant to show its face so soon after the merciless storm's last lashes. Several clouds still hovered, almost like a rear guard for the blizzard.

"Momma!" Sonny's repeated calls echoed in Lorraine's foggy mind. She'd spent most of the night tending to her husband, the dogs, and Dex. Toward daybreak, she'd finally drifted off as the wind died down to an exhausted whisper. "Momma, Daddy's trying to get up."

Lorraine opened her eyes to see Ike falling off the bed with only a blanket on. His shakes thumped against the wooden floorboards, his body mostly a bright pink. She sprang from bed and wrapped her arms around him as he shivered on the floor. A glance at his hands showed an angry red color. They weren't good, but better. She hesitated to uncover his feet. Pulling the blanket aside, she gazed at his stumps, no longer frozen but still white. Or were they coloring some? A light gray?

"Jessie, help me get your father over to the fireplace." Between them, they hefted Ike onto the still-warm hearth. Lorraine set about rebuilding the fire, which had warmed the house so well last night. Orange coals still hid under black ash, and soon she had the fire blazing again. Jessie dragged a chair up, and they piled woolen blankets over him as he sank into it, shaking.

"Sonny, how are the dogs?"

"Rowdy's better than Penny, Momma. She's not movin' much."

Jessie sat on the bed, arms around her dog, which looked smaller somehow, curled in her lap. "She's not as young as Rowdy, Momma. I'm so scared."

Lorraine eyed her ten-year-old, who held her nearly-as-old dog tight. They'd grown up together, and Penny went everywhere with her, even to school in Cottonwood when the weather allowed.

Lorraine stoked the fire higher. Wasn't hard to figure why her husband turned back with the dogs. The cattle were important—they kept the place going—but he had to live with her and the kids every day. No cattle, maybe no ranch, but no dogs, no peace. As she rubbed his feet, she knew she had to get Ike into town to see Doc Early. Had he brought back the hay wagon last night? "Ike, honey, do you feel up to talkin'?"

"Sure."

The man never was much for conversation, but right now, she'd have to work to pry more than one-word answers from cracked and bleeding lips. "Where are Buster and Bert?"

"Out there." He swiped at his short beard with a shiver.

"So, they stayed after the herd."

He nodded. "Pushin' cattle toward the forest."

Lorraine imagined all sorts of trouble with that. How could they tell where they were going? Had they even reached the trees? She worked on his calves, close by the morning fire she'd set as soon as she got up. His legs were still pale strangers. "Ike, is the wagon outside?"

"Downrange, due south. Left it."

She had to get that buckboard. "The horse?"

Ike stared into the fire and shook his head. "Good horse."

Dex was up this morning, so she'd watered and fed him stale carrots. She should shoo him back out of the house, but where would he go? The barn doors were snowed shut, and no telling when she could get them open. Ally was all right in there, wasn't she? And the two other horses. Probably. She ran a hand through her hair and gazed out the front window. The blizzard left its white footprint everywhere, with near ten-foot drifts anywhere something slowed its assault. The front porch hid under several deep mounds, but the door was mostly clear.

What to do? Ike needed a doctor, and Buster was still out somewhere with Bert. If she got the wagon, she could take Ike in, but she'd need Raven. She eyed the drifts blocking the weathered barn's double doors. No way to clear those, unless … "Jessie, get your winter coat and boots on and pile all the wood into that bin by the hearth. Grab that broom. Ike, I gotta go get that wagon. I'll be back soon as I can."

She buttoned her heavy coat and tugged gloves and boots on. Sweeping matches and a flint into her pocket, she pushed the door open wide as a small pile of snow tumbled in. She pulled the kerosene canister outside by its leather grip and grabbed the shovel from the front porch—thank heavens she'd thought to retrieve it from the barn when the storm started hammering. With one hand holding the kerosene and the other on the wooden bin's leather handle, she and Jessie started across the short distance to the barn. Snow came almost to the knee, but she urged her daughter on. The hardest part wasn't the still-numbing cold—dragging the box as it sank partway into the snow was worse. They would hurry around to the front and shovel-sweep as much away as they could, then heft the basket again. Trudging through the snow stole almost an hour— precious time she wasn't sure Ike had.

At the barn, she splashed the pieces of wood with kerosene, and the two of them threw the dripping logs onto the large drift blocking the opening where the two doors met. Her throat tightened as most disappeared into the nine-foot pile. She struck several matches on the flint and threw them onto the wood she could still see. They flared and spawned a wintry duel between hot flames and cold snow. She set about attacking the barrier with the shovel while Jessie dug furiously at the pile with the broom. The fire melted the drift partway—not to the ground, but it was enough to climb up on.

As she stood atop the mound, Lorraine jammed the shovel handle between the double barn doors. With all her might, she levered the sturdy wood back and forth until the doors stood almost a foot apart. Thank heavens Ike kept the rails greased. A man who always cared for what he had. "Jessie, help me!" With their feet against the edge of one door, they pushed against the other, which gave way easier than Lorraine expected. They dropped to the floor inside, and she called to Ally. Ike's horse pawed at the straw in the bottom of her stall. "Not goin' with me today, girl. Gonna take your sister."

"Jessie, water the horses while I get Raven tacked up." Lorraine fastened the bridle with the long leathers, yoke, and harness on the horse. No room for a saddle—how was that going to work? Better to do this inside the barn than try it on the open range. Pretty mare, almost as good-looking as Ally, though she'd never said that to Ike. At the thought, her husband's pink body and white feet flashed to mind. Why'd he light out after the herd in that terrible storm? She shook her head, but she knew why. The herd was the only thing keeping this, and all the other spreads around here, going. The fall yearling sale hadn't been good, either. Their ranch was already struggling, and now this storm. And Buster. How could an old man like him survive that fury?

"After I ride out, close these doors behind me and hurry back to the house. Keep your Pa's feet close to the warmth and blankets around him and the dogs. Lead Dex out back here to the barn and feed him, too. I'll be back as soon as I'm able." With that, she pushed through the drift outside and headed south on Raven as fast as the deep snow would let her. The land before her stretched as if it didn't have a care in the world. How could it? She was carrying it all. Her worries were as thick as the storm's flurries had been. Ike and his feet, Buster and Bert. Was anything left of the herd? Could she even find the wagon? Damn this ranching!

She rode in a light snowfall that must have only annoyed the drifts. The storm—harsh as it was—had transformed the rough landscape of the Park basin into graceful, gently rounded hills. The silence stood in harsh contrast to last night's howling hell. How fast life changed. Her life. The McAlisters seemed to reel from hard luck to worse luck. They were due a break, and this wasn't it. She'd ridden this range for years, but today the land was a stranger. With no landmarks, it was hard to figure out if she was still heading south. The only tracks to be seen were the ones the horse plowed. Where was the wagon?

A snow-covered mound appeared ahead to the left. She only noticed it because everything else was flat. Before Raven even plodded close, she knew it was the horse Ike told her about. Poor thing didn't have a name to be remembered by. They had better-looking horses over the years, ones that were smarter, but none that ever worked harder. Something always in short supply. She tipped her hat and nudged Raven's flanks. Took a few to get Raven going, but going where? Was she going to be stranded out here, too? The trees on the east side of the Park looked small from here. Lumpy, snow-covered against a sunless, glistening white.

How much farther could Raven go and still make it back to the ranch? Another bulge ahead, but there was only one horse missing … oh no! As soon as she spied this one, other lumps seemed to spring to sight. How many head had they lost? She put a hand to her brow and scanned the surroundings. Off to her left in the distance was a grayish spot, and she reined Raven that way. When they got to the buckboard, Lorraine swung off. Raven pawed at the snow while she tried to heft one of the wagon's buried rails. Maybe the wind firmed the snowpack because she couldn't free it up. After agonizing minutes trying with no success, she swept the buggy seat clean and sat down. Hitching was usually a two-person job for a reason.

When she'd regained her breath, she rubbed her eyes hard. Going back without the wagon wouldn't do, not if she wanted to get to town. Think. What could free up the rails? She jumped down from the bouncy seat, grabbed Raven's traces, and backed the horse up against the front of the wagon between the two submerged rails. She put the blanket she'd been riding on Raven's backside between the horse and the wooden front. Tying the leathers to a metal flange, she clambered back up on the buckboard. With all her strength, she yanked the reins back and yelled, "HYAH! BACK! BACK!"

The horse smacked against the buckboard, inching it backward. "HYAH, HYAH!" Then a few more inches—that should have been enough to loosen those rails. She dropped into the wagon bed and felt around under the snow with her gloves. There. The stable rake they always kept in the buckboard to fling hay off. Hurrying around front, she attacked the snow covering the wooden shafts. They wriggled, but the snow still held them captive. She tugged Raven forward slightly, then grabbed hold of a rail and tried to heft it up to the harness. Not high enough. No! She couldn't be this close and fail. Clasping her hands together, she sank to her knees in the snow and prayed for strength.

Laying a hand on Raven's yoke, she struggled to stand and strained with both hands on the wood again. Halfway, but no higher. She didn't have the strength anymore. Her body shook with the cold and the effort—like her husband's last night. She screamed and gathered herself for one more try. Lifted the rail again, but this time laid it on her bent knee to catch her breath. If she lifted it high enough, she could slide the rail into a leather slot on the harness, then secure it. With both gloves underneath, she heaved. "AAAHHH!" There it was, next to the hole, but now she needed Raven to back up. Hurry! "Raven, BACK!" The horse backed toward the wagon, and Lorraine slid the rail into the harness. She draped her arms over Raven, heaving for breath.

When she recovered, she stood over the other rail. This should be a little easier, but … oh no! Even if she got the rail up, she couldn't secure it unless Raven moved forward, but then the other rail would drop back into the snow. Hands to her face again. Her father's voice echoed in her head. "Trying's for cowards. You ain't a coward." Her feet were starting to numb, standing out here for as long as she had been. Raven's legs—her whole body, for that matter—had to be suffering as well.

The other rail rose more easily in Lorraine's grip but was still inches away from the slot. Might as well have been a mile. Maybe if Raven moved a little left, it would work. She grabbed the horse's bridle and guided her that way, then raised the rail again. As she pulled Raven back toward her, the horse straightened, and the iron ring inched toward the end of the rail. Just as it touched, the other rail gave way.

Lorraine screamed into cold nothingness and sobbed.

A shot rang out over the empty landscape. She didn't know who it was but drew and fired her pistol into the air. A horse appeared in the distance with … two riders. She squinted against the blinding white. Buster and Bert! As they neared, Buster lay slumped forward with Bert's arms wrapped around him from behind. Hallelujah! Lorraine's joy was immediately tempered by a closer look at her listless friend. The man was no stranger to bitter cold, but had this storm finally killed him?

"I'd say you're a sight for sore eyes, Bert." She paused as a tear fell down her cheek. "Is he … dead?"

"No, ma'am."

"Then what's all that blood on him?"

"Long story. Not his."

"Can Buster hear me?"

"Don't think so, Miss Lorraine. He's pretty froze up. Glad to see you, too. When I fired that shot, I was hopin' to find Mr. Ike. Is he okay?"

"No. I been tryin' to hitch this horse up to that wagon, so's I could wagon him to Doc Early's, but nothin' doin'. Don't know as how I could have busted through all that snow to town, anyway. So, I'm gonna need you to fetch Doc back to the house to tend Ike—and Buster, too. After we get him settled in, you hightail it to town."

They pushed through the snow back to the ranch house, where Lorraine and Bert eased the timeworn man off the spent horse as if he was a statue. The day was fleeing, but a pale sun had brought faint warmth with it. The horses could stay inside the barn. Besides, Lorraine wasn't sure the ranch house floor could hold any more without buckling. The two of them carried a limp Buster inside and hurried him under the bed covers.

Lorraine didn't know who to check on first. Ike sat by the fire, which had worked itself up to heating the whole house. His feet had turned a faint pink, and he rested them on the warm hearth. When he saw Buster, he tried to stand, but his legs wouldn't let him. Rowdy paced near Penny, nestled at Ike's feet. A good sign that she lifted her head when Lorraine came in. Buster lay still amid the commotion. As she fussed over her old friend, Lorraine said, "Jessie, did you check on Ally and the others in the barn?"

Her daughter nodded. "She's okay, and the others—cold, but still standing. I fed and watered them, just like Daddy said to. Had to break up the ice to do it."

Lorraine put a hand to Buster's neck. "How's Penny doin'?"

"I'm scared, Mama. She hasn't gotten up yet, and her breathing's shallow. I just don't know."

"Try to get her up—the longer she stays down, the worse it'll be. Get some water in her if you can."

Ike struggled on all fours to the bed and called Rowdy. He lifted the covers. "Under here, boy." He scooted the dog in next to Buster while Lorraine wrapped several hearthstones in blankets and placed them around the unconscious man.

"He doesn't look good, Lorraine."

She put two fingers to his neck. "Gray face, pulse thready. Can't tell much now; have to wait 'til he warms up some. Maybe he'll come out of it, but he isn't as strong—or young—as you." She glanced at Bert. "You thawed out a little?"

He nodded.

"Best thing you can do right now, then, is go get the doc. There's a canteen hangin' by the door and a food pouch in the icebox. Take that mare in the last stall—not Ally—yours is wore out. But if you push the horse too hard through this snow, she'll founder. Can't have that. I need you to get there and back. Do this for me, Bert. The sooner you leave, the sooner you're back again, so hurry." She waved him out while Jessie shut the door behind him.

"Where's Sonny?"

Jessie pointed to a lump next to Buster. Lorraine lifted the bed blankets to see her son snuggled up against the old man. She ran a hand along Buster's cold torso and felt for a pulse again. With a hand to her brow, she said, "Don't know how much longer he has. I'm gonna get in next to him."

Ike limped back to the hearth and worked his way down to a seat. The sharp stabbing in his feet and his quarrelsome hip were nothing compared to the prospect of losing one of the only friends he'd ever had.

Chapter Four

February 1870

Lorraine McAlister stared at the doctor as she buttoned her dress. His nose was deep in a large book titled *Remedies*. Old Doc Early. He seemed to have become a part of his age-old office furniture, peering over glasses perched on his nose. Even when he was young, he must have been old. Doctoring in Cottonwood for as long as she could remember. He delivered both her babies and healed her up when one … She pulled her sleeves farther down over the rashes on her wrists.

Early looked up. "What other things are ailing you besides those welts on your arms?"

Lorraine rubbed a chill away. "What doesn't? My joints are all achy. One minute I feel feverish, then shivery. And this winter cold doesn't help. What do I have, Doc?"

"Never knew you to complain about anything, so this'll bear some looking into." He started to say something, then buried his nose again as he flipped pages. With a shake of his head, he glanced back up. "I ain't quite sure what it is, Lorraine, but it appears you got a bushel of it. I have an idea, but what I'm thinking of I see mostly in miners. In the meantime, let me get you something to ease your pains." He worked himself up off his stool and fished through a messy stash of glass bottles on a faded wooden bureau. "Here's some laudanum."

"How often should I take this?"

"You'll know."

"Well, how much should I take?"

"Spoonfuls 'til you can't read the label." He took his glasses off. "Come back and see me if you don't start feeling better soon."

As she left the small, dusty room, she looked back to see Doc studying the book and shaking his head slightly. Outside, Bert stood with the wagon at the ready. She said, "Did you get to see Hannah?"

He stared down the hard-packed street at the dress shop. "Said she was busy. And was going to be for a while."

"Sorry about that." Lorraine winced when she started to step up to the bouncy seat.

The young man reached an arm out and boosted her up. "You all right, Miss Lorraine?" Worry shrouded his face and tinged his voice.

"Of course, Bert. Let's go, please." He snapped the reins, and they almost lurched off the seat as the horse jumped away. Lorraine's hand flew to the bouncy seat's curved iron arm. "But you keep drivin' like that, and I won't be."

As they trundled south, she gazed at the Park's soft landscape. Aspens and cottonwoods had shed their yellow finery along the banks of the South Platte a while ago. Fair winds had tumbled gold leaves to the ground, as if the earth was donning nightclothes and shedding everything it didn't need for the long winter ahead. Crisp, dry days starched with full sun ruled the basin now. The deep blue sky seemed even bigger this time of year. She couldn't imagine a more beautiful setting. So lucky. And they still had a remnant of the herd. Thank you, Lord.

A smile crept over her face despite her aches and pains. "No need to rush home." But her achy knees told a different story. Maybe they should hurry.

Bert glanced her way. "Yes'm."

They crested the rise that sloped down to the flat basin where the ranch lay.

"Would you stop here for a moment, Bert?"

He pulled the horse to a halt.

Lorraine untied her bonnet and shook her hair loose. She craned her head so the afternoon winter sun shone directly on her face, the warmth a momentary extravagance. Bert sat motionless. She closed her eyes, her mind filled with a vision of small yellow summer flowers waving to her from the hillsides.

The horse's whinny broke the spell.

"Time to be goin'." She bow-tied the bonnet under her chin again while he snapped the reins. Not quite as hard this time.

The ride to the ranch wouldn't take long now. This time of year, the roadbed was dry and firm. What was she going to tell Ike? He knew something was wrong, even though she'd tried to hide her pain. Trying to walk through the stiffness almost doubled her over at times. She rarely went outside anymore, usually shooing him and the others away with a wave of her hand and a halfhearted smile. No doubt Buster and Bert noticed, too. She'd always done for others. Never did much for herself and had a hard time accepting help, especially from those closest to her. Like Ike. Another of what he called her "perversities."

"Bert, I need a favor." She clutched her heavy coat tighter as they rode.

"Anything, Miss Lorraine."

"I need you to lie for me if Ike asks you where I was." She glanced sideways at him.

Bert drove on for a few minutes, then drew the wagon to a halt. He rubbed his forehead. "Sorry, ma'am, but I can't do that. I'm afeared of Mr. Ike enough as it is—if he found out I'd lied to him, I don't know what he'd do. Buster says if you fib about small things, what's to stop you from lyin' about things that matter?" He shook his head. "Ask me anything else."

Warmth surged up her neck. "You're right. I shouldn't have asked that of you. Would have put you in a terrible position."

"Won't tell him a lie, Miss Lorraine, but that's different than not tellin' the whole truth, and nobody can say otherwise. I'll work at stayin' out of his way. Okay?"

"That sounds like a good idea."

The McAlister ranch was about an hour out of Cottonwood, and it spread ahead on the brown plain. From a distance, the place looked like someone cleared a meager area around a few structures, which the surrounding land refused to let get any bigger. A small patch of lighter brown showed beside the house, where her garden drooped. Cold nights had turned summer green to winter brown.

Two dogs rushed their way, barking joyfully. Both mutts, with Penny, the smaller one, in a limping run. Lorraine shook her head. Jessie's pleas won out years ago. Almost like their daughter planned it. During a trip to town, she found a stray she lured to the wagon with some food she also 'found.' And that look on her face. Clever girl.

But Penny had been a blessing, along with Rowdy, who wandered onto the ranch a long time ago like he owned the place. Turns out he might as well have. The two couldn't have been more different—Rowdy, lop-eared and tall, and Penny, stocky and short. But no puppies in the years since, their days taken up by playing and guarding. They circled the wagon as it rolled, barking excitedly.

"Like I said, I would appreciate—"

"Don't have to ask twice, Miss Lorraine. I may be dumb, but I'm not stupid. What's goin' on is between you and Mr. Ike." He nodded, then flicked the reins.

She said, "Looks like you got somethin' on your mind."

"Might not be anything you want to hear."

They neared the ranch. "Out with it—you're about to burst."

Bert drew the horse to a halt. "Just think you're shortchangin' your husband if you don't level with him about whatever it is. I know I wouldn't want my wife keepin' secrets from me."

Lorraine took a deep breath. With a wave of her hand, she said, "Let's go." Her sight blurred. She and Ike had always been honest with each other, leaned on each other during hard times—and there'd been so many.

Honesty was one of the few things life hadn't stolen from them. Yet.

Chapter Five

Late Winter

Buster was the first to see them coming, or at least to notice that someone was coming. Three blurry images rode toward the ranch from the north under the afternoon sun. Even at a distance, he could tell they weren't horsemen, bouncing as if in a contest to see who could pop up the highest. When they were still a way off, Buster yelled toward the barn. "Ike! Come on out."

The rancher looked out of the small tack room with a shoeing hammer in his hand. Wasn't room enough for a forge, too. "What're you fussin' at me for, old man? I'm doin' the blacksmithin' you're too darn ornery to do. Not sure why I keep you around anymore. You can't even hardly walk these days. Guess I'd be in a fix with Lorraine if I was to shoo you off, though."

Buster waved the back of his hand at him. "You get yourself in tussles with your wife all by your lonesome. Don't have nothin' to do with me. Come over here, willya?"

Ike put the tool down and wiped his hands on a thick, dirty apron. He came outside and limped toward the corral where young Bert worked on a lower rail.

Buster had a hand cupped over his eyes to shade the bright winter sun. He stayed in its warmth as much as he could these days. Chilblains were always lurking, just waiting for him to get even a little cold again. He pointed north. "Take a look-see."

The riders were close enough now that Ike could make out three men in dark suits with heavy riding coats.

Buster said, "You know 'em?"

"Can't say as I do. Don't recollect seein' any of 'em before. Mighty strange. Never seen the like out here. A man's gotta intend on ridin' here to end up here." Without looking his way, Ike said, "Bert, you heeled?"

"Yessir, Mr. Ike."

The young man still wouldn't call him 'Ike' even though he'd been here at the ranch for nigh onto eight years. The best shot of the three. "Free up your Colt but leave your hands loose—these fellas don't look like they're comin' to make trouble. And call Rowdy." Bert was the best whistler of the three, too.

Ike swiveled to see Jessie and young Sonny playing with her hoop in the mostly barren yard. Lorraine always planted a summer/early fall garden, but the plot was past its prime now, as browning corn stalks bent toward the earth beside the house.

"Jessie! Take your brother inside, please."

Bert whistled, and Rowdy came and sat next to him. With his size, he looked like he'd be a good watchdog, even though the worst he'd ever do was lick someone to death.

When the three strangers pulled up by the front of the house, Ike nodded. "Afternoon."

The one in the middle nodded back. "Are you Ike McAlister?"

"Been called other names, but yeah. And who would you all be?" He looped a thumb over his belt.

"Good. You're the man I came to see."

"Not sure why you'd ride all the way out here, mister, but if you're plannin' to stay for a spell, how about y'all get down from your mounts? Don't fancy a crick in my neck."

The three swung off. The older one in the middle had an air of prosperity about him—fine clothes, a gold watch chain tucked into a vest pocket, fancy-tooled boots. Ike wiped a hand over his dusty shirt and tilted his hat back. The other two riders worked for the string tie in the middle, no doubt. They were unsmiling, eyes shifting to take in the surroundings. One held a bouquet of flowers that didn't square with the wary look on his face.

"My name's Stilwell, Thomas Stilwell." He said his name like it meant something and flipped a lazy hand at his men. "These are my associates." The two stood motionless, hands at their sides. "Is there somewhere we can talk, Mr. McAlister?" He scanned the ranch with a slight lift of his chin. "Perhaps inside your … sturdy … house?"

Ike's neck burned. True, the ranch wasn't much to show for what had it been—eight, nine years now? But Lorraine kept everything spotless and made the place a fine home for him and their two growing children. They had everything they needed, and that had always been enough. He kept telling himself that. A home for Buster and Bert, too.

He stared at Stilwell. "Almost sounded like you were chewin' on somethin' sour the way you said that. Or did I get that wrong?"

"Uh, no, Mr. McAlister, certainly nothing of the sort. I apologize if I offended you. That was not my intent at all. If you prefer, we could talk right here."

Ike was about to agree when Lorraine's voice rang out from behind. "Ike! Bring our visitors in the house, please, and out of the weather." A west wind was stirring darkening clouds. With a bit of luck, the gusts would bring a welcome storm to this dry land, but the fickle sky had teased so many times before. The high basin was bedded down as winter claimed the browning hills of his South Park home. Could be another heavy snow, too. Never could tell what was coming. He smoothed his short beard with a calloused hand, his worn cotton pants loose on his tall frame—and squinted at the visitors.

Buster glanced at his friend, leaned on his cane, and stepped forward. "Gentlemen, you heard the woman. Won't you please follow me?" He put a hand on Ike's back, turned him in Lorraine's direction, and forced him toward the house. Bert tarried behind to tend the horses as the group stepped up the short stairs into the house.

Inside, the two men took their hats off and held them by the brims like fig leaves, while Stilwell stood chest-out like a preening rooster. Lorraine forced a smile. "You all got a mite dusty ridin' here, and I'm guessin' from your clothes that you ain't from up Como way or anywhere else in the Park."

Stilwell said, "No, ma'am, we're from Denver but brought our horses on the South Park railroad and rode here from there. Como, that is."

"Well, fine. Why don't you all come sit at the table, and I'll fix coffees?"

"Thank you, Mrs. McAlister. I believe I'll take you up on that." He turned, and one of his men handed him the flowers. "I took the liberty, Mrs. McAlister …"

"Yes?"

"To bring you these chrysanthemums, although they could never match your beauty." With a look from him, the two sidekicks backed away from the table.

Lorraine raised her eyebrows. "Why, thank you, Mister …?"

"Stilwell, ma'am. Thomas Stilwell, at your service." A swoop of a plumed hat was all that was missing.

"Very thoughtful, Mr. Stilwell." Lorraine turned to find something to put them in and came up with a tall glass she filled with water. As she placed it on the small table, she turned the slight crack in the 'vase' away. She eyed Ike and motioned to the table. He worked his way down into a chair across from Stilwell while Buster brought a steaming china cup over. She carried the last ones and sat next to her husband, with Buster on the other side.

"And your associates, Mr. Stilwell?"

"Uh, Mr. Strothers and Mr. Dobbs."

Lorraine nodded their way.

Ike sized him up. Looked around forty, maybe forty-five, a gray tone working its way through black hair. He'd been working on the paunch for some time, judging from its size. As he sipped, the man seemed soft around the edges, like the give in an old mattress that had once been firm.

Ike said, "What can we do for you, sir?"

His wife broke in. "Pardon our manners, Mr. Stilwell. I'm Lorraine McAlister, and you've met my good-lookin' husband, Ike. Buster's to my right too, which I find a comfort. What brings you out here? We're a long way from Denver."

Ike half-smiled. His wife always did have a way of getting to the point.

"Not as far as it used to be with the South Park running now. Well, still as far, but not as long anymore. And that's what I'd like to talk with you about, Mr. McAlister—the railroad. Would Buster mind showing my men around outside?"

Ike said, "I believe he looks pretty comfortable right where he is. But your men can join Bert at the corral if they're of a mind to."

Stilwell cleared his throat. "I've heard you weren't too fond of the idea of the railroad running right through here a few years back."

Ike took a long sip, then placed his cup carefully back on the table. How did the man know about that? "That about sums it up. And it's running through Como now instead of here."

"Yes, and you played a big part in that. Word is you're a pretty influential person in South Park."

Ike shook his head. "I'm just a small rancher tryin' to outwit the elements day by day. Sometimes they win, and sometimes I get the upper hand. Either way, you play the cards you're dealt."

"Oh, Mr. McAlister, hardly. You seem to have a way with people, getting them to do your bidding. Like you did with my railroad."

Ike clasped his hands in a white-knuckled grip in front of him. *His* railroad? "Years back now."

Stilwell sported a smirk. "Only a few years, and people have a way of remembering things, don't you think?"

Ike took another sip so his mouth wouldn't betray him.

Buster broke in. "Mister … uh … Stilwell, don't seem likely you came all this distance by accident, did you? A body kind of has to want to get here to be here."

Lorraine smiled her pasty smile, one her husband had seen often. "Yes, Mr. Stilwell, we're all interested in why you and your men have come. Won't you tell us?"

"Yes, quite. As you may know, I serve as president of the Denver, South Park, and Pacific Railroad, which has just come into South Park by way of Como—as you said. We recently had the inaugural run of the railroad through this section and are quite proud of the business it's going to … the way it's going to improve the lives of everyone around here." He swept an arm in a grand arc. From the look on his face, if words could puff a chest, those would have swelled his.

Ike drummed his fingers. "That's already gettin' to be old news, Mr. Stilwell." He looked back over his shoulder at the two men standing behind him. "Read about that in the *Cottonwood Courier* a ways back. Now, if there's nothin' else, I got work to do."

As Ike rose, the visitor did as well. "A moment, please, Mr. McAlister. I have an offer I hope you'll be interested in."

A glare from Lorraine, and Ike sat.

"You may not know that we—the railroad—have a … security problem." Stilwell twirled one end of his too-big-for-his-face graying mustache. "Yes, I'm afraid we're the target of thieves. Some of our equipment has been purloined"—he dragged the word out—"from our yards and our routes." Tension etched the man's face. "And so, that's why I'm here. To see if you would be willing to join forces with us."

"Join forces?" Ike looked around the room. "There ain't nobody here but me and Lorraine, and two tired hands."

Buster grinned. "He means 'hired.' By the by, I been meanin' to mention that. 'Hired' means you pay somebody, don't it? I ain't been paid for years now. Figure I got me a right smart sum comin'. Got plans to stay warm on a beach in Mexico. Just wonderin' when I can expect all that back pay?"

Ike smiled under his beard. The old coot. He always did have a way of easing things. "About the same time as you get your next raise."

"Well now, that's somethin' to look forward to. That'll sure get me out of bed in the mornings here on out."

"That right? Then I should have given you one sooner. Get you up earlier." Ike couldn't hide his grin anymore.

Buster's laughter echoed through the small house.

Lorraine rolled her eyes and turned to Stilwell. "Why don't you tell us about this offer?"

"Come work for me at the South Park, Ike. You'll be handsomely paid." He pivoted to Lorraine. "Your two children, Jessie and Sonny, right?"

Lorraine scrunched her napkin. How did he know that?

"They're in school in Cottonwood?"

Lorraine's eyes widened. They went when the weather cooperated. "Yes, why?"

"Because they could be going to a real nice school in Denver, with all the advantages a big city offers both you and the children."

Ike glanced at his wife. "We like it here just fine."

"And I understand that blizzard nearly decimated your herd. How many head did you lose?"

A flush warmed Ike's neck. How did he know that? "We're still okay unless another bad one comes." He'd never wanted to punch a man in the mouth as much as right now.

"Well, no matter. What I'd be paying you would allow you to restock your herd and—"

Lorraine interrupted. "Let us talk about this, Mr. Stilwell, will you? How can we reach you?"

"Why don't you let me transport you both to Denver in one of our luxurious passenger cars? I'll put you up in the finest hotel in town, the Centennial, and we can discuss it further in my office … would you let me do that, ma'am?"

Ike clenched his fists. "Like my wife said, we'll be in touch."

"Would you like to know how much we'd pay you, Mr. McAlister?"

Ike glanced at Lorraine, whose face revealed nothing. She rose, which brought conversation to a halt. The men did the same.

"Thank you for stopping by, sir." She nodded to the others, walked to the front door, and opened it.

Bert stood outside by the horses, reins in hand. "I watered and fed 'em, Mr. Ike, like I knew you'd want."

The young man who kidnapped his pregnant wife, Lorraine, years back had grown into a reliable helper. Took a particular interest in working with Sonny, teaching him how to rope and ride when Lorraine would let him.

She stood on the porch as the men walked out. "Thank you, Bert. That was quite fast."

He beamed. "Mr. Ike says you can do a job fast or slow, long as it's done right. I like fast better."

"That's my husband. Hand those horses over to our guests, will you? These fine gentlemen are needin' to get back to Como." She smiled at the railroad man.

Stilwell's companions didn't move until he nodded, then all three mounted up. He touched the brim of his too-wide hat. "Thank you, Mrs. McAlister, for a most pleasant visit. Nice to meet you, Mr. McAlister, and see your ranch. I look forward to hearing from you soon. And I trust you'll be discreet about our visit?"

Ike stared back silently.

As they turned to leave, Buster sidled up next to him and whispered, "Don't know about them three, Ike. Somethin's makin' my neck itch, and—"

Ike glanced at his friend. "You should probably sit this one out, Buster. No sense wadin' into the middle of a muddle."

"You know I can't do that. Your troubles a ways back was what saved me from drinkin' myself to death. So, the way I figure it, some of the fixes you get in do me good. Not many, but some. And this feels like it might be one of 'em."

Chapter Six

Ike watched the railroaders go, their dust lazing in the cold afternoon air behind them.

Lorraine called from the porch. "You weren't very friendly, Mr. McAlister. What was that all about?"

"Stilwell rubbed me the wrong way. My gut's always steered me straight, and I reckon I won't ignore it now. Him talkin' about our money troubles!"

"So, what are you thinkin'?"

"I'm thinkin' you shouldn't have invited them in."

Lorraine glared at her husband. "Don't be turnin' this back on me, mister. I never could tell you what to do, Ike McAlister." But as she walked back into the house, she wondered. What *would* her husband think of working for the railroad instead of himself? Would he even consider it?

Ike limped to the tack room and set about doing work that didn't need to be done. Things always seemed to clear up some when he was pounding on a piece of metal. Stilwell lived in a different world, one he knew little of and one he'd never had a hankering to find out more about. The rhythm of the clanging bought him some distance from his changing world. His children were growing up, Sonny almost five. What had he accomplished since the War? And Lorraine. Married her away from the Cottonwood bed and breakfast, which had provided for her. Not always well, but she'd owned the place all those years ago. His younger brother, Rob, gone too. Gritty Kansas rides with him after the War, chasing so-called guerrillas. Nothing but killers and thieves who deserved what he and Rob served up. But sheriffing in Cottonwood took Rob several years ago—far too early.

His and Lorraine's small spread had never done very well, in either good times or bad. The bad stretches he expected—that's most of what life dealt out here. The good times … well, they didn't seem to come around very often. Lorraine was his constant, though. Without her, who knows? Maybe he'd have been a drifter signing onto cattle drives in the spring and drinking away his wages the rest of the year. Maybe even a highwayman. Likely never would have had his own place and probably no children. That stopped his wandering thoughts … he couldn't imagine life without them. His hammering grew louder.

***

As her man disappeared into the barn, Lorraine had no doubt he was chewing on the man's fine clothes, sleek horse, tooled saddle. But Ike had always been more than enough for her. In her eyes, their ranch was plenty good and the house a beautiful home. The children, well, they were an undeserved blessing. Wanted to have more, but the good Lord didn't see fit. She turned back to the house, a hand to her side. Whatever that pain was, as she thought on it, had been there a while, lurking in the background but reminding her always. She wiped her brow and cleared the cups from the worn kitchen table.

"Children, outside with you before it's too dark to play. And feed the dogs, Jessie."

Another glance outside. Buster was holding forth with Bert about something in the corral. Those two had been drawn to each other ever since Bert came to be with them. One, an old drunk, now sober, who poured his life out for too many years in treacherous high mountains that ringed the Park to the west, and the other, a foolish young man who made a big mistake kidnapping her. A mistake Ike gnawed on like a bone before Lorraine made him agree the boy could stay. Ever since, Bert had sought his approval like a puppy dog looking for a warm lap to curl up in. No longer a youth, Bert had proved his mettle time and again. Wrangled pretty good, too. A keeper. A second chance that had turned out.

Lorraine gazed north toward Cottonwood, where Ike's sister, Sue, lived. The town hadn't grown much since she came here years ago from Denver. Back then, Lorraine's boarding house barely got by, but it was where she first met Ike, so it would always hold a special place in her heart. Bert usually went with her on trips to town for supplies these days. Wasn't that far. After shopping, sometimes she'd seek Sue out at the old boarding house. She'd taken it over when Lorraine left for the ranch. Her husband, Hugh, the sheriff, was usually gone when she stopped by, lawing around town somewhere. Lorraine smiled. Known around town as the "Professor." A good man, and he'd sure fooled them years ago with his English accent and airs.

On those trips to town, Bert hung around The Sew Pretty, the dress shop where Hannah worked—unless they were scrapping. Those two had been off and on these past years. Why hadn't they gotten married? Heavens knows Bert wanted to. Hannah still struggled with her past, though. Maybe she'd never work through those hurts since she'd watched Lorraine cut her wicked father down on Cottonwood's main street years ago. Didn't seem like time had mended that wound. Maybe it never would.

"Mama! Come look!" Sonny had the breathless charm of youth. He pulled her out of the house, she stumbling slightly. His small hand pointed with excited fingers as they stood together with Jessie. "Look at that!"

The Good Lord had painted the western sky with bright oranges tinged with gray borders bleeding into swatches of blue. Happened most nights, but still, she'd never taken it for granted. Jessie grasped her hand, and they stood while the heavenly canvas changed before them. The colors softened as if to wave goodbye and disappeared behind the ramparts, safely tucked away until tomorrow. A lighter gray swept across fading daylight, somehow a proper color for the Painter to end the day with.

Lorraine reached down to her son and hugged him lightly. Soft tears streaked her face as she straightened to pull Jessie close, too. What gifts. She turned to go back inside. With hands to her knees, she climbed the front steps.

What was wrong with her?

Chapter Seven

Buster crouched as he pulled Ally's foreleg into a bend. It was easier to get down these days than back up. The storm had been gone now almost a week, but it had nearly done him in, and his hands shook with a life of their own. Lost most of the feeling in his feet, too—not that they weren't heading that direction anyway. He rubbed a hand over the horse's taut leg while Ike pounded away in the barn. He shook his head as he put the leg down, careful to use his body as a shield between his friend and about the only horse he'd ever seen Ike on. He worked his way back up and swept a hand over Ally's chestnut neck, now flecked with gray. Another long stroke over her back with a brush. Ike never said much about the mare's warhorse days. That senseless War past almost fifteen years now. So many men … Ally nudged his hand, and Buster wrapped his fingers around the apple in his pocket. She always knew. So smart. He drew it out, and the apple disappeared.

He glanced back at the barn where Ike worked away. His best friend—pretty much his only one—spent a lot of time there. Always looked like he was working, and he was, but Buster knew Ike was mostly figuring. He pursed his lips, then released Ally back into the corral. Ike's horse, Ike's decision about that leg. He closed the corral gate with a light pull. No way he was going over to the tack room. Ike had probably seen him examining Ally anyway. He scratched at his neck as he searched for some way to look busy. Bert was at the water pump, and he tottered that way. The hammering stopped, just like Buster figured it would.

Ike's irregular strides sounded behind him. Couldn't mistake that *thump-thump, thump-thump* gait. Headed toward the corral. Buster wiped at the trimmed beard he kept tidied up for Lorraine. No doubt he'd been a mess when she first saw him years ago. Being a drunk would do that. He still had nightmares about that deadly winter mountain trek years back. Those foolish, headstrong settlers. Should never have agreed to take them in such harsh—still couldn't erase the sight of that sightless child from his head. But being taken in by Ike and Lorraine had sobered him up. Saved his life, just like they'd straightened a wayward Bert out, too.

His mind said, *Don't turn* to the sound of the steps, but his body didn't take the hint.

***

The corral gate creaked open, and Ike limped to his horse, his arms full of hay he dumped in her wooden peach basket. He rested a hand on Ally's muzzle and ran his palm along the winding scar on her side, still visible in the waning light. Hair was scarce around it. She bobbed her head as she always did when she thought they were off on an adventure, but he kept a steady hand under her neck, her eyes—brown pools of pain—never leaving his. He told her how pretty she still was and worked himself down to a kneel. When his hand circled the left fetlock, he felt the heat. He rubbed up and down the leg.

"What'd you go and do, girl?"

But he knew. She'd kicked out in distress in her stall during the storm. Wasn't hard to see the new gouges at the bottom of the wooden gate. Ally had always healed quickly, but that leg looked like it was going to take some time. Still a strong horse with a spirit not to be denied. The leg didn't need binding—Ally was smart enough to know not to stress it. Seemed like whatever he was thinking ended up in her head, too.

Damn storm. Almost killed him and Buster, and Penny too. Left its mark on all of them, Buster most of all. The man had almost shaken the bed—and the house—apart for two days after. Had a stiffness about him that hadn't been there before. Rheumy eyes that looked like he'd been drinking. Cussed old man. He'd *told* those two to head back in with him, but hearing had never been Buster's long suit. Wasn't his hearing that kept him after the scattered herd that day, though—it was his heart. The man had always been loyal, something hard to find in this harsh land. Never had known someone so set in his ways, but Lorraine also said the same about her husband more than once. A short chuckle, and he looked toward the ranch house.

His wife tried to hide her pain, but she couldn't keep it a secret. Her wrinkled forehead, fake smiles, and stilted walk all added up to something. That in a woman who'd never complained about the hardship of anything. Every time he started to ask how she was, she either waved him off or changed the subject. Used her favorite phrase to do it. 'Nothin' ain't nothin' to fret about, cowboy.' How many times had he heard that?

He brushed Ally's coat and rummaged through memories of when he first 'met' his wife. Not exactly the usual *Howdy* do, *ma'am*, seeing as how she'd shot at him, which made Ally rear and dump him on his bad hip. Should have known then to steer clear of Lorraine Blanchard, but as he looked back, those cards were already dealt. And a fine hand it turned out to be.

He gave Ally a pat on the rump after she finished eating and admired her as she walked to that favorite spot of hers nearest the house and the children. He turned back to the barn, his mind awash with questions. Never had spent much time thinking on things outside of the ranch, but this one had him buffaloed. What was Stilwell all about? Ike and the railroad had never seen eye to eye, and now the man was offering him a job as head of security. Why? He'd never done anything close to lawing, had never considered it. Brother Rob had, though, and paid with his life. He didn't intend to do the same. Cottonwood brought joy to the McAlisters over the years, but the town had also cruelly sliced at the family.

Buster came in and headed for his horse, the gray that didn't look like much. But then, he'd always said they were a good match in that way.

"You thinkin' of goin' for a ride?"

The old man nodded as he drew his saddle off a wooden rail. "Figured to. Care to join me?"

Buster's way of saying he had something on his mind, so Ike reckoned he ought to hear him out. They saddled up and rode west along the rolling hills of the Park. He gazed at the brown landscape, then lifted his eyes to the snowy ramparts rising almost to the top of the western sky in the distance. A far cry from Kansas. Colorado had taken hold of his heart and become his home. What had it been, eleven, twelve years since he'd come here to settle up with that killer Manning and his gang? The man who shot his father in Lawrence and left his mother to die. But he'd met his end on the street in Cottonwood. Fate has a way of catching up with everyone.

He eyed his friend. Buster stared straight ahead, not saying anything, but talking nonetheless.

"You got somethin' to say, spill it straight."

"You ain't said much since Stilwell left, Ike."

"Not much to say."

"We both know different. You been chewin' on his words."

Ike rubbed a hand over the back of his neck. That much was true. "Don't know what you want me to say, Buster."

"What's the sense of bein' friends if you never tell me nothin' important?"

"Things are a swirl right now."

"You gonna take him up on his offer?"

"Why'd he come see me, after me fightin' that railroad he says is his a ways back? And now to go to work for them?" He shook his head. "Can't make heads or tails of why he'd want me. There's others do security in Denver—Pinkerton's boys and the like."

"Why you still gnawin' on it, then?"

"Gnawin's one thing, swallowin's another."

"What're you thinkin' of doin', Ike?"

There it was, finally out in the open between them. "Don't rightly know at this point, but reckon I've only got one choice. May not be the smartest thing to do, but I know it's the right thing."

"Smart don't matter when it bumps up against right."

"Denver's a chance to take care of this family in a way I ain't never been able to do before, Buster, and when you've never had money, it looks pretty good. And Lorraine could get some proper doctorin'. I may not have much, but I do have them."

Buster nodded. "Then you got plenty. I started out with nothin', and I still got most of it left."

Talk died away, like everything that needed to be said had been. They traveled in a winding loop that took in most of what day there was left. This time of year, when the sun started down, it skedaddled in a hurry.

"I'm startin' to chill up, Ike. Let's get back to that warm house of yours."

"Guess it's gonna be yours and Bert's now for the time bein'." As he eyed his friend, he knew he didn't have to worry about the ranch.

They turned and headed for the house. The dogs barked him a greeting while Lorraine brought cooked-up canned peas from her garden to the table.

"These are the last we have 'til spring, so I thought I'd better fix 'em 'fore they get all mushy." She kept her eyes cast down, hiding the pain in them.

Ike bent over and lifted her chin, his gaze holding hers hard. "How're you feelin'?"

"I'm fine, just a touch tired."

He worked to a seat next to her. That wasn't it, that wasn't what was bringing her low. "Tell me true, Lorraine. What's wrong with you? And don't tell me 'you're fine' anymore." He sat down next to her. "What is it?"

She put the peas aside and rested her hands on the table, her bottom lip trembling. "I don't know, Ike. I shoulda told you before, but when I went into town the other day, I stopped in to see Doc Early while Bert did the shoppin'. Doc says he's not sure what I got, but the way he said it led me to believe he has an idea. Said to come back to see him in a week." Her cheeks flushed. "Sorry."

"For what?" Ike stood, his arms spread wide.

"You don't need a cripple for a wife right now. Things are bad enough as it is, what with losin' so many head recent. Won't have enough breedin' stock come springtime. That'll hit hard next fall in the yearling sale. What'll we do then?"

"You're talkin' about next year? You should—"

"I'm thinkin' about this family, Ike, and what's ahead of us. I don't like what I see, and I know you see it, too. You're just too prideful to admit it."

He leaned forward and took her hand. "What're you sayin'?"

"I'm thinkin' about that offer Stilwell made. Don't know why he did it, but makes sense, considerin'. I know you been thinkin' on it, too. Talk to me."

"Is that what you want?"

"Bert and Buster know how to run things here. I'm thinkin' there's a reason they were both spared in that storm—so's they could do exactly what I just said."

"Sounds like you got this all figured out."

"I been percolatin' on it some."

She'd just said what he'd been thinking but hadn't had the courage to bring up. "The only reason I'd consider it would be to get you better care. Big city—probably got docs all over the place. Heal you right up."

"But you hate cities."

"And I love you."

"Well … the children would have a real school there. Others to play with, too. I'm guessing you'd make good money—"

Her look said she left something unsaid.

"Like I never have before, is that what you were gonna say?" His neck burned, but he pushed back the anger behind it. There were more important things in play here than his feelings.

She reached across the table and took his hand.

Whatever life was about to throw at them, they'd face it together.

Chapter Eight

The three men rode into the small town of Cottonwood as evening clouds escorted the rising moon. Stilwell walked his horse down the middle of the dusty main street, past what looked like a boarding house, and up to a saloon called Wildfire. "We'll be stayin' overnight, boys. Next train'll come through Como about midday tomorrow. Drinks are on me." They dismounted and strode inside, swinging doors flapping behind them. When Stilwell walked in, heads turned, as the Wildfire didn't usually have customers as well-dressed as him.

He scanned the place. "Dobbs, go grab that table next to the poker game. Lucky, get us some whiskeys. Better yet, get a bottle." Wasn't much to see through the smoky haze—cowboys' night out, from the looks of it. His glance came to rest on a saloon gal. Prettier than any he'd seen in Denver. What was she doing in this dreary town? A sharp woman who could have her pick of places to work, so maybe there was a reason she was here. Hiding out? Her hair was brownish and done up, not like the other girls, who wore theirs down, using their long hair as an invitation. A woman that pretty had to work at fitting into a place like this.

She was young, but her makeup made her look older than her years. Stilwell watched as a steady stream of customers angled her way, only to be sent packing after a minute or so. If she didn't want company, what was she doing in here? He stared until she lifted her head from a whiskey and her gaze swung around the room. Her eyes swept past him to the bartender, who brought her another. She raised it to the last customer she'd shooed off, and he nodded back.

Stilwell motioned to the barkeep. "Who's that woman?" He didn't have to point her out; the bartender knew who he was asking about.

"Miss Tibbie."

"Tibbie? Never heard a name like that before. How'd she come by it?"

The bartender shrugged his shoulders and asked if he wanted another.

"Yeah … sure." Stilwell couldn't tear his eyes away from her.

As the barman walked away, he said back over his shoulder, "Her parents."

"Her parents, what?"

"Where she got the name."

"Sounds like there's a story behind it."

"We've all got stories, but from what I've seen, she's likely got more than most."

He waved the man off and sat with his men. "Lucky, ask her over here."

"Uh, boss …"

"Do it."

The sidekick rose and approached the woman, who gave him a steely gaze in answer to his question. Lucky raised his hands in the air as he came back to the table. "She said—"

"I could tell what she said. Sit down." Stilwell rose and walked over. He took his hat off and stuck a hand in his silk vest pocket. "Ma'am, I'm visiting from out of town and wondered if I could buy you a drink?"

She looked right through him. "Yes."

Stilwell motioned to the bartender. He started to pull a chair out when daggers flew from her eyes. "Uh, do you mind if I sit?"

"I said you could buy me a drink—didn't say you could sit down. That chair's taken. All of them here are."

"So … waiting for someone, huh? Stands to reason a beautiful woman like yourself wouldn't be alone."

"As you say, waitin' for someone …" She stared until he turned back to his table with a slight bow.

Dobbs said, "Thought you'd be sittin' over there or bringin' her back here. You don't come away empty-handed on much you go after." He elbowed Lucky with a grin, which quickly disappeared under Stilwell's stony stare.

He rubbed his eyes. "Getting late, boys. Time you went and got us rooms. Two. One for me, and you figure out the other. Try that boarding house we passed on the way here. I'll be along directly."

"Do we gotta, boss? We wuz just gettin' limbered up here. And this string tie's stranglin' me. Can I—"

That silent stare told the answer. The two rose and left by the open front doors. Stilwell swigged his glass and strode past the saloon girl to the poker table. "How's a visitor get into this game?"

No reaction. Hard-bitten faces stared at the cards in their hands.

He'd take a softer tack. "I'd like to join if I may." He scanned to see who was losing the worst and handed the man a golden eagle for his seat. The bleary-eyed townie grabbed the twenty bucks and hurried off to the bar. Stilwell pulled out a wad of money just long enough so that everyone saw it as he sat. He waited until the hand was over and placed two fifty-dollar bills on the wooden table in front of him. "Will this be all right to start, gentlemen?"

When he'd cleaned out the last man, he rose and tipped his hat to the circle of scowling faces. One of them said, "Wouldn't advise comin' back, mister. Your luck might run out somewhere along the line."

Stilwell nodded as he swept winnings into his hat. "Sounds like good advice. Been a pleasure, I'm sure." As he left the saloon, he flipped the leather loop off his Colt and headed for the boarding house, alert for any night sounds behind him. When he got there, he looked the place over. Tired—like the rest of the town. Losing the railroad to Como hadn't helped Cottonwood prosper, which meant there were likely rooms available most every night. Ha. McAlister's chickens had come home to roost.

A well-dressed man greeted him as he entered.

"Good evening, sir. We are pleased to have the pleasure of your company."

Stilwell regarded the tall stranger, his strange accent and manner.

"Pardon my manners. My name is Hugh Walnutt, sheriff here in Cottonwood. This is my wife's boarding house, so welcome." A slight bow.

An Englishman here? And the law in this forlorn place? Fine jacket, nice string tie, nothing out of place, but no badge showing. Never would have figured this. Stilwell nodded. "Thank you. Is my room ready?"

"Here is the key. Upstairs and to the right, second one down. Your fellows are next door and already settled. They said you would pay." A short chuckle. "My wife, Sue, sets breakfast at seven. Shall we call you?"

"Not necessary, thank you."

***

Morning brought bright light that reduced the linen curtains on his bedroom window to nothing. At least the sun hadn't abandoned this place like everything else had. Stilwell splashed his face in the washbasin and dressed, making sure his clothes made a fitting appearance. He checked his gold watch and placed it back in his vest pocket. Dusty though he was, at least he was the best-dressed—huh

… maybe not. That sheriff came to mind. Any man who looked like a dandy must not be much of a lawman. Either that or he was someone better left alone.

Stilwell came down to the dining room just as a handsome, youngish woman laid a platter on the sturdy wooden table— steaming eggs, some sort of meat, probably venison, and fat biscuits. Hot coffee. He nodded to her.

"I'm Thomas Stilwell, ma'am, and this is a fine place you have here. I'm guessing this breakfast will be as agreeable as my visit to your fair town has been so far." He said it in such a way that if he'd had a hat, he would have doffed it.

She glanced sideways at him as she poured coffee. "Morning, Mr. Stilwell. I'm Sue Walnutt, proprietress. I hope your sleep wasn't fitful."

"Not in the least, Mrs. Walnutt, thank you."

His two men filtered in and sat on either side of him, neither acknowledging Sue. Stilwell upbraided them.

"Where are your manners, boys? Introduce yourselves to our hostess."

They mumbled their names.

"Excuse them, please. They aren't often in the company of ladies, and I'm afraid this trip has taken a toll on our hygiene."

She smiled, but it didn't reach her eyes.

When he finished, Stilwell patted his mouth with his napkin. "I was looking forward to seeing your husband this morning, ma'am. I understand he's sheriff of this fine town."

"Has been for a while."

"I understand that, too."

"He's already up and gone, sir. Lawing don't wait for nothing."

"So I'm told. Thank you for your hospitality, and we'll be on our way."

The other two rose with Stilwell and nodded. As he neared the front door, the railroader turned back.

"By the way, did I hear that you are Ike McAlister's sister?"

Sue almost dropped a tray as she lifted it off the table. "Why, yes; you know my brother?"

"Met him for the first time yesterday at his ranch, and a fine place it is."

Her face held a question she wasn't asking. Maybe she could help convince McAlister, though.

"Told him I'd like him to come work for me." He smoothed his mustache.

She set the platter down. "Work for you? What do you mean?"

"Yes, I represent the Denver, South Park, and Pacific Railroad, based in Denver. I believe you have heard of us?"

"But that's the railroad—" She stopped. Wouldn't do to air out the family's laundry with a boarder.

He waited, and when she didn't finish, he said, "And we just completed a new leg to Como. Quite an accomplishment."

He stood puffed out like he'd swallowed a balloon.

"Likely we'll have the track to Fairplay finished soon, too. Goes some of the way now. I plan to get it there before next winter. Could use a good man like your brother."

Sue wanted to say lots of things in reply but just nodded.

"Ma'am." He swung his large hat on and, with a perfunctory bow, excused himself, his men in tow.

The ride to Como took short of an hour. Stilwell drew his stallion up at the sparkling new railroad roundhouse and dismounted.

A soft snoring came from the station master's office as he approached. He smacked his leather riding crop on the desk, and an old man behind it nearly fell backward off his chair. Stilwell squinted.

"Who're you, and why are you sullying my office?"

The white-haired man wiped a hand over his weathered face. "This your office? They said it was just gonna be me here."

"Not any longer. You're fired. Strothers, you take over."

"But, Boss, I'm goin' back to Denver with you."

"Not anymore. Get yourself comfortable. I'll have your things sent. Besides, I need someone to tell me what's going on here, so you'll be telegraphing me every day."

"But I don't know nothin' about messagin'."

"Then maybe hire this old fella here. Could be he knows telegraphing better than he knows how to stay awake. And where's that train? Should be coming through about now." He checked his gold fob watch.

The old man shuffled away until Stilwell stopped him.

"You there. Any messages today about the train?"

He looked back over his shoulder. "Not sure what you just said. Along with sleepin' too much, my hearin's gone bad. I got a good memory, though—it's just short. Reckon you don't need a worn-out old codger like me. I'm sure your young fella can handle the learnin'."

Stilwell rubbed his chin. "Wait … just wait a minute. No need to hurry off." He strode over to the man. "Is there anything that might help your memory?"

"Now that you mention it …"

He had no reaction to the dollar Stilwell produced, but a five-dollar bill got his attention.

"Remember anything now?"

"Uh-huh. Got a coupla messages earlier. Somethin' about a hold-up west 'tween here and Fairplay."

Stilwell squinted when the man said no more. "A hold-up? Did they make off with anything?" Today was a weekly silver run from the mines this side of Fairplay.

The man pursed his lips. "Not sure I remember."

Stilwell held out another fiver, and the man ignored it. Ten dollars later, he said, "Wire mentioned a shipment of silver or some sort that ain't there anymore."

"Damn!" Stilwell whacked his hat on his pants.

Just then, the telegraph keys clacked to life. Stilwell fastened his gaze on the man, who stared back.

"What's that saying?"

"Not sure I can hear it this far away, but then again, I don't work here no more."

"Yes, you do! Now tell me."

The man craned his neck. "Don't that beat all. Fairplay says the robbers took off with the cache south, which would put them somewhere just to the west of us now. Wouldn't be surprised if we don't see 'em crestin' that hill there 'fore long."

Stilwell looked west and scanned the railroad bed just coming to life.

"Get back in there and tell Denver."

"So, you hirin' me back? How 'bout a raise?"

Stilwell nodded, eyes still fixed on the western bluffs. Without turning, he said, "What's your name?"

"Just."

He turned. "That short for Justin?"

"Nope."

"What's the last name?"

"Desserts."

Chapter Nine

Lorraine took a long look around the small ranch house. Would this be the last time she saw it? The bed where Jessie and Sonny had come to be. The mattress was lumpy but filled with tender memories. She stepped out onto the porch as Ike loaded the last of their belongings into the buckboard. They left the old, broken-down wagon out on the range as a reminder of nature's power to amaze and cripple. Ike had painstakingly built a new one as winter continued to fight him. The dogs circled near, Rowdy leaping into the buckboard. Ike lifted Penny in as well. She had plenty of heart, but the old girl didn't have much jump left in her legs.

"Why don't you leave Rowdy here to look after us fellas, Ike? Somebody has to. Take Penny, 'cause Jessie wouldn't stand for nothin' else."

Buster's words held truth. Ike called the dog off the buckboard.

Lorraine's small garden seemed to wilt even more as she stared at it. It never produced much of anything, just a few greens she fussed over to keep some color around the house. Every year, when the peas and tomatoes ripened, she procrastinated in picking them, wanting living things around as long as possible. She even felt a little melancholy canning the vegetables back in the fall, knowing winter was right around the corner. She left them too long last fall, as usual, and the big storm did the rest.

"Are you ready, Lorraine?" Ike took her by the hand as she stepped down the stairs one at a time. She limped to where Buster and Bert stood wide-eyed. With a quick hug to each, she said, "I'll miss you both more than you know." Ike led her around to the bouncy seat up front, boosted her by the waist, and wrapped a heavy blanket around her.

"Wait. Please." Small tears glistened on her cheeks as she rested a hand on the new buckboard frame.

Jessie reached out from the bed. "Are you okay, Mama?"

"Yes, dear. Just some dust." She nodded, and Ike snapped the reins. The horse pulled the McAlister clan away with a rocking gait over scrabbly ground. Lorraine wondered if the jarring ride was mocking her. She worked so hard to make the ranch a home all these years, and now a single wagon held all that was dear to her.

As they rolled along, Lorraine held tight to the wrought iron rail that bookended her seat. Every jolt coursed through her, while tingling fingers and legs mocked her. Constant cramped muscles bore the brunt. She never heard from Doc Early about what this was, meaning he probably didn't know either. All she wanted was some rest from it. She had been so tired lately.

Recent conversations with Ike had been surprising. He was the one pushing to start anew in Denver and leave the ranch to Buster and Bert. He had been the one who said he'd leave Ally here; she wouldn't do well in a big city. He was the one who talked about better schooling for the kids. He had never mentioned the real reason, but she knew. His eyes always reflected Ike's true feelings, and she saw her pain in his. She had almost refused to go, knowing how much the ranch meant to him. Her, too, but his gentle persistence had broken through her unspoken fears. Illness had stripped away most of what it meant to be a mother or wife anymore, the two things closest to her heart. And that helpless look her husband carried these days tore at her soul. She knew what he was thinking. His face always said more than he did.

The trip to Denver that Stilwell hosted went well and made her more comfortable about moving there. He feted and regaled them and finally seemed to win Ike over. Her husband didn't said much, but she was used to that. She also knew him well enough to recognize that his silence held a different edge this time. Something lay underneath it that he wasn't telling her. It took two weeks of him cajoling her before she agreed. And she thought he'd be the one dragging his feet.

***

Ike would never have figured it. The visit Stilwell arranged hadn't been too bad, all in all. The man put them up in the Centennial Hotel, the best in town, and the railroader was nothing but gracious. Ike had seen some big cities during the War, but Denver was different—wasn't all shot up. Bustling. New. Had an energy to it he'd never seen before, except when nature had a bad day—which happened often out on the Park. Most of all, Ike wanted to know if Lorraine liked the city. See what her eyes said. Stilwell even brought in a schoolteacher who patiently answered her questions. The man was smarter than he looked.

He always believed there was a time and place for everything, and now was the time for this move—for his wife and children. Wasn't exactly sure how his herd was going to make it through the winter. With fewer cattle now, though, maybe he had enough hay stored. Ranchers aim to run out of winter before they run out of feed. And Buster couldn't afford to get chilled again, so the winter workload would fall mostly to Bert. Ike shook his head as they wagoned, but the young man had proven himself these past few years. He should thank him for his good work, but he had a hard time parsing out compliments Bert's way. The image of a near-dead Lorraine Bert kidnapped years ago still flew through Ike's head on and off. Why couldn't he let that go? A failing on his part, as Lorraine reminded him often enough.

Anything Bert still didn't know about ranching, Buster could teach him, so things would probably be all right here. Maybe. No one but him had ever run the ranch, creating a small doubt that made his stomach a touch unpleasant. It didn't really matter, though, because he'd let nothing get in the way of their move. He prayed, but what if there wasn't a doctor in Denver who could heal Lorraine? What then?

The land reminded him of riding these hills with Buster. He owed the man more than he could repay, but that was true of most of the people he knew. His friend had encouraged Lorraine about the move several times these past couple of weeks. She likely listened to him as much or more than she did her husband. Buster had broken through somehow; Ike would have to ask the old trapper what he did so he could try the same sometime. Buster always spoke from the heart.

Truth stood on its own two feet, even if a body didn't want to hear it, and never knew there was such a thing as a lie.

But the decision was made, and now they were on their way to the Como train station.

At Cottonwood, they pulled up at Sue's boarding house. No telling when they'd see family again. Ike lifted Lorraine off the front seat and helped her to the front door. Before he could even knock, Sue came running out and flung her arms around her sister-in-law.

"Oh!" Lorraine muffled a painful cry.

Sue stepped back. "I'm so sorry, Lorraine. I didn't know you were hurting so much."

"I ain't that bad off, just that jostlin' on the way here."

"Well, come on in and set a spell." Sue guided the family to the front parlor. "Ike, would you please fetch us a couple of coffees?"

Her brother came back with two lukewarm cups. "Is Hugh around?"

Sue said, "I know he's in the office today; you could probably find him there."

"I'll be back soon enough, all right?"

Lorraine waved him out.

Midday sun warmed him as he crossed the street to the sheriff's office and jiggled the door open. That latch never did work right. "You awake, lawman?"

Hugh Walnutt rose from behind his desk and stuck his hand out with a big smile. "Englishmen are always early risers." He motioned to a chair. "What brings you here, brother-in-law?"

"Passin' through on our way to Denver. Wanted to let you know we're movin' there."

"I say, moving to the city? But you are a rancher, Ike."

"The ranch is in good hands." Likely.

"Even so, why are you uprooting your family?"

A question he wondered about often enough. He didn't want to lay it all on Lorraine's illness, so he said, "I'll be workin' for the railroad."

"Would that be the same one you contended with all those years ago? The one that tried to bully people and buy all the small ranches around here?"

"One and the same." He enjoyed hearing Hugh's proper English diction, so foreign to everyone else.

"That seems contrary, I must say. You will be doing what, then, may I ask? I did not know you knew anything about railroading."

Another question he'd been asking himself. "They tell me I'll be the head of security." Ike rolled tobacco in a cigarette paper, licked it closed, swiped a match on the rough desk, and lit it. "I may need some pointers on what I'm doin' from you."

"I am at your service." A short bow.

"Things change, Hugh. Hope you and Lorraine will come visit us."

"Excellent! Another adventure. I am—how do you say?—in!"

More like misadventure. What was he getting his family into?

Chapter Ten

April 1870

Ike climbed the wide granite steps that led into the handsome stone railroad building. Hard to miss this place. The marbled lobby was canopied by a majestic rotunda painted with a mountain scene—mountain lions, wolves, and bears. Matching white marble stairs rose in a winding fashion to a second story. As he climbed, he ran his hands over smooth brass railings that looked like they'd been shined this morning. At the top, he recognized one of Stilwell's men who'd called on him at the ranch.

"Welcome to Denver, Ike, and the Railroad. Uh, may I call you Ike?"

Ike nodded and shook his hand. The man gestured to the right. A thick green carpet, the color of money, ran down the hall—a first for his boots. Everyone else in the building wore shoes.

The man—what was his name?—showed him into an office with two large windows framing a view of the Rocky Mountains to the west. A blinding afternoon sun, backdropped by an intense blue sky, warmed the room. This had to be the man's office. A grand golden oak desk and matching swivel chair took up most of it. Pictures of local city scenes hung on the wall. Or … maybe this was the previous security chief's office—someone he knew nothing about at this point. Maybe he'd try to rectify that.

"Welcome to your office, Ike. How do you like it?"

He glanced at the thick rug. "Much too nice for a busted-up wrangler like me." He eyed the man. "I ain't too good with names. Remind me of yours."

"I'm Dobbs, Ben Dobbs. I help out around here."

Helps out? "Mind if I ask doing what?" That sounded rude the way he said it, but he let it lay there.

"I do a little bit of everything, and there's been a lot of that lately."

The way he said that gave Ike pause. Maybe it was his tone or the smug look on his face.

"Let me know if you need anything." Dobbs touched his hat brim, turned, and disappeared out the door.

Ike eased himself into the wooden chair in front of his desk. Wasn't ready to claim the large upholstered one behind it yet. A far cry from the timeworn ranch furnishings that had served his family well. How much did a man really need? All this? How about a roof that didn't leak in a hard rain, windows that kept some of the cold out, and a wife and children who warmed the house? A vision of Lorraine climbing the short stairs to their home flashed through his mind. He'd done this for her, moved them all, like she'd done for him and the family for so long. Didn't know how long he was supposed to stay in the office—did he have regular hours? But he needed to see Lorraine. He grabbed his hat from the ornate brass hook and headed toward the Centennial.

All in all, the move had gone better than he thought it would. The company found them a home not far away, bigger than anything he'd ever been in, much less seen. Would be ready for them to move into soon. He could walk to work now. Stilwell had also taken time to introduce Lorraine to his doctor. He owed the man for all that but wasn't sure how he felt about being in someone's debt. He'd gone with her to see him, but this doctor didn't seem to have any better idea about what ailed her than Doc Early. The only thing he'd said was that she needed rest.

"That's all I've been gettin'." She shook her head and lay down on the dark velvet divan in their hotel room. Finally, she shooed him out of the room and told him to go back to work. "I'll be fine here, Ike. Got the children—them and you's all I need. Go on now."

He snapped back and wiped his brow with a new linen hanky embroidered with a picture of a train.

Back at the railroad office building, he marveled at how tall it was. Four stories, imagine that. People he didn't know had been coming and going for weeks as he fumbled in his office for something to do. No Stilwell yet. The lettering on his door was barely dry when someone called his name from down the hall.

"Mr. McAlister. Ike McAlister!"

Ike stood in front of the desk as a young man hurried into his office.

"Courier, sir. Your ranch's been attacked." He held out a piece of paper.

The words were barely out of the youth's mouth when Ike snatched the telegram and hurried past him into the paneled hallway. He raced down the back stairs two at a time, even with his bad hip. Sprinting into the brilliant sunshine, he semi-ran several blocks to the Centennial Hotel.

"Hello, Mr.—"

The desk clerk's words bounced off his back as he rushed up the stairs to find Lorraine. He threw their room door open and … no one. Downstairs, he leaned into the man. "Where is she?"

"I … um … I'm not sure. She left about an hour ago."

"Where would she go?"

"Maybe the millinery, where they sell dresses and hats. Or maybe …" The man's voice drifted away.

No, that wasn't Lorraine. She'd never complained about things she didn't have like other women did. Always took the most joy in her family and her faith. And now she was in a strange city fifty-some miles distant from their ranch in South Park. And he'd taken her away. Truth be told, Ike wasn't eager to leave either, but what was wrong with her? The railroad's hefty offer had just cinched the move.

All that vanished as he searched for her. Should he get the kids from their new school or find Lorraine first? As he hurried down the street, glancing side to side, he clenched and unclenched his fists. Read the damn telegram again.

Western Union spread in large block letters across the top.

Ike McAlister

Ranch attacked Stop Raiders Stop Buster hurt Stop Hurry Stop

Bert

The paper shook in his hand. He stared at it as if it was in a foreign language. Buster hurt? How bad? Couldn't be good. His old friend had grown more crickety the past few years. He rubbed a hand over his face. Think. Looking for Lorraine was taking too long. He stopped the first man he saw on the wooden plank sidewalk. "Where's the telegram office?"

"Turn around, go a block, take a right, and you'll see it on the left."

Ike thrust the telegraph door open and roused the startled clerk.

"What can I do for you, sir?"

"Send a telegram to Cottonwood in South Park."

The dispatcher laid his hand on the brass tapper. "Yes, sir, go ahead."

"Send it to Bert at the McAlister ranch. Say, 'I'm comin',' and sign it 'Ike.' That'll be enough to get it where it needs to go." Ike threw a dime on the man's desk and hurried out the door for the hotel.

In the lobby, he pointed a finger at the clerk. "See to it my wife gets this telegram. Tell her I'm leavin' for the ranch."

At the railway station, he checked the schedules. No train for South Park until tomorrow—one a day. He yelled to the stationmaster. "Where's the stables?"

"Just head down thataway long enough and you'll smell 'em. 'Course, could be cattle you're smellin' too—stockyard's not far off either. Anyway—"

The man's words faded away as Ike lit out in a limping run. At the livery, he cornered a man pitching clean straw into a stall. "Need a horse, a good one that won't give out on me. Make sure. Saddle him and be quick."

The stable hand led a mare out of another stall, heaved a saddle off a rail, threw it on, and cinched it. Fastened the bridle. "You wanna buy her or just ride?"

Ike said, "How much?"

The man rubbed his chin, eyeing Ike up and down. Ike figured he was taking in his new clothes—a nice suit with a black string tie.

"Well, this is my best horse, and that saddle's just come from a rich widow. Said it was the best one she'd ever seen. Fine tooled leather, it is."

Ike pitched a five-dollar bill to the man, most of his first month's pay. The stabler caught it but didn't look at it. Ike said, "That's all you're gettin'," and led the mare out. A quick stop in the mercantile for a canteen, water, and dried jerky, and he'd be on his way. Matches, too.

The way to South Park was one he remembered even after all these years. Follow the South Platte west, then push along the foothills that rose in the distance. Up and over Kenosha Pass, the high mountain gateway to the Park—his and Lorraine's home all these years. How long had it been? Almost fifteen summers since he first came to Cottonwood after the War. Several of those memories still needed more fading.

The mount ran sound as they loped toward the distant hills that fringed the city to the west. No doubt Lorraine would have a piece of him for setting off without her—a large piece, and rightly so—leaving her to corral the children and figure out their next move. She'd be up to it, though; always had been the one taking care of the family.

As he rode, his mood darkened. He wouldn't have made her and the kids leave their home just for some job dangled in front of him. In a big city, too, and now someone attacked the ranch. Wasn't Indians. His friend, the Ute chief Rain Water, must have warned other tribes away because there had been no raids in recent years.

"Damn!" His shout echoed in the thin air.

He'd taken off with no thought except getting to the ranch as quickly as possible. Had forgotten to grab his Colt from the hotel room but did pack some oats from the stable.

How long would the ride take? His mind raced along with the horse.

The sun balanced on top of the western heights ahead. It would only teeter a little longer, which meant less than an hour of daylight left. He'd never liked night riding, a holdover from the War. When the sun sank this time of year, it did so in a hurry, along with the temperature.

What would it dip to tonight? Twenty? Maybe twenty-five with no weather.

At least he'd been smart enough to bring the heavy winter coat from his office. But once again, he'd spun into action without much thought, like Buster said he tended to do. He could hear the man's slow drawl in his mind. 'Use your head, Ike.'

How badly was his old friend hurt? He wasn't that strong anymore. Too many bitter mountain winters had exacted a harsh price.

But he better not have died on him.

The route grew more jumbled as the horse left the wide Platte basin and trotted along the base of the rising hills. A bushel of diamonds masquerading as stars littered the early evening sky. In the dim moonlight along the heights he rode, cool nights had ushered in a blanket of brown.

His thoughts whirled back to the ranch.

Had it only been a few weeks since he'd packed the family up and taken the train—now his train, he guessed—to Denver?

At least he'd gotten Lorraine out of there before more bad weather came. Seemed like good timing, with heavy winter snows still ahead.

But as he rode, he wondered.

Had that ever been a good plan?

He eased the mare upward at a diagonal along the sloping hills to his right. He'd feel better higher, looking down on things. The rushing waters of the South Platte below to his left would be his guide.

Night closed in fast as he climbed, and by the time he reached the hilltops, the little light left was scurrying away in a hurry.

His neck flushed. He shouldn't have left without finding Lorraine and telling her himself, not letting her read the telegram alone.

That truth added to an already bitter taste souring his mouth as his mind pivoted back to the attack.

Dusk drove the landscape into darkening shadows. Scrubby plants clung to uneven ground among the lodgepole pine forest that spiked the hillside. The mare leaned into the slope—Ike as well.

Granite formations bulged as they passed, as if to gulp their share of the thin air. He guided the mare around the detritus that calved off the large rocks and lay splayed across the forest floor.

He laid his left hand on the horse's neck, then patted her buckskin coat as they navigated the rise to their right.

Riding a different mount was a new experience that sparked anew one of his many regrets—leaving Ally behind.

Qualms seemed to pile on top of each other as he got older.

But his horse wasn't one to live in a city. She'd lived running free and was meant to go out the same way.

Lord willing, the raiders left her alone.

A noise below grabbed his attention.

Somewhere in the murky distance, riders galloped beside the riverbed toward him, their hooves clicking on river rock.

Maybe the same riders who hit his ranch.

Who else would be out here this late at night?

Not likely they'd seen him, as high as he was.

How many? Three, maybe four.

How should he handle this?

Couldn't just let them ride by, whoever they were.

He pulled the mare to a stop—a little too hard. Her left foreleg slipped, and they lurched downhill in a crazy dance.

As the horse pitched forward, Ike spun off and hit the ground hard.

The bullet in his hip reminded him it was still there.

That War still had a long reach.

No way he could stop the stumbling animal's descent—catching his breath and finding some cover was about all he could manage.

The horse would have to fend for herself.

Muffled voices echoed from the valley walls below.

He was hidden no more.

Chapter Eleven

Lorraine hobbled through the aisles of the large dress shop with a hand on the tables. So many pretty outfits. And all the bolts of cloth, bursting with color. But what was she doing coming in here? She'd never done anything as bold as this. Women in plumed hats and long dresses glided throughout the store, fingertips lightly traveling over silk taffeta gowns. Another sight she'd never seen before, and a far cry from the mostly browns of their ranch. The only dress shop in Cottonwood—the only other one she'd seen—The Sew Pretty, paled in comparison. She shouldn't be out walking around, but today was a good day, which meant she didn't hurt as bad. She did a few back-and-forths past the window before turning the doorknob and easing in through the door. Maybe she could blend in without anyone noticing.

"Why, hello there!"

No such luck. A smallish woman hailed her from across the shop with a raised hand. For someone so little, she moved fast. Silvering hair done up in a bun, and she wore a broad smile as she approached.

She came to a halt in front of Lorraine and looked up. "Hello, dearie, how can I help you?"

Lorraine didn't want help; she just wanted out. "Um … I just came in to look, is all."

"Well, that's why we're here. Why don't we take a look together at some new things I've just gotten in? My name's Agnes, by the way." The woman took her by the arm and pointed the way.

"I really don't have time today. Perhaps I could come back?" She tried to hide her limp.

The storekeeper glanced at her. "Will you be bringing your husband in? There are so many people in town who want to meet him."

How did the woman know who she was? "I … don't … um—"

Lorraine felt the woman eyeing her up and down.

"Come over here, honey. Sit and have a cup of tea with me, won't you? Sometimes I get lonely with all these women in my store wrapped up in themselves."

The words weren't out of her mouth before Lorraine felt a hand to her back, gently guiding her forward.

They headed toward a small alcove at the back of the store. Several finely dressed ladies sniffed as she passed.

The woman said, "Come, come, don't mind them. They keep me in business. Aren't those hats something, though? Whoo!"

Lorraine smoothed her flower-print dress and put a hand to her simple, embroidered collar as she walked. A familiar warmth rose upward from her neck. Dowdy. She knew the word—had never felt the feeling before.

"Let's sit here, shall we?" Agnes sat in one of two cushioned chairs, and Lorraine eased herself into the other. What was the woman doing? A black pot lay on the table between them, along with two saucers and cups.

"Let me pour, all right?" Dark tea streamed from the fancy china spout. "Sugar? I like two lumps these days—used to be I'd drink it without any when I was younger. Helps me mask my other pains now."

There. The woman's sweet smile again. Lorraine relaxed her grip on the chair's arms.

"No, thank you. Never been partial to sugar in much of anything, so haven't missed it."

"Have you found lodging yet outside of the hotel, Lorraine?"

"Yes, but turns out it's not ready. How do you know so much about me, ma'am?"

Agnes took a sip and grinned. "Call me Agnes, please, or Aggie if you prefer. I'm harmless, but I'm a hopeless busybody—know most everything that goes on in this city. So, let's get back to you, dearie. Tell me about the children."

Lorraine stopped being surprised and sat back in the chair. The pain in her knees eased, and the black tea warmed her throughout as she sipped. Felt so good.

"Well, Jessie—Jessica—is almost ten, and Sonny five." She took another sip. "I'm afraid she hasn't taken the move well. New school, new surroundings, no friends." Wasn't hard to figure why her firstborn longed to return to the ranch. "Sonny seems to be doin' some better, but I think it's easier on boys somehow. Always has taken after his father."

"Children adapt. How are you doing?"

"I'm gettin' along. Don't know what to do with myself most of the time, though." She gripped the chair arm and smiled a small smile. "I believe you're one of the few people I've spoken with since we came." Another sip warmed her. "My husband—"

"Yes, tell me about Mr. McAlister. Heard he's been brought in to tighten things up at the South Park."

"The South Park?" And what did 'tightening things up' mean?

"Oh, that's just the name people hereabouts call the Denver, South Park, and Pacific Railroad. Easier, isn't it?"

"Yes, I suppose. I'm not sure what you mean by 'tightenin' things up,' though."

"Oh, fiddlesticks. Just an old woman spouting off with nothing else to do, I am. Don't mind me." She took another long sip and avoided eye contact. When she put the cup down, she said, "Heard they made him a mighty nice offer."

Lorraine's turn to take a long sip. It *had* been surprising that the railroad would pay Ike that much money. Back in South Park, they'd always had what they needed, but that was all. Money didn't matter to her, but Mr. Stilwell kept raising and raising the offer. Couldn't figure it.

Agnes glanced at her sideways, the cup held to her mouth. "There are stories that he worked against the railroad when it was supposed to start through South Park years ago. That true?"

Who was this woman? Did she mean harm?

"Lots of things happened a while back. Stories are just stories, aren't they?"

Why all the questions? She glanced at the woman's hand where a wedding band would have been. Empty, but with a slight indentation on the ring finger. Maybe it was time to leave.

"I have to get some errands done. Thank you for the tea and your fine company."

The shopkeeper didn't move to get up. "And how is your husband adapting to the city?"

That stopped her. A question with an answer she hadn't figured out—the man was a master at hiding his thoughts. She often had to pull them out, like a hammer yanking a rusty nail out of an unwilling board. How *was* he adjusting? She let the woman's question hang in the air.

Agnes took a last sip and set the empty cup on the table next to her. She rose with a hand out to help Lorraine up.

"Don't mind me. I'm a nosy so-and-so, but I don't repeat what I hear. It's how I've stayed in business here for so long. The things I could tell you." She fluffed a hand in the air, took Lorraine by the arm, and guided her past the high-fashion women on their way out.

On the wooden sidewalk, she said, "How long have you been dealing with this pain?"

Her heart thumped. "Is it that obvious?"

"Your eyes give it away as much as your body does. Why don't you let me walk you to your hotel? The Centennial, isn't it?"

Before Lorraine could respond, Agnes turned back to the customers primping in her store.

"I'm afraid we're closing early today, ladies. I do hope you'll allow me to pamper you another day."

When she'd ushered the last ones out, she pulled a key from her frock and locked the front door behind her. She slid her arm through Lorraine's again.

"This way, dearie."

When they neared the hotel, someone shouted her name.

"Mrs. McAlister, wait, please!"

She turned to see the hotel desk clerk hurrying toward her at what must be high speed for a man of his years.

"Yes?"

"I was gonna wait until you came back, ma'am, but thought I'd better start lookin' for you. Uh, your husband wanted you to see this."

The clerk held a piece of paper out. Looked like it had already been folded—and unfolded—more than once.

Lorraine opened it and read. And again.

What?

She skimmed the words a third time and squinted at the clerk. "Where's my husband?"

"He took off, ma'am."

"Where?" Her heart thumped.

"I reckon he's headed back to your ranch, from what he said."

"But no train's left town recently, has it?"

"No, ma'am, ain't one headin' west agin 'til tomorrow."

Her heart sank. "Then … he's ridin', isn't he?"

A nod.

"Damn him!" Several ladies stared as she limped into the lobby. "Mind your own business!" She turned toward the staircase.

Agnes put a hand out. "Lorraine, what do you have in mind?"

"I'm goin' after him." She grabbed the handrail and pulled herself up the first step.

"What about the children?"

That stopped her. They couldn't go with her. All the worries she'd stowed away these past few months burst forth, and tears streamed down her cheeks.

Agnes put an arm around her waist. "I have an idea. Would you mind hearing me out?"

Lorraine wiped at her nose.

"You and I know you're in no shape to travel right now, and your children need their mother. Would you consider—be willing to—come stay at my house while we work some things out? You and the children would be welcome company. It's a big house for a widow like me—lonely, too."

Lorraine sat heavily on the staircase with her head in her hands. "I don't know what to say, don't know what to do. Ike's goin' back to the ranch? What's happened?"

"Now, don't fret about that right now. Let me help you upstairs, and we can pack your things while I send my helper, Olivia, for your children. I can have the hotel clerk take your belongings to my place—would that be all right? Okay?"

Without waiting for a reply, Agnes took her by the arm and started up the stairs, Lorraine's cheeks wet from weeping.

Chapter Twelve

The evening's dark was Ike's friend. Rushing waters echoed rhythmically in the gorge as he listened to the voices below and tried to sort out who they were—and what they were going to do now that they had his mount.

"This here horse musta had a rider, Nate."

"You figured that out all by yourself, did you?"

"Uh … yup, but the saddle helped. We gonna try and find him?"

"Yeah, dummy. No reason a man would be out here at night unless he was up to somethin'—like us. Check the horse for any markin's that say where he came from."

Silence. Then, "Nothin', Nate."

Sounded like three of them to Ike's ear. Likely the ones who attacked his ranch from what they said.

"You two ride up the hillside here. I'll go on ahead some, then up."

"Ain't sure about that, Nate. Horses is pretty tuckered out from all the ridin' they been doin' tonight. Got ourselves busted up some back there, too. That one old man … 'Sides, we already done what we came for. Maybe we oughta let it go and head straight for Denver."

"No. Loose ends tend to unwind, and this here feels like a loose end."

Their voices drifted up to Ike in the night air. That's all he needed to know. But how bad did they hit the place, and how were his friends? He'd settle up with these outlaws, but now he couldn't do much except hide. As long as he didn't move, he had a chance. He pushed into a small bush and lay still. Stickers. Bad choice, but moonlight tended to hide things that weren't moving. He'd never figured out why that was but was grateful for it now. Couldn't leave his bad leg extended—might be too easy to spot—so he inched it in and cupped a hand over his mouth against the pain.

Someone scrambled over loose rock in the distance ahead. Far enough away for Ike to stretch his leg some—just as another man cocked a weapon right below him. Rifle from the sound of it. Don't move that leg an inch. Would have to work to do that anyway—the thing was numb. Probably couldn't even stand without falling down. At least he'd drawn his pistol while prone. Hadn't taken the time in Denver to grab his gun belt with his worn Colt, though. Only thing he had was the small Webley the Company gave him. Another mistake among several he'd made recently. Small enough to carry around in his suit pocket, but didn't pack a punch like the Colt.

He trained the short barrel on the night sounds coming closer. There. A rider stood facing him, silhouetted against the dim moonlight, scanning the surroundings not fifteen feet away. Had he seen him? He must have. Ike considered. He could drop him—the Webley could shoot at least that far—but that would bring the other two, and he could hardly move. No, better to stay put and take his chances.

Shouts from a distance. "Ain't gonna find him in this dark, Nate. Probably already gone, or maybe he—"

Then again, might just as well settle up with them now.

Pow!

The Webley split the night air. A tumbling sound followed as the tracker dropped from sight. Was he dead? Now he'd done it. The other two would be bushwhacking their way toward the shot. He struggled to a shaky stand on one foot while he tried to will feeling back into the other leg. He stumbled over to check the man, knowing that made him an easy target. There. He reached down and felt for a pulse—dead.

A man's voice wafted his way. "You get 'im, Nate?"

Ike yelled a muffled, "Yup," through his cupped hand. Wasn't sure if the two bought it, but he'd find out soon enough. He worked his way to a prone position next to the same shrub, the leg tingling now as he flattened.

A fine time to be caught without his rifle. Even in the cool dark, he wiped sweat from his eyes. He yanked the cussed string tie off and waited. Never did like anything around his neck. Clouds blown by a building north wind drifted across the heavens, and the moon played a game of peek-a-boo. The skittering light would be to his advantage—about the only one he had lying on this cooling hillside.

Dark pine needles lay everywhere and served to soften the sound of the approaching horses, but one of the riders' voices came clearly. "Nate! Where are you?"

Should he answer or let them stray into range? He cupped a hand over his mouth again with a muted, "Here."

"Where? Keep talkin'. Can't see nothin' in this blamed dark."

He'd said enough. Now they'd have to get themselves killed without more of his help. And he was ready to oblige. He cursed himself as he lay. Should have grabbed the dead man's pistol. Wasn't thinking straight.

The night riders dismounted among the pines.

"Where are you? Hey!"

Not far away now. They rustled through low shrubs that sheltered beneath tall lodgepoles. Ike rested his arm on a small granite rock and gripped the pistol with a sweaty hand. The Webley was new to him, but considering its size and load, he'd have to lure both raiders close before firing.

Near now. A man appeared out of the gloom, rifle angled in front of him. Ike waited for the second hunter, but only the one stepped toward him, scanning left and right. Not close enough.

Where was the third one? If Ike dropped this hombre, it would tip the other off. The rifleman closed in, then stopped and knelt. Ike couldn't see what the shooter was doing, but he had to be near the man Ike killed.

"Duncan! Nate's dead! Over here!"

Not good … but maybe it was, because it would bring the third man into the open. But maybe it wasn't, because Ike was outgunned and any surprise gone.

Sounds to his rear. Don't turn, don't twitch. Looked like the other rifleman circled and came up almost directly behind him. The man nearly stepped on his bad leg as he passed by. When he'd cleared, Ike scraped his boot over the scree, and the man turned. Ike dropped him, which sent the last one crouching out of sight. Not much chance of getting out of this now, with only his peashooter. Silence lay over the hillside like a shroud. Only thing Ike could do was wait until the last man made a move—gave himself away.

A night wind picked up in the wrong direction. Bad timing. He didn't need any sounds he made carrying to the last man in the still air. How many times had Buster hectored him about that? The old coot better be alive.

The night's silence gave way to crunching sounds ahead. Gravel underfoot. Was the raider—yes, he had to be leaving. The noises faded. Was probably scrambling downhill for the horses.

Ike struggled up, hefted the dead man's rifle, and tried to keep the sounds within earshot, but couldn't hear past his own stumbling. No matter. He'd keep heading downhill until he reached the river and figure things out then. Needed to get there before the outlaw galloped away.

How much farther down did he have to go? In between his limping steps, he caught a sound ahead. Hurry. His boot heel gave way on a small rock, and suddenly he was down, tumbling over and over before ending up on his back against a middling rock, leg on fire. The rifle lay somewhere behind him, wrested from his grasp during the fall. He brushed at a cut on his cheek and struggled up as a shot rang out in the night air.

Nowhere close, but he got to a stand just as the commotion of thudding hooves rose from below. He hurled a rock at the retreating sound, then collapsed to a seat on the sloping hillside.

Couldn't do anything but stay for the night now. How bad were things at the ranch? And Buster, that old rascal. Probably tried to take on the night riders—would be just like him.

A gimpy Ike took nearly an hour to locate his mount. Poor horse had tumbled down the slope toward the rushing river and stood by the waters, eyeing him like, what was *that* all about?

He dropped the horse's reins, undid his thin bedroll, and scraped rocks away from a level spot.

A long night just got longer.

Chapter Thirteen

Lorraine rubbed her eyes open and gazed around the fancy bedroom. Gauzy drapes—and the sheets—were they linen? Where was—oh! The woman in the dress shop. What was her name again? And the telegram that turned her world upside down yesterday. Served Lorraine right for being somewhere she shouldn't have been—that hifalutin shop. She had no business in an expensive place like that. And where were the children?

Those thoughts were interrupted by a knock on the door, followed by a small woman who bustled right in, carrying a tray.

"About time you woke up, missy. Thought I was going to have to come in here and check for a pulse. Now, sit up, won't you?" The woman's bright smile matched the sunlight that streamed through several windows.

Lorraine passed a hand over the fine fabric bedspread. "I never oversleep—I mean, at the ranch with the chores and all." Lorraine let the words drift away as she pushed herself up, and the woman placed the tray across her legs. A round silver top hid her breakfast. The china tray itself was nicer than anything she ever had at the ranch house.

"Well, I'm glad you did today, dear. You look like you needed some rest."

Did she really look that bad? "I should be gettin' up and lookin' after my children—"

"Oh, they're fine, playing with my cats downstairs."

Lorraine placed the tray to the side. "I'd like to see them, please. Thank you."

"After breakfast." She put the tray back.

Clearly, this woman wasn't going to be deterred.

When Lorraine finished, Agnes said, "You don't remember my name, do you, sweetheart? I can see it in your eyes."

Lorraine eased from the bed and fumbled her dress on over her chemise. "Um …" She straightened up and tried to hide a grimace. "Actually, no, I don't. Sorry."

"I thought as much. You had a lot on your mind yesterday. It's Agnes, by the way—Agnes Franklin. Just call me Aggie for short, because I'm, well, short!" With a chuckle, she said, "Let's go find those children of yours."

"I'll just be a second, if you don't mind. Where …"

"The outhouse is in the backyard. Can't miss it. I try to keep it tidy, but sometimes drifters use it at night, so watch yourself."

When Lorraine limped back in, she took a quick look in the silvered mirror in the hallway. Had she ever been this pale? Never mind, couldn't do much about it anyway. She brushed her hair. The house was grander than anything she'd ever seen, but that didn't take much. How did—didn't matter.

Downstairs, Agnes led her toward a large room. Lorraine could hear the children from here. She walked slowly into the paneled library, and they ran to her, their squeezes sweet agony. Tears seemed to pop from her eyes.

"Momma, you're crying." Jessie wiped at her momma's cheeks.

"I'm just so glad to see you, is all."

Sonny drew close, and Lorraine pasted a wan smile on. She shooed the children over to the warm hearth and whispered to Agnes. "What do you hear about my husband and the ranch?"

"Haven't heard a thing, dearie, but they say no news is good news. I expect this is where we should lean on the Good Lord."

How could she do that when He felt so far away?

Lorraine eased into a velvet-upholstered chair and motioned to the children. Waiting had never been her strong suit, but what choice did she have?

Those thoughts were cut short by Agnes. "Guess I know what you're thinking; you don't seem the type that waits for things to happen. Ranching and all would likely have seen to that. So—"

"Ma'am, there's someone here to see you and Miss Lorraine." Agnes' helper stood in the doorway and motioned toward the front door. "But I'm not sure you—"

"Out with it, Olivia."

"Um, it's Mr. Stilwell, in the front portico, ma'am. Should I escort him into the—"

"No. Leave him there. I'll go out to meet him."

The woman stood with an uncertain look on her face. A nod from Agnes, and she curtsied, then disappeared.

"You just set a spell there, Lorraine. I'll attend to this." With a finger to her lips, she swept down the hall.

Lorraine wasn't going to miss this, so she worked her way over to the open door. With a hand to her ear, she leaned into the hallway. The house's high ceilings tended to echo sounds, which should have made their conversation easy to hear, but with the children's noisy chatter, she had to work at it.

She didn't know Stilwell, having only met him a couple of times, but she'd already been around Agnes long enough to know she wasn't happy to see him. The woman's tone reeked of disdain she hadn't heard before. Something was between them, but what?

She only caught snippets. Soon, Agnes ushered Stilwell out and closed the heavy front door hard.

Lorraine shuffled as well as she could back to her chair just as her friend returned. She wanted to know more about their relationship, so she prompted Agnes. "That was nice of him to stop by. He seems like a regular sort."

Aggie looked like she'd just sucked on a lemon. "Not so much. The man's mean, but not around me. Said he dropped by to say hello, as if the last nine years he's never visited were nothing. And what he did to my husband. Man's got a syrupy way about him, don't you think? Never did care for that—on my flapjacks or people."

Lorraine kept silent. Better to let Agnes get out what she wanted to.

Her host peered at her, waiting for a response.

An uncomfortable silence followed. Lorraine couldn't look away. Finally, she said, "Uh … I just met him that one time—out at the ranch when he offered Ike the job here."

Agnes lifted an eyebrow. "Don't really know your husband, but can't figure a reason that puffed-up railroader would traipse all the way out your way to do that. Ike's a rancher, isn't he? What in the world does he know about steam railroading?"

She poured tea, and they stared into the fireplace's flames, the question lingering unanswered between them.

Lorraine took a sip, called the children over, and hugged them. There. That was better. They always managed to whisk worries away when she wrapped her arms around them, leaving cares to creep back in when they wiggled out.

Agnes poured again. "Strange visit, if you can call it that. He seemed fair interested in you, though—asked how you were doing— and you only met him a couple of times? Saw you peeking out into the hall, listening."

Why would he ask about her? And how did Agnes 'see' her?

She shook her head. "Huh. Never knew him to be the neighborly type. Usually has his toady do his bidding. What's his name? Never can remember." She handed the teacup and saucer back to Lorraine. "Think Stilwell had a brother—maybe a half-brother—but he died a few years back. No one else close to him I know of."

Lorraine sipped, and her stomach quieted. Seemed like it was out of sorts most of the time now.

As she sat in the snug living room, it felt so good to have someone wait on her.

And damn that Ike! Just like him to leave her to worry like this. Surely nothing would happen to him—would it?

Chapter Fourteen

Morning brought a harsh reminder of just how cold the night on the Pass had been. Ike snugged his buckskin coat tighter. It crinkled and cracked as he struggled to a stand by the South Platte, still in the grip of winter's icy crust. Frigid water assaulted his senses when he splashed his face. He wolfed down a cold breakfast of jerky and turned to the task of getting on his horse—which promised to be one of the hardest things he'd do today.

The horse must have wondered what he was doing back there, but Ike finally gained the saddle, bad leg out of the stirrup. The rutted road down the west side of Kenosha Pass presented almost as much danger as the dark did last night. Jumping on a horse and riding over unfamiliar ground wasn't the smartest thing he'd ever done. No sun on his back yet—looked like it was going to be late greeting the day. Galloping made no sense until it was lighter, although he wanted to race. For once, he was using his head.

At the bottom of the Pass, the Park leveled off to rolling hills that both revealed and then hid the faint lights of Como. As he passed through, he scanned the large railroad roundhouse going up and reined the horse south on the dirt path to Cottonwood. Change was coming to the Park on winter winds. Something he'd never looked forward to, the good and the bad it brought, but that seemed to be the way of things. Change hadn't been good for his friend Rain Water and the Utes, just pushed them farther west over the years. And he'd never have thought Sue's coming to Colorado would turn out as well as it had. But Lorraine and the children had been the best change in his life. Blessings he didn't deserve.

He reined in at the doctor's office in Cottonwood—someone he'd no doubt need if the attack had done what he thought it might have. Hastening in, he stared at a young man behind an old desk. "Where's Doc Early?"

The youth rose. "Passed away a couple of weeks ago."

"Sorry to hear—a good man. Have someone who knows how to doctor meet me at the McAlister place."

A faint, "She's already there," trailed after him as he ran out. What did that mean? He galloped along the familiar road to his ranch—heart in his throat as he rounded the last bend before his spread, searching for any movement.

An eerie silence shrouded the wooden ranch house. Ike reined to a halt out front with a thudding dismount, ignoring his bad leg. The front door stood open at an angle, off a hinge. "Buster! Buster!" He rushed in to find his friend sprawled on the cold floorboards, a young woman wiping his face with a cloth. Bert pushed up from a nearby chair, pain pinching his face.

"Bert! What happened?"

The young man stood for a moment, then slumped back into the chair. "Don't … rightly know, Mr. Ike. They … hit us fast, burst right through the door. Hardly had time to even look up before one of them butted me in the stomach, then knocked me upside the head." He held a hand to a bloody ear.

Ike knelt by Buster and glanced at the woman tending him. "How is he? And who're you?"

She didn't look up. "Name's Tibbie." After cutting away his torn shirt, she ran a hand along Buster's bleeding arm. "I can't get him to say anything other than moans. They hit him on the head pretty good. Maybe the butt end of a rifle. Hasn't made much sense since."

Whoever she was, looked like she knew what she was doing. Ike stared at his friend and pursed his lips. "Don't worry about him, his head's the hardest thing he's got. He'll be fine." Maybe saying it aloud would convince himself it was so. He bent down, his mouth near Buster's ear. "Can you hear me?"

The old man opened his eyes. "I'm … old, not … deef. Your breath … woo."

Ike stood with a finger pointed at his friend. "You old faker. Shoulda known you're too ornery to kill. Time you quit slackin' off." The man had more sand than anyone he knew. "Okay if me and Bert gentle him onto the bed?" A nod from the woman. He hoped Buster couldn't see the worry framing his face. Looked like his friend—just about his only friend—was busted up some inside, too, which was something he couldn't help with.

When they'd settled Buster in, Ike stepped out onto the front porch and squinted into the distance, Bert limping just behind. "Keep that rifle handy, son. Don't think you'll need it, but never know what these cowards might still have in mind."

"There's five of 'em, Mr. Ike. Three busted into the house 'til Buster shot one and I put a round into the one with a torch. Then they started hightailin' it. The bodies are around somewhere. One was groanin' outside somethin' fierce 'til he wasn't no more. I put the torch out, then crawled back inside and passed out."

"You did good, Bert. Real good." Ike squinted. "You say there was five?" He'd run into three on the trail here, and counting Buster's dead man, that only added up to four. Where was the man Bert shot? Must be the barn. Ally. He limped there only to see a body lying outside her open stall. He nudged the man with his barrel, then checked for a pulse. Dead. He stepped over him to see his horse backed against the far wall of the stall, front leg pawing the ground. Ike approached, saying, "It's me, girl. It's all right now." Her wide eyes radiated her frayed nerves. With a hand to the soft hair under her neck, he tried to calm her. Running a hand over her flank, he felt along the long scar where hair was scarce. His hand continued to her rear leg, then ran down to her hock, then to the dried blood on her hoof. All looked okay. His warhorse had been in worse situations. Ike squared away her feed and water, then closed the stall door behind him. He dragged the man out of the barn and left him next to a pile of dirty straw outside. The young woman stood on the front porch, wiping a cloth over her brow.

He said, "How long you been here?"

"A while. Came when your man found me at the boarding house after he sent you the telegram."

His sister Sue's boarding house. Hadn't seen her or her husband Hugh for some time now. He touched his hat brim. "Name's Ike McAlister."

Tibbie said, "I guessed who you were."

Bert came out of the house bent over some. "Sure glad you got here, Mr. Ike. Was hopin' my telegram would find you in that big city."

Ike nodded. "Pardon me, ma'am—uh, Tibbie—but still can't figure why you're here." He wasn't ready to give any strangers a pass today, even if it did look like she was helping.

"Well, since Doc died, I've also been doin' doctorin' in Cottonwood. Got some medical know-how, and no one else was steppin' up, so here I am."

Made sense as far as it went. He limped back into the house and started mixing up a potion Lorraine used when the kids were sick. Tibbie came in as he gave a small glass of it to Buster.

"What is that, Mr. McAlister?"

"Just somethin' we been usin' around here when needed."

"May I see it?" She smelled it and put it on the kitchen counter. "He's not sick, he's injured, and there's no room for both of us tending Buster, so if you want to stay, I'll leave."

Ike felt like he'd been caught raiding the cookie jar. "Uh ... I guess it oughta be you, with your healin' skill." He walked over to the bed. "Not sure how you do it, but you keep managin' to get yourself froze or beat up half to death. Just lie there and do what she says. Think you can stay out of trouble for a while?"

A wan smile. In a soft voice, Buster said, "Call this trouble? Pshaw. Ain't nothin' of the sort. Git."

The crinkle around Buster's eyes made Ike feel better about leaving. Not good, but better. He walked out to the porch. "Bert, you recognize any of 'em?"

"No, sir."

"I'm goin' to Cottonwood then. Can you handle things here?"

"Yes, sir."

"Like I said, I don't expect you'll have any more … visitors … today. Rats and cowards skedaddle when you shine a light on 'em. Miss Tibbie, would you like to ride back with me?"

"Thanks, but I'll stay here—need to do some more bandagin'—and watchin'."

He looked toward the barn. Should he ride Ally or take the horse he came in on? He rubbed the back of his neck. Looked like her hoof was good … but no sense pushing it. He'd be sure to be back soon and would saddle her for a ride then. "Uh, Bert, uh … mind helpin' me on up?" Embarrassing, but the leg had tightened considerably since that tumble on the Pass. The young man steadied the gelding while Ike double-pumped his way up and into the saddle. Soon, he was trotting the well-used path to Cottonwood.

Wasn't more than a few minutes into the ride when sounds of clip-clopping came his way. He guided the horse off the trail and waited behind a tree. Whoever it was couldn't be up to any good, and there was no way he was going to let him—likely a him—pass unheeded. Started to unloop the Colt he kept at the ranch but thought better of it. A rifle would give him more range, so he unsheathed his

Winchester instead. A shotgun would do nicely right about now, but he'd never carried one. Maybe he'd start.

As the rider came into view in the distance, Ike levered his rifle and fired skyward. "Stop right there, mister. State your business."

The rider's horse reared, then, "Is that you, Ike?"

The Professor's familiar English lilt. "Yeah, it's me, Hugh. About time you got out here, Sheriff, but I coulda shot you." He put the rifle away. Had to admit, nerves were making him jumpy as a hump-backed cat. Nighttime raids will do that.

"I was endeavoring to find out what transpired at your ranch. After I heard about the assault from the telegraph operator, I remained in town to determine if the brigands were inclined to ride back through or head south. When they did not appear, I departed Cottonwood for your ranch. And here I am—surprised to meet you here, I must say."

"That's two of us—and I saw 'em. Saw more of 'em than I wanted to. Three night riders were ridin' the Pass headed for Denver when I ran into them. Only one of 'em rode away." Ike rubbed his hip. It never had been worth a hoot since the War, but lots more fared worse than him. "I was just comin' your way, wanted to check on you and my sis."

"She will certainly be very glad to see you. It has been several months, if memory serves. Mind you watch yourself, though. She keeps her pistol at the ready inside the boarding house, especially now. I would suggest you announce yourself while still at a distance."

"Good to know, Hugh. Me and you got some catchin' up to do later, though. I'd like to pick your brain on some things."

"I am at your service, Ike. I will be traveling to your ranch now to assess matters. Are your friends uninjured, I hope?"

"Buster's in a bad way, but that ain't nothin' new. Still the toughest bird I know. Bert's busted up some, but he'll be okay. And there's a woman out there by the name of … uh, Tibbie. Know her?"

"Indeed. The saloon keeper brought her to town about a month ago, and it appears she has a modicum of medical knowledge as well. A fortuitous circumstance owing to the unfortunate passing of the doctor."

"Well, that's comin' in handy now. Did they hit town, too?"

"It seems not. I cannot think of a reason why they would target your ranch only, but it appears that is exactly what they did."

"I was wonderin' on that, too." Ike nodded and nudged his horse toward town.

As he drew near the boarding house, he shook his head. Hadn't seen his sister near enough lately, and with his brother gone these years now … She'd always been the strongest of the three. Sure, he and Rob had gone to war, but she cared for their parents and kept the home and the family newspaper business going. Worst, when Quantrill ransacked Lawrence, she dealt with their folks' deaths alone. Never whined about the hand she had to play. And the gumption it took to take off on her own for Denver, searching for their parents' killers. The toughest of the McAlister clan, for sure. The hard times he'd had were nothing compared to the way she'd pushed through life's grittiest stretches.

He pulled the gelding up at her front porch and worked himself off. Memories flooded his thoughts as he gazed at the two-story place Lorraine owned before Sue did. Both women managed to make this house a home in a land that seemed to go out of its way to strip away everything nice—and everyone of families. The freshly painted appearance was almost like a jab at him, a reminder of how long it had been since he'd visited.

He kept Hugh's advice in mind. "Hello, Sue! Don't shoot your last brother."

He stiff-legged up the front stairs and knocked on the wood and glass door. A flurry of noise inside was followed by the door's quick opening. Sue rushed out and wrapped her arms around him. Even afternoon sunlight shaded by the porch couldn't hide her flaxen hair—curly since the day she was born. He hugged her to him.

"Oh, Ike, I've been so afraid when I heard about what happened. How are Buster and Bert? And what about Ally? Who would do such a thing? And why?"

"Buster's busted up again, but he's been worse off than this. Bert's okay, and Ally seems sound. The 'why' doesn't merit figurin' at this point. Time enough for that later. How's my little sis?"

"Getting by. Sometimes I get a bad feeling out here in the Park, though. I worry about Hugh, being sheriff and all, like Rob was until … but enough of that. How are Lorraine and the children?"

Ike shrugged. "Wish I could say 'good,' but she doesn't seem to be gettin' any better, and the kids, well, I don't get to see them much with the new job."

"Been meaning to ask you about that job. What is it you do?"

Sue's familiar directness—one of the things he liked best about her. Not that he hadn't been wondering the same thing himself. "Not sure I know yet. Things don't seem to be very fleshed out."

"So those fancy Denver doctors haven't been able to help Lorraine feel better?"

"No, they haven't. Uh, can we go inside? It's a bit cool, and I'd like to sit down."

"Hip been acting up?" Without waiting for an answer, she said, "Well, Jessie and Sonny couldn't be doing too well with their mother still hurting and you trying to figure out what you do."

That was about the long and short of it. She grabbed his hand and pulled him inside. Place looked different. He eased into an unfamiliar chair in the front parlor.

"Done some redecoratin'?"

"Yes, Ike." He could hear the irritation in her voice. "A while back now. I'll get you some coffee, or would you like tea?"

The tea was a dig at him as she left the room. She knew better. There was a burr under her saddle, but he'd never been very good at figuring out what the women in his life were thinking. And Jessie was getting old enough to be annoyed at him soon, too.

Sue brought in a steaming cup of coffee. "When's the last time you ate a meal?"

When *was* it? "Uh … a while ago, I guess."

She said, "Too late for breakfast?"

"Never too late for that."

"Then get some of that hot coffee in you and come sit at the table." She left, and soon an irresistible aroma of bacon drifted from the kitchen as he came into the familiar dining room. He worked himself down to a seat, leg stretched out. Hadn't realized how tired he was until he sat. New table, too. Life had a way of moving on whether he wanted it to or not. Not much was the same around here. And where had the peace he'd always found living in the Park gone? Even during bad times. That smell of bacon and eggs was still real, though. Pancakes, too.

Sue served, then sat across the table watching him eat. She wore a familiar frown, and he guessed what was coming. Maybe keeping his mouth full could keep him from talking.

"How can you stay in Denver with your wife not doing well and never seeing the children? Makes no sense, Ike."

"I see them some." Another forkful of flapjacks. Sue had never been able to have kids and had always taken a special interest in her niece and nephew.

"Can Lorraine care for them?"

"Not so much these days." He'd just said what he didn't want to admit.

"Well, I'm coming for a visit, so you better get on back there."

Ike stopped eating. Sue had never been out of Cottonwood since she first came here, what, ten, twelve years now? Except for getting kidnapped by Manning's gang years ago. And no use trying to talk her out of coming, considering the set of her chin.

She leaned toward him. "Why don't you let me bring the children back here with me when I visit?"

Take the kids? Where'd that come from? He wiped a cloth napkin across his mouth. "That's so far from happenin', I don't even know what to say."

"Is it? What do you think Lorraine would say?"

"She'd say the same thing. Would likely be upset you even thought it, much less spoke it."

But it appeared his sister wasn't going to be put off. "But you just said they're not doing well there."

Ike didn't know how to answer that, so he let it be. Time to change the subject. "Uh, just ran into your husband out on the trail. Surprised, I was."

"He said he was going to your place. That's what sheriffs do when something bad happens, brother. But now you've got some food in your belly, so it's time to go on upstairs and get yourself cleaned up—I can smell you from here. I'm going to run a tub."

Ike lifted an arm and sniffed as she left. Funny thing was, he never could tell when he stunk, but his wife always seemed able to. A losing proposition both ways. He finished his coffee and stepped up the stairs. By the time he lumbered in, Sue had the cast-iron tub half full with water heated on the room's potbellied stove.

Even pulling off his long johns hurt. Another reminder he wasn't as young as he used to be. It took a while to fold his lanky body into the oval bath, but the warmth of the water loosened his joints until he could lay his head back on the rim.

Sue hollered from downstairs. "Use soap, and shave while you're at it!" She always did have a way of getting her point across. Couldn't remember the last time he'd done this—just relaxed. Didn't know what to do with himself.

The warm water encouraged him to slow his mind and gather his thoughts. Taking time to think things out had never been his strong suit, but he'd been blessed in life. He and Lorraine had always been able to figure the way ahead, yet doubts dogged him as he lathered. The last thing his wife needed right now—a husband unsure about what to do.

A sudden vision of Lorraine danced in his head. What was it? Was something wrong? He couldn't tell, but his neck itched, and he pushed up out of the water, hustling his clothes on. Needed to get back to his family instead of returning to the ranch. Buster and Bert'd be all right now, right? A clean shirt from Sue lay on a chair. He donned it and finished dressing, then hurried downstairs.

His sister met him with a hand up, stopping him. "You need the rest, and your family will still be there tomorrow. And you don't want to be going back over that pass at night again. Shouldn't have done it the first time. And no sense looking for your horse right now."

Ike knew his sister well enough to know there was no getting around her. Besides, he could use a good dinner and blessed sleep. Still, he wondered about the 'why' of the raid. Who was this enemy he'd never seen coming?

He had an idea this wasn't the last time he would run into whoever it was.

And them into him.

Chapter Fifteen

Stilwell placed his felt topper carefully on the brass hook in his office. A muted gray, the type the local swells wore. He twirled the sumptuous brown leather chair with a finger. A paneled office. Thick carpet. Life was good. With luck, the railroad would turn a profit for the investors soon, and he'd been smart enough to take a small percentage of earnings as his cut. He'd be able to work for himself and spend his days in the upscale men's club. He eased his hands into his vest pockets and gazed out the second-floor window onto the bustling streets of a new city. Shiny black canvas buggies with silk fringes atop plied muddy, wintry streets, although the weather had been more accommodating of late. Mingling with the wealthy—all he ever wanted.

But not quite all.

There was still that one last loose end to handle. As the years piled up, what started out as only a painful memory had hardened into his relentless fixation.

Stilwell let that go for now and relaxed in his chair, spreading his fingers wide across the felt pad atop the lacquered mahogany desk. "Dobbs!"

The toady appeared at the open doorway and ambled in. He started to lower himself into an overstuffed chair, but Stilwell stopped him. "You won't be here that long. Tell me how things are going."

"You mean with the railroad or that other thing?"

"You know which I mean." Stilwell lit a large cigar.

"Things are set there. Have the housemaid workin' the plan."

"When can I expect to see results?" Smoky rings drifted above Stilwell's head.

"Need me to speed things up?"

Stilwell shook his head. "No … that would be too obvious. Besides, I want to hurt them more. Drag it out. Leave things be for now." He triple-tapped his cigar on the ashtray. Patience had never been his strong suit, but he'd make an exception now. "How are those Chinamen doing on the track?"

"Well, the roundhouse foundation is outta the ground some, but work's been slow—basin's real cold. Nigh onto ten thousand feet there. They got no winter gear, and I hear there's lots of frostbite."

"Sounds like their own fault." More cigar O's and another tap-tap. "How many are there now?"

Dobbs shrugged. "Hard to say 'cause they're always movin' around, and I ain't sure anybody's countin'. Want us to?"

"Just get more up there. Search Chinatown and hijack some if you have to—or should I say shanghai? Past time that stretch to Fairplay was done." By rights, that should be *his* silver being teamstered out. "Work them longer, too." He could imagine the displeasure on his bosses' faces now.

Likely too boastful when he said the track would be done soon. The workers' fault, though, not his.

Dobbs pursed his lips. "Uh, not sure about doin'—" A hard stare from Stilwell. "Yes, sir."

Stilwell held a hand up. "If you have to, scour the opium dens down there. Just be careful who you run into. The, uh … incident wasn't that long ago. There might be someone you look familiar to. Take Strothers and anybody else you need."

"Ain't nobody gonna recognize us with bandanas coverin' our faces." He put a hand to his stubbled chin and rubbed. "Only be an issue if we get in a scrap and I have to drag some of 'em out. One of my men breathed a cloud of that stuff last time and got stupid there."

Stilwell stared at Dobbs. "Don't get stupid. Our sheriff will still only go along so far." A flip of his hand, and the conversation was over. Now for matters closer at hand. He brushed at his lapels, lifted the hat from the rack, and walked out of the building.

He'd plotted this for years, but now it seemed like things were at a standstill. Time to force the plan forward—patience be damned. The day was taking on the same gray hue as his mood. He shook his head. After all the things he'd done for the railroad, the owners were still pulling his strings like a puppet.

The meeting with them hadn't gone well. The president didn't ask him to sit down as he reclined behind his desk, swirling his ever-present glass of bourbon. Never offered him one, either, and if there was a time he could have used a drink, that was it. The man raised questions about the former security chief—the one who … died. Could hardly remember his name anymore, even though it had been fairly recent. Fry … Freeman … Franklin, that was it. He'd already buried that memory, just like he buried the man. Turns out the roundhouse foundation had been a convenient resting place for a body. Even if the workers had seen something, nighttime dimmed eyesight—not that any of them could be understood anyway. Wasn't just the Chinese, but Irish and Italians, too. He couldn't decide which he loathed more.

Besides, who'd believe any of them now that thick concrete covered the roundhouse floor? Nice of the railroad to provide that handy "headstone." All of which allowed him to fill the man's job with McAlister. Always nice when a plan worked out.

Had to push the track farther west every day—roundhouse could wait. Past time to go there himself—hadn't been since his visit to McAlister's place. Besides, a trip to South Park meant he could check on the McAlister part of his plan with his niece. He strolled to Agnes Franklin's house, twirling his fancy cane.

The housekeeper answered his knock with a surprised look on her face as she stood in the open doorway.

"Get me Mrs. McAlister. And tell Mrs. Franklin I have a present for her guest."

The young woman stepped out onto the porch and closed the door behind her. "What are you doing here?"

"Just a friendly visit to the wife of one of my men. Is she feeling any worse?" His voice held a hopeful note.

"Maybe, but I cannot talk. Wait here." She disappeared into the house, and soon Agnes stood in front of him.

"Why, Mr. Stilwell, I declare. Two visits in as many days. To what do we owe the unexpected pleasure?" She dragged that last word out.

"Oh, I was simply taking the air and thought I'd stop by to see Mrs. McAlister, since I wasn't able to yesterday."

"You seem to have taken a sudden interest in her welfare. I wonder—why is that?"

"No particular reason other than I feel a certain obligation to the McAlisters, having persuaded Ike and his family to move here. At the South Park, we like to take care of our own." He jiggled the gold fob on his watch, which hung in a satin vest pocket. The look on the woman's face said that hadn't rung true, so he'd try again. "As I told your housekeeper, I have a gift for her. May I come in?" Had to see how ill she looked. The short woman straightened.

"No, you can't. With her husband gone right now, I'm standing guard."

Damn woman. Had a flinty stare that let him know there was no getting around her.

She raised an eyebrow. "Leave whatever you brought with me. I'll make sure she gets it and knows who it's from."

He wiped at his bare chin. Dammit. He'd never run across a woman who radiated a more formidable air, even one this short. He tried to smile as he pulled a wrapped package from his coat pocket. "It's just a small token of … my respect. I hope she likes it." A silver watch. Wasn't as expensive as it looked. But no doubt she'd never had one before. Who needs a watch on a two-bit ranch like that?

The woman eyed it with suspicion. "Something she needs, I'm sure," she said with a *hmmph* in her tone. "If that's all—"

"Will you give her my best wishes for a continued recovery?"

The woman rolled her eyes as he doffed his hat and bowed.

Back at the office, he summoned Dobbs. "Keep an eye on that woman's house. Let me know if you see her or that McAlister woman outside, got it?"

"Yes, sir."

"I'll be gone a few days in South Park. Strothers still there?"

A nod.

"Wire him to meet me at Como with a horse and provisions tomorrow."

The next day's train climb up Kenosha Pass was balky, and the engine spewed a fearsome amount of black smoke. Maybe because it was secondhand—a new locomotive being out of reach. The line hadn't produced much yet, but the teamsters around here were up in arms about it taking their business. Ore production from Fairplay and its surroundings promised to make whoever captured it beyond rich. That'd be him. But smelters were popping up there, a direct threat to the railroad's ties with Denver-area smelters. Another thing he'd have to take care of. All in good time.

When the train finally lumbered into Como, he took a few moments to inspect the roundhouse floor. Good and thick. An eerie silence lay over the site where hundreds of workers toiled. Rhythmic *clicks* of picks were about the only sounds piercing the thin mountain air.

"Mist Stiwll!"

He turned to see the newly scarred face of his lackey, Strothers. The man was hardly understandable with his misshapen mouth, but he'd gotten it in loyal service to him. Franklin had put up a good fight, which stood to reason. Stilwell was kind of irritated—he deserved more recognition from his bosses than he was getting. "Strothers."

"Din' know yous comin' 'til telgram."

What had they ever done before the telegraph? "I didn't want you or anybody else to know." He surveyed the track west. "Why aren't you farther along than this by now?"

"Woulda, buh cain't unnstan' th' fellas. Tell 'em whado'n they do't bad. Gotta rip up'n do agin."

Stilwell considered. The workers probably didn't understand much English, much less the way Strothers spoke. He needed to send Dobbs to take over here—or maybe McAlister. No … better that it's Dobbs. He had other plans for McAlister. Needed to keep him near. A flush warmed his neck as he thought of the man. His time was coming.

He strode to the telegraph office. The same old man sat in the same old chair that looked as old as him. Awake this time. Didn't look up.

"Huh. You here to fire me again?" He shook his newspaper like it had fleas.

Stilwell said, "Never mind that. Send a telegram to Denver."

He put a finger on the tapper without putting the paper down.

Stilwell imagined the operator under the same concrete floor with the former security chief. "Send it to Dobbs at the railroad."

"There's several railroads in Denver now, way I understand it. But then, I'm old and—"

"Listen, old man, you know it's the South Park." He paused and took a deep breath. "So, send it to Dobbs AT THE SOUTH PARK. Pack your things and get out here. Now. End."

As Stilwell walked away, the operator finished sending the telegram, then paused and clicked some more Morse code. Stilwell only picked up a couple of words, but he got the message.

Chapter Sixteen

The next morning, Ike gave his sister a peck on the cheek and rode for Como. The ride brought back desperate memories from years past, like a nighttime raid on Como by Kelly's murderous gang that most didn't come back from. Not much had changed for the better since. Seemed like there was always someone who wanted what someone else had. The town shimmered in the lifting fog ahead—laborers already on the line. Chinese, with their strange headgear, and others from somewhere in Europe, he'd heard. Hard way to make a living. At least they knew their job—he still hadn't figured his out.

Ike pulled up at the Como depot and scanned the few low buildings. Almost eight years since Kelly's raid, and the town still hadn't grown much. The railroad would change that. Stock sheds, probably blown apart in the last storm, were still being hammered back together. And when was the next train to Denver? He'd load his horse on and ride in the cargo car.

He'd only ridden the train once, and that was to come to Denver at Stilwell's invitation. He looked left and right down the small main street. Thank heavens there was someone in the telegraph office. Lorraine must be worried sick—and angry, he knew that much. Inside, an old man puffed away on a pipe. Ike leaned over.

"Need to send a message."

He looked up. "This would be a good place to do that."

"Send it to … uh, the Centennial Hotel in Denver."

"Who to?"

Ike rubbed his eyes. Yeah, a name would help. "Lorraine McAlister. Say, Am okay, heading back on the next train. See you soon. That's it."

"Who from?"

Wasn't hard to tell he'd never sent a telegram before. "Just say 'Ike.' Uh, Love, Ike."

He walked out onto the street and eyed the legion of workers and their handlers. One boss in particular caught his eye. Couldn't tell what the man was yelling, but he was laying a club or a bat on the backs of a couple of Chinese laborers. The two dropped where they were. The bully loomed over the immigrants and kept kicking them with the toe of his boot. They lay with arms raised, as if to say, 'No more.'

Not much had ever riled Ike like he was now. He limp-ran over, left hand on his pistol grip. His ears rang as he neared the man.

With a surly expression, the line boss said, "Whadda *you* want?"

Ike kept coming, fist clenched.

"Stop right there, mister, ain't none—"

Before he could finish, Ike's big right fist smashed into his mouth, staggering the man, bright blood covering his black beard. He dropped the club and reached for his gun, but not before Ike slammed a shoulder into his middle, driving both of them to the ground, Ike on top. He punched the man in the face again, and all the fight went out of him. With a hand wrapped tightly around the bully's shirt, Ike dragged the dazed man to his knees and hovered over him.

"I oughta use that club on you, you coward!" His voice rang out over the high basin. Workers and overseers stopped and stared.

"Now get the hell outta here. Leave your gun belt and rifle. Best you head west and don't stop till you hit the ocean."

Ike dusted himself off as the man staggered away, the bully's bluster gone with his pride. Workers looked away when Ike stared. Heads down, they went back to work. Picks clicking on rocks clanged over the land as Ike heaved the club far into a ditch. Time to go home. He limped to another overseer nearby. The man backed up.

"When's the next train to Denver?"

"Hard to tell," he said, backing up more. "Schedule's one thing, train actually comin' is another. Guess they're still workin' things out." A face of fear. "Uh … Who are you?"

"Name's McAlister. They tell me I'm the new security chief."

"Yessir. Hope you have better luck than the last one." One more step back.

"Yeah, heard he died, but haven't heard much more than that."

"Don't surprise me they didn't tell you nothin'. I wouldn't have either. Wouldn't have been a good way to get you to take the job."

"You know what happened?"

"Heard he got stomach-shot in an alley down Chinatown way. Painful way to go."

"Who told you that?"

"Uh …"

"Never mind. What was he doin' there?"

"Ain't sure about that, either. If anybody knows, they ain't sayin'. Never found out who, either."

"You mean who shot him?"

"Yeah. Word is he had some trouble with them Chinese, but I never saw it, and I been doin' this for as long as they been layin' track in the Park. There's stories about folk goin' into parts of Chinatown and never comin' out. Reckon he was doin' somethin' he shouldn't have, somewhere he shouldn't have, the way I figger it."

"Thanks."

Staying out of Chinatown was going to be hard to do. Ike had an itch to find out more, and he usually scratched his itches. From what he could tell, sounded like the man just vanished. Trying to get the lowdown about it from folks he worked with hadn't produced anything, either. No memorial service, far as he'd heard. Did he have family in town? Ah … forget it for now. There were more pressing things to worry about. Like Lorraine.

He turned at the sound of his name.

"Ike! Ike McAlister."

Stilwell. The man looked more puffed up than usual. "What are you doing here?" He looked surprised.

"Raiders hit my ranch. I rode this way quick as I could. Still figurin' things out, like who they were and why my place." He watched for Stilwell's reaction. The man was probably a good poker player.

"My word! I hadn't heard that. I hope everyone is all right."

"More or less. They'll heal in time." Buster was so damn crusty-hard, and Bert was young. Ally would make out, too—she always did. "What brings you out this way?"

Stilwell placed his cane in front of him, both hands resting on it. "Curiosity. I had heard of some trouble with the workers here, and I wanted to see for myself. But then, I guess you already knew that, being our security chief and all."

Ike squinted. The man had a backhanded way of speaking, not plain like he was used to. Or proper like Hugh. He could use his lawman brother-in-law's help figuring things out right about now.

"Nope. Don't know anything about that. Was just settlin' into my office when the raid came. Been out here the last couple of days runnin' things down."

"Such a shame. I'm sure you'd rather be back in Denver with your wife, what with her miseries. By the way, how is she getting along? Have the doctors been able to help her?"

Something about the way he said that was peculiar. "She's holdin' her own." But that was about all. And there hadn't been any answer to the telegram he'd sent her a while ago. Maybe it hadn't reached her—but maybe it had.

Ike peered down at his boss. "How about we go back on the train together, and you can fill me in more about my job."

"Plenty of time for that, but I will not be going back right now as I still have some business to conduct here."

Before Ike could say anything, Stilwell turned and strode away. Business? What could he be doing out here?

As Stilwell retreated, a familiar itch spread up Ike's neck. He followed the railroader but hung far behind as the man disappeared into one of the town's two saloons. With an eye on the place, he tried to mix in with people walking back and forth across the street. But blending in wasn't one of the things he did best.

What was Stilwell really doing? The man had lackeys to run things out here.

The saloon doors swung open and closed with customers time and again, until finally, a flap produced Stilwell. The man paused on the wooden sidewalk and gazed around like a banker. He tugged the bottom of his gold silk vest and patted his round stomach. A kid walked a horse up, and Stilwell flipped him a coin. Guess he shipped his horse here from Denver. The youth helped Stilwell mount up, and several grunts later, the man settled in the saddle. He yanked the horse's reins and headed south out of town. Hmm. Why that way? The only thing in that direction was Cottonwood … and his ranch.

An oncoming train pumped black smoke high across the Park basin, and its shrill whistle split the air. Ike hesitated. He wanted to follow Stilwell—but also figured he had been away from his family long enough. As Stilwell grew smaller in the distance, Ike turned toward the Como station.

Had he made the right choice, letting Stilwell out of his sight?

Chapter Seventeen

Lorraine leaned back against the fluffy bed pillow as Agnes pulled the down comforter over her shoulders.

"There, now. That's much better, isn't it?"

She put a hand out, beckoning to the two treasures in her life, grasping the children's hands in hers with a slight squeeze. "Go on back downstairs and make me somethin' pretty, okay?" No school today due to a swirling storm. Just as well, as neither child had taken to their new teachers or classmates. But it was still early in the term. Give it time. Give herself time—to heal, to become a wife and mother again, not this shell that pain had taken prisoner.

Agnes fluffed a couple of pillows and almost whispered, "The doctor will be here directly."

"The doctor? Why is he comin'?"

"Just a checkup. Doc said he wanted to see how his herbals were doing." Her cheery tone couldn't mask the worry in her eyes. "How are you feeling this morning?"

"Much better, thank you." She was getting good at lying. "Have you heard from my husband?"

"Why yes, this telegram came a while ago. I just didn't want to wake you." She handed Lorraine the slip of paper.

Lorraine gazed at the telegram, then held it out to Agnes. "I'm sorry, I can't … a little dizzy. Would you mind readin' it for me?"

"Why, certainly, sweetheart." She patted Lorraine's hand and scanned the page. "It says, um—" she ran a finger over the words, "that he'll be on his way back soon. That's about all."

"Did he say anything about how things were at the ranch? How Buster and Bert were? Ally?"

"No, but I'm sure no news is good news."

Aggie sounded confident at least. Lorraine muffled a groan as she turned slightly in bed. "Does it say when that came?" She didn't know much about telegrams, first one she'd ever gotten.

"Why, it was delivered this morning, so it should have been sent yesterday. Your mister's only been gone a couple of days. He'll probably be back today."

"I hope he'll use his head this time and take the train." She still couldn't figure why Ike left the way he did. Nighttime was always treacherous in the mountains, riding or not.

"The train isn't real reliable yet. Schedule is still a bit loosey, so he might not ..." She paused, then left the rest of her thought unspoken.

Lorraine caught her drift—no telling when Ike would be back. She lay against the soft pillows, something she never had at the ranch. Never missed them, but then, hard to miss what you never had. The plump bolsters served as a pointed contrast to her hard life. She eyed her host, a woman she only met a couple of days ago.

"Why are you so nice to me? You don't even know me."

Agnes tut-tutted her way out of the bedroom and called back from the hallway. "I know you plenty. I'll be back directly. Think I hear the doc."

Lorraine tried to break through the fog that seemed to be her mind these days and swept her arms in front of her as if to do so. She picked up muffled conversation from downstairs. Her ears weren't working all too well, either. A slap to one of them produced no help, just a ringing that made hearing that much harder. That was silly. The sound of footsteps on the polished oaken stairs came her way. Agnes guided the doctor into the bedroom. A comical sight— a short woman with a hand on a tall man's back, nudging him forward.

Bedside, Agnes pointed a finger at Lorraine. "Just look at her, doctor. A body doesn't have to have any medical smarts to know she's in a bad way, and you have to do something about it." She stood with arms crossed, craning her neck up at him. "And we aren't leaving until you do."

The doctor rubbed a hand across his chin and stared down at Lorraine.

"What's the matter with me, doctor?" Lorraine winced as she shifted to look up at him. "My palms and the soles of my feet—"

By the doctor's face, she could tell he wasn't sure. He hadn't helped ease her aches and pains, and now he stood there with an 'I don't know look.'

He ran fingers over the small bumps that showed on her feet and hands. "Does it hurt when I do that?"

Lorraine stiffened in bed, raising herself slightly on painful elbows. "Well, it ain't the best thing I've felt today, so you can stop anytime." That drew a frown from Agnes in return.

The doctor peered closer as if he were examining her for bedbugs. "Would you mind unbuttoning your bedclothes at the neck some?"

The only man who'd seen her chest was Ike, and she hesitated. Besides, it wasn't her neck and chest that hurt—it was just about everywhere else. Her hand went slowly to the top button, then she stopped and clutched the fabric together, finger joints throbbing.

Agnes patted her on the arm and nodded.

All right, all right. She undid the top button, then the next one— and stopped. That would have to do.

The doctor adjusted his glasses and wrinkled his nose as he leaned in and drew the clothing slightly apart. A swipe at his mustache and he said, "That's fine, Mrs. McAlister, you can button back up now." Easier said than done with the way her fingers worked these days. Lorraine fumbled with the buttons until Agnes reached in and helped.

"I am sorry you are in pain, ma'am. I will do everything I can to help you recover."

"Hmmph. You haven't done anything so far." Agnes had a way of saying what she was thinking.

Lorraine wondered. The elderly doctor almost sounded like he left an if I *can* unspoken. How come every doctor she ever met looked like they were on death's doorstep? And they all wore whiskers—but then, most of the men she knew did, too. What would it be like to kiss a smooth-faced Ike? Her mind wandered back to the ranch as Agnes saw the doctor out.

Ike's short telegraph had been reassuring, hadn't it? Her mind drifted.

The children. She called out. They must have been on the stairs, as both came rushing in almost before she got their names out. She motioned them up on the bed, Penny at the side of it.

Jessie's eyes radiated her concern. "Mama, are you all right?"

Lorraine smiled—her first true smile in a while—as the children snuggled into her. They always had that effect. "Don't worry about me. Tell me all about you. School starts up again tomorrow. Are you excited?"

Jessie's slight pause told her all she needed to know.

"Have you met some nice kids?"

Jessie's bottom lip quivered. "Yes, Momma."

Lorraine's heart stopped. She'd been so concerned about herself that she hadn't spent much time with the children. "Would it be all right if I went to school with you tomorrow?"

How was she going to be able to do that? No matter. She'd do it.

"That'd be fun, Momma! Come on, Sonny." Jessie grabbed her brother's hand, and they bounced off the bed together, Penny their constant companion.

At least the children seemed happy—but then, not really. Lorraine could put up with a lot if they were—not much if they weren't. She looked over at Agnes, who'd come back into the room.

"You've had a lot of excitement, so I'll just let you get some rest." She eased the door closed behind her as she left.

Tears flowed down Lorraine's cheeks. She'd already been *getting* a lot of rest.

Was she dying?

Chapter Eighteen

After settling his horse in a cargo car, Ike eased into one of the new passenger seats. Thick blue carpeting ran the length of the car. No one else was on board, so he straightened his leg on the seat opposite, and his hip decided to stop irritating him for a while. The ride to Denver would give him time to figure out his next move—time to plan instead of just reacting, as he was wont to do. Those raiders at his ranch were killers, not just bandits or thieves. Why his place? And they must have known he wouldn't be there since he'd been in Denver these past few weeks.

The train lurched up the incline to Kenosha Pass as billowing black smoke signaled its passing. He didn't even know how a railroad engine worked, guessing that steam played into it somehow. Settling back against the dark leather seat cushion, it had become clear by now that he was on his own in whatever this job was. No training, no guidance offered, which made it all the more puzzling that Stilwell hired him for something he wasn't qualified for. The man didn't strike him as an idiot. Ike had seen the dark underbelly of life often enough to know when it was staring back at him. Whatever he'd gotten himself into wasn't just staring, though—it was glaring.

Rhythmic chugging lulled him into a shallow sleep, only interrupted when a conductor in a smartly pressed black suit shook his shoulder.

"Not many people taking the train yet, young man. Mostly animals and loot from Breckenridge's mines. But we're here—Denver Station."

Ike hadn't been called a young man for some time and couldn't remember when he'd felt like one. All he'd put his body through the last couple of days came to a head when he tried to get up.

"Need some help there, sonny?" The conductor smiled as he reached out to steady Ike.

"No, I'm fine." He used the seat's arm to push himself to a stand. "How do I get to the Centennial Hotel from here?"

The old man said, "Two blocks up and two over." With a touch to his ornate hat, he walked to the next car.

Ike offloaded his horse and set off for the stables first, then limped his way to the hotel. The clerk's eyes widened when he walked in. "Are my wife and children here?" He placed a hand on the stair's baluster.

"Uh, no, Mr. McAlister, they ain't been here since you left. A short lady with a loud voice took 'em."

"Whaddya mean, took 'em?" Lorraine didn't know anyone. Had he come back to find his family gone? Where would they even go? Just then, someone called his name. He turned to see a young woman with her hands clasped in front of her.

"Would you please come with me, sir?"

"Do you know where my family is?"

"Yes, my mistress is hosting them. My name is Olivia, Mr. McAlister."

"Lead on." Who was this lady, and what was he getting himself into now?

As he limped outside, she glanced at him and said, "Perhaps we should get a buggy." She hailed one.

When they arrived at Agnes' house, a little woman met him in the portico, smiled, and pointed to the stairs. Olivia asked her, "Should I take some food or tea up to her? She seems to like my tea."

"That might be refreshing, but maybe after a bit."

Before Ike could start upstairs, though, the children ran from down the hall, wrapping their arms around his legs and pinning him right where he was. What a joy.

"Daddy, we missed you so!" Small tears wet Jessie's cheeks and ran down to her grin. He swooped them into his arms and took one step at a time up the winding staircase.

Lorraine sat up on the bed to meet him, arms outstretched. She buried her face in his chest while he hugged her lightly. A wince, then a lingering kiss, and she leaned back against the pillow.

Ike stuttered as he sat next to her. "I'm so …s-s-sorry I didn't tell you anything before I left."

Her eyes glistened. "You're here now, that's all that matters."

The worry he'd kept bottled up spilled onto his face as he sat next to her. Didn't need to ask how she felt; he could tell just by looking. How her eyes squinted in pain when she lay back. The short woman came in, and Ike rose. He reached a hand out.

"My name's Ike McAlister, ma'am."

She grasped his hand between both of hers. "As if that's something I didn't know. I'm Agnes Franklin, and it's been my privilege to have your family here the last couple of days."

Lorraine broke in and related how that came to be. Ike shook his head. The Lord truly did work in mysterious ways.

"Thanking you for taking care of my family doesn't seem like enough, Miss Franklin."

"It's missus, and call me Agnes, please. They've been fine company for an old woman who doesn't have many visitors these days. My husband …well, not important right now. I'll let you all catch up." She walked out.

Sonny sat in Ike's lap, Penny's paw draped over his leg.

"Tell me about the ranch, Ike. Is everyone all right?" Ike saw the pleading on his wife's face. "I've been so worried."

He said to the children, "Why don't you two scoot back downstairs and play?"

Jessie started to protest, but he put a finger to her lips. "Please. I'll come see you in a minute."

When they'd gone, Lorraine tugged on his shirt sleeve. "Tell me!"

"Well, everything's sorta okay, all in all. Buster and Bert are kind of busted up, but they'll be all right. Five of 'em hit the place, but only three left." He decided against telling her just one made it back to Denver after Kenosha Pass. "When I got there, some woman was doctorin' them. Said Doc Early passed away a couple of weeks ago. Bert said she works in the Wildfire. Saloon gal." He shook his head. "They should come out of this okay. Ally's fine, and she got a lick in, too. Put one of 'em down."

"Who was it attacked the ranch?"

"Wish I knew. The one raider I did see sorta clear wasn't anybody I recognized."

"And why, Ike? Why did they do that?"

Another question he had no answer to. What he did know was that it wasn't an accident. They picked his ranch to hit—specifically.

"Not sure, Lorraine. All I know is nothin's gone right since we got here." He didn't want to admit it, but she wasn't any better—worse if he was honest. He'd change the subject. "Who's this woman?"

"I told you, Agnes is a dear person I met the day you left. Couldn't hide my pain from her. She invited us to stay and wouldn't take no for an answer. I don't know what we would have done without her. I'm hurtin' … more … Ike. You know that—I can see it in your eyes."

"What are we gonna do, honey?" His wife always seemed to have the most common sense, but that never nettled him; they'd proven to be a good pair over the years.

"Somebody's after us, and they're still out there." She paused. "How many of 'em did you kill?"

He never could bluff her. "Caught two dead to rights on Kenosha Pass on my way to the ranch. Shoulda got the third, but he got away. Looked like he was headin' this way."

She laid a hand on his. "Stands to reason there's somebody else behind the raid—the kind that don't do their own dirty work. One thing I know for sure—we're not going to let them win at whatever game they're playin'. And if they want to come after us, I say come on!" She lay back, a thin film of moisture glistening on her forehead. "And past time for you to take a bath!"

Ike decided not to mention he'd taken one yesterday. He smiled. That was more like it. There was the woman he'd fallen in love with. He took a hanky from the bedside table and patted her forehead, leaving a kiss on it as he left.

After cleaning up, he drew on a coat and walked to his office. Spring was sure taking its own sweet time this year.

As he stared at the black lettering on the glass of his door, he could still make out the outline of the previous security chief's name. The funny thing was, no one had mentioned him since Ike came to work. The only time was when he'd asked. A formidable woman who worked for Stilwell just down the hall had given an odd response when he mentioned Franklin's name—she just stared at him. He decided not to press it, though—he was the new guy, and no telling what alarms he might set off if he pushed further. That little voice in his head had mostly steered him right over the years, and he figured he should heed it now as well. But still, the mystery nagged at him.

One killer still roamed free.

Chapter Nineteen

Bert brought the weathered ranch wagon to a halt in front of the mercantile in Cottonwood. He eased off, head still pounding. His right leg kept fighting him as he walked into the store. The raider who'd whacked him across that knee found the right spot. At least he had something in common with Ike now. From his bed, Buster told him to go for supplies, although the man wasn't healing quickly or well. Supposed it had to do with his age and how often he'd stared death straight in the eye—and death blinked. One day the ghoul would win, but not today. Bert wasn't going to let that happen. Crazy old coot.

He knew the store well, having escorted Lorraine on her trips to town, so he headed for the bags of flour stacked on the floor. A familiar voice rang out from the counter.

"Why, Bert, it's so good to see you."

Constance Emery, who owned the store, motioned him over. He hesitated, then headed in that direction. She practically purred from behind the worn wooden display case.

"Dear me, but I heard about what happened out at your—I mean, Ike's ranch. And Lorraine's, of course."

She fanned herself, then leaned forward. "So, you got shot?"

Without waiting for an answer, she said, "Your head is what I heard. And Buster, too. How is he?"

Without blinking an eye, she switched subjects.

"Speaking of hearing things, I haven't heard how Ike and Lorraine are getting along."

Bert said, "And the children."

"Well, of course, the children, too. So how are they? Lorraine?"

There it was. She had never said more than two words to Bert before, so it was clear what she wanted to know. Wasn't his place to talk about them, though. He'd learned a lot from Ike just by watching him go about his business.

"Doing as well as can be expected," and he shut up.

Truth was, he wondered how they *were* doing. Ike never said much, and Lorraine hadn't been in much shape to.

"I'll collect a few more things and be on my way."

He gathered bacon, eggs, lard, and more bullets in a burlap bag before bringing everything up.

Constance said, "A very good shopping trip, yes indeed. I'll just throw in a can of peaches for Buster. I know how he likes them so."

Bert nodded a thanks. Seemed like every cowhand he knew was partial to peaches for some reason. But the less time he spent here, the better.

She totaled up the supplies.

"Should I put this on Lorraine's tab? It's … um, getting larger. Not that she needs to pay anything now, seeing how that's just one of the ways I've always been … willing to help folks out where help is needed. And right now, looks like they need a lot of help."

She stared at him as if expecting a response to her largesse.

Bert reached into his jeans pocket and fisted some dollars out. He pushed them across the counter to her, not willing to let her have anything to badmouth Ike or Lorraine about.

He grabbed the bag and turned to see Hannah walk in the door. Last time he'd seen her was a couple of months ago in The Sew Pretty. She always gave him baked goods for Lorraine, but she'd made it clear in so many words she wasn't interested in him anymore. She pretended not to see him, but he knew she had.

Well, he wasn't going to go out of his way to talk her up, either. Besides, he'd never known what to say to her, so he kept walking toward the front door when he heard her call his name.

"Bert Quincy, aren't you going to say hello to me?"

Hannah stood with hands on her hips, facing him.

His short "hello" was followed by Constance waving a hand as he left.

"Say hello to Lorraine for me."

Back at the wagon, Hannah's footsteps sounded on the wooden walkway behind him.

"You don't have to be rude, Bert. I've never done anything to merit that."

She practically huffed that last bit out, but she was right about the "never done anything" part. There had always been an awkwardness when he visited her dress shop, standing, holding his hat, and not knowing where to put his hands. Waiting for her to look up at him. Hadn't been that long ago that she'd been encouraging him during his visits.

What changed?

"Didn't mean to be rude, ma'am. Please accept my apology."

"Did you just call me ma'am?"

He'd never been good at reading women and didn't know how to handle her challenge.

"Sorry, just trying to be respectful. Excuse me, but I'll be on my way now."

He labored up onto the bouncy seat, snapped the horse's reins, and the wagon responded with a slight lurch.

Don't look back.

Couldn't get out of here quick enough.

As he drew away from the store, the tightness in his chest loosened, and the pounding in his head grew fainter.

He wagoned by the Wildfire Saloon just as a young woman pushed out through the swinging doors. When she saw him, she raised a hand in greeting, then hurried his way, waving for him to stop.

That's what's-her-name—Tibbie—who doctored him and Buster after the raid.

Was he going to run into all the women in town?

Hadn't seen Ike's sister, Sue, yet, though, so maybe not.

He drew the wagon to a halt and reached to set the wooden brake but stopped. Didn't intend to be here long enough to need that.

"Hello. Bert, isn't it? Sorry I didn't get your last name when I was out at your ranch. Excuse me … I'm a little out of breath."

"Yes, ma'am. It's Quincy, and it's Mr. Ike's ranch. His and Miss Lorraine's."

She wore a gaudy green dress with sequins sunlight sparkled off of. A bit of a shock after she'd been at the ranch in her worn overalls and straggly brown hair.

"You can call me Tibbie. Everyone does, among other things. I saw you goin' by and wanted to find out how you and Buster were doin'. Didn't get his last name, either."

Now that Bert thought on it, he didn't know his friend's last name. Never had come up in any conversation.

"Both of us doin' fine, ma'am. Still a little sore, but that could be from chores, too. Buster's not up and about like he oughta be yet, but he's tough. He'll be fine."

He wished he believed that.

"I'll come take a peek in a day or two. Can you keep him goin' till then?"

A good-looking woman.

"Yes'm."

Man was too tough to die.

He touched a finger to his hat.

Early spring brought muddy roads and rocky footing, so the ride home took longer than it should have. Worst season of the year. Seemed like the longest, too.

Almost like it was winter, winter, winter, spring, summer, summer.

By the time he got back, dusk had chased the sun away, and stars struggled to life in the darkening sky.

Bringing in an armful of the store-bought goods, he found Buster bent over at the small kitchen table, wheezing, his bearded face red.

"Buster!"

The old man lay sprawled, head resting on an outstretched arm.

"What the heck are you doin' out of bed?"

"Man's gotta move his bones, or he'll set up like stone."

He lifted his head and eased back in the chair.

"And mine've already been gettin' stoney for some time, young'un."

"You shoulda waited for me, you old … I don't even know what to call you."

"Just don't call me late for dinner."

His chuckle broke the tension.

"Want me to help you back to bed?"

"Why would I want to do that? Just came from there, and I'm too old to start goin' backwards at my age. Just catchin' my breath— I'll be fine right here."

Bert shook his head and got a glass of water.

Buster put a hand up.

"I don't need no water."

"Ain't for you."

Bert took a couple of sips and put the glass down by Buster's chair.

"Got a little dry in town. Um, by the way, the lady what treated us wants to come out and see you. See if you're still breathin' regular."

Buster smiled.

"You mean that pretty one with the brown hair? I don't remember a lot about the raid, but I remember her."

"Not worth talkin' about. You seem to be gettin' along pretty well."

"From the look on your face, that's more'n I can say about you."

Bert hesitated.

"You remember that gang I used to run with—the one that convinced me to kidnap Lorraine all those years ago? When I lost this finger?" He pointed to the missing digit on his left hand.

Buster nodded. "Hard to forget somethin' like that."

Bert hadn't forgotten it either, nor Lorraine's grace in forgiving him. "I swear, when I was in town this morning, I saw some of 'em, includin' the one that put me up to it."

"What would he be doin' around here now?"

"Not sure. Don't seem like there's anything around here for him to steal, like gold." Bert passed a hand over the bandage on his forehead. "And that's likely the only thing they'd be anglin' after. Surprised he ain't takin' down trains around Como."

Buster took another sip of water. "Must be somethin' else then. Need to figure out what he's after, and soon."

Chapter Twenty

Ike woke the next morning in a strange bed. He reached over and lightly laid a hand on Lorraine's hip. At night, she fidgeted a lot, trying to get comfortable. Jerky movements from bad dreams. Kicked him sometimes—always swore it was by accident. After he helped her up for breakfast, he tried to suggest they move back into the hotel, but Agnes wouldn't hear of it, to Lorraine's silent relief.

Agnes had arranged for the children to be schooled by an in-home teacher, common for the wealthy of Denver. Ike found their host busy in the kitchen.

"Uh … Miss Agnes, can I speak with you?"

Agnes nodded to her helper, Olivia, who was busy preparing lunch. The woman swished out. She closed the door and, with a smile, said, "What's on your mind, Mr. McAlister?"

"I wouldn't mind if you called me Ike, and you've done more'n I can thank you for, ma'am. I just wonder how I can pay for our stay here." He'd never liked being beholden to anyone. Would use his first paycheck to square things.

"Not about money, Ike." She finished cutting up a chicken and put it in the wooden icebox. "Your family does like chicken."

He nodded. "Thank you." Guess he'd ease back into how to pay her another time. "Never had many cluckers on the ranch. Those we did, we ate when we could catch 'em. 'Tween us and the coyotes, they didn't stand much of a chance. I guess varmints are varmints, whether they're in the Park or here in town." How was she going to react to that?

"I've known plenty of those in my day—the good Lord seems fit to allow more around here all the time. As for you and your family, I figure you're the ones doing me a favor. Haven't had another person to care for in a while now. Feels good. Better than some of those phony customers of mine who think the bigger the hat, the grander the lady. There's nothing about a hat that makes a woman a lady. Not one like your wife, anyway. You're a lucky man, Ike McAlister." She started on potatoes.

He'd known that for a long time. He rubbed the back of his neck. "How do you think … how's she doin'? You've been around her more in the last two days than I have in the last week."

Agnes placed the knife carefully on the counter, followed by both hands. She shook her head. "Her color isn't good. She can't be getting any better looking the way she does. I see a glaze—a dullness—in her eyes I don't like, either."

"What's the doctor say?"

"Not much help. Says to keep using cold compresses on her forehead, as if that'll cure what ails her. Gives her some pills that taste like sugar. And yes, I tested them. My guess is he doesn't know what she has or how to treat it."

So, he'd uprooted the family from their home and brought them to Denver so Lorraine could heal up, and now the doctor didn't even know what she had? Faith had sustained him during tough times in the past, but now it felt like what he did have was slipping away. And the way the job was supposed to ease the family's money predicament was turning out to be a sham as well—hadn't been paid since he arrived. Stilwell said he'd take care of it and held out a twenty, which he declined.

More and more reasons to return to the ranch were piling up, but he wasn't made to cut and run. Letting his family down wasn't in his makeup, and no one was going to drive him away. If he left, it'd be on his own terms. Lorraine saw troubles the same way, too. He decided not to tell Agnes he was going out to find out more about her husband.

Where was this Chinatown anyway, and how far away? He could search city streets on foot but wished Ally was here. Things were always better riding her. Who to ask? Needed to be a little careful. Wouldn't do to have word on the street bandied about what the new guy was doing. Ah, the stabler. About the only person who wasn't a total stranger. Maybe he could offhand a question to the old man.

The white-haired owner didn't look up from his seat when Ike strolled in. He'd just finished off a bottle and sat swearing up a storm.

"Bad day, mister?" Ike eased onto the whiskey barrel next to him. He pulled out a plug of tobacco and offered it up.

"Never touch the stuff—about the only thing I don't," the man chuckled. "Never did anythin' for me, but I do miss the only excuse I ever had for spittin'."

Ike chuckled. "Sounds about right." He bit off a chaw.

The stabler squinted at him. "You're the fella took one of my horses the other day."

"Yup. Hope I brought her back in good shape."

"Fine horse like that needs a good gallop now and again, like you gave her. Still had a twinkle in her eye when I led her back into the stall." The stabler turned the bottle over, and the last drops drained out. "Can't quite figger why you're here, Ike McAlister. Yeah, I know who you are. Didn't come by just to say hello, did you?"

Was it that obvious? "Uh, guilty. Need to do some traipsin' around in Chinatown. Never been there. How do I—"

"Huh. Last thing you oughta be doin', sonny. People goin' in there got a way of not comin' out."

"So I've heard. Like Franklin?"

"Franklin? Fella that worked for the railroad?"

"Yeah, like him." Did that sound casual enough?

"Odd thing, that. Never recovered the man's body, or so they say."

A little itch popped up on the back of Ike's neck. He looked sideways at the old man. "You think there was some funny stuff?"

"Nobody's sayin' nothin', which makes me think there's somethin'. Why'd you want to … never mind, none of my business."

Just as well the stabler didn't finish that question. Ike wouldn't have known how to answer it because he wasn't exactly sure why he felt the need to run this down.

"So, how do I get there?"

"Best you go on foot. Horses disappear there too—sometimes for food. You can always tell. It's got a tangy taste that, once you've et it, you never forget it." He rubbed his bearded chin and pointed north. "Uh, less'n a mile thataway. Topside of the city. Uh, you'll know it when you reach it, always somethin' cookin'." The man's eyes glassed over, and his chin took aim at his chest.

Ike leaned on a cane as he walked the city's side streets. He'd head north but not in a direct line. Why'd he feel the need to hide what he was up to? He peered left and right, a habit that had served him well over the years. Town was growing, that's for sure. Wooden skeletons of new buildings rose to either side, even as Denver was still surrounded by open land as far as the eye could see. Never had cottoned to cities. Most of what he'd seen of them was the aftermath of war's devastation and death.

That was one of the things he liked about the West, though. New starts were everywhere. Why hadn't his and Lorraine's worked out so far? Didn't know what he expected with the move, but this wasn't it. Did life ever work out like it was supposed to?

Dead ahead, an older section of two-story brick buildings rose, bookending both sides of the street. The road narrowed, and people stared out from dirty windows, mostly women. A man lurched his way and grabbed his arm, mouthing something nonsensical. Ike shook the man off. Wasn't sure if he wanted a handout or was trying to pull Ike into the decrepit building he stumbled away into. Maybe he'd need his cane for more than just helping him walk.

Garbage odors he didn't want to smell tingled his nose. The dingy block could use a good scrubbing. A hard rain would help, but this part of town needed more than that. Grime here seemed to have spread almost like a fungus. Was he even going the right direction? There weren't a lot of people he passed that he wanted to stop and ask.

Catcalls kept his head on a swivel and his eyes darting. Maybe he should have started earlier in the day, as daylight was fighting a losing battle against hazy air. And what *was* that rotten smell?

Three scruffy men closed in on him from ahead. Ike always had a head for trouble, whether he was getting in or out of it, and now his neck itched like crazy. He slowed—couldn't have run from them anyway. The sounds of battle rose in his head, and he stopped, feet spread and hand gripping his cane tightly. He knew exactly how he'd use it. Swing the curved end up between the first thug's legs, then swipe across the second's face. The third he'd figure out as things went.

As they neared, the men split to either side, eyes locked on him from under low, grubby hats. Which to take first? It'd be the one on the left, the side he had the staff clutched in. They closed, wooden clubs drooping from their hands. Closer. Another step, and he'd lunge left.

A sound from behind. Blackness.

Chapter Twenty-One

Agnes bustled around the bedroom, busying herself with nothing that needed to be done—rearranging towels by the sink, adjusting the curtains, checking the oil level in the lamps. Lorraine watched from bed as her host fussed about, but the woman kept facing away. Sniffles.

Finally, Lorraine said, "Aggie, whatever are you doing? You ain't been talkin' me up like you usually do. What's the matter? Tell me true."

Her host cleared her throat and turned. Lorraine saw the red eyes, the splotchy face, and sat up. "Agnes! What's wrong?"

The woman shook her head, wiped her eyes, and stood with head bowed at the bottom of the bed. "Didn't know any way to tell you."

"Tell me what?" Lorraine leaned forward, heart racing.

Agnes put a hand to her forehead. "It's Ike. He's … um, well, disappeared."

"What? That doesn't make any sense. He was just here. You saw him."

"A woman at the railroad office said he left there yesterday afternoon and didn't show up this morning. And he didn't come home last night. Did he tell you where he was going?"

"No, and I didn't ask. I just thought he was goin' back to work." Lorraine kicked herself as the news sank in. She should have noticed he wasn't back last night, but it was rare enough that she slept the night through. "I need to go find him; help me up, please."

The small woman stood ramrod straight by the bed, hands on her hips. "No."

"I said, help me up, dammit."

"No, I won't. You got the heart to go after him, but not the body, so you'll just stay right where you are."

"You're a heartless … wench." She almost spat the words.

"You bet I am, and right now, this wench isn't going to let you get up."

Tears filled Lorraine's eyes, and her shoulders slumped. "But I have to …"

Agnes came and put a hand on Lorraine's arm, patting it. "You're in no condition, and you know it. I've already notified the sheriff, so there are people out looking for Ike right now."

Tears streamed down Lorraine's face. "Thank you. I didn't mean … I'm just—"

"I know, dearie. I'd feel the same way you do, but it won't help the children to have both of their parents in danger."

"Do you think Ike's in danger?" Lorraine's heart leaped as she said it.

"Much as I'd like to say no, I think yes, probably. A man like your Ike isn't just going to disappear on a whim, not with you and the children here."

As Lorraine started to say something, Agnes said, "I'll let you know if I hear anything, and I'll send the children up to see you when school's over. Olivia should be here with them soon."

A flood of emotions warred inside Lorraine as she watched Agnes leave. She'd just called her gracious host heartless, but most of all, her husband was missing. He wasn't dead, was he? She'd always done for the family, and now she couldn't even get out of bed. What good was she to anyone, herself included? Hadn't been for a while, either.

***

Bert checked on Buster one last time and headed for the barn. How was Ally doing? Next to Lorraine and his children, that horse was Mr. Ike's prized possession. She'd shown her mettle during the raid, disposing of one of the outlaws by herself. He'd already gotten rid of the dark-stained straw scattered just outside her stall. The best way to get on Ally's good side was to do what Mr. Ike did. He reached out a handful of shrunken carrots to Ally that she didn't eat.

Tending Lorraine's withered vegetable garden wasn't what he or Buster were best at. Maybe if he got some fresh ones in town or from Ike's sister Sue, that'd perk Ally's appetite. As he patted the horse front to rear, though, he wondered. He didn't know that much about horses, only what Buster taught him, but as he eyed the warhorse, he knew enough to suspect the problem might be more than fresh vegetables.

He stared at the rear hoof that ended the outlaw's life with one kick. Looked all right, didn't it? Bending down, he trailed a hand down her rear leg to the hock, scared of what he might find farther down. Was the horse favoring that leg? He traced down to the fetlock but knew before he touched it that it would likely be warm. Heat spread into his palm as he wrapped his hand around the leg and lifted it to examine the hoof. Damn! Ike's horse got hurt while he was in charge. He made sure Ally had plenty of water and feed, then headed for the ranch house.

"Got a problem, Buster. Ally's hurt her leg—I mean, hoof— and I don't know much about fixin' those."

Buster lay in bed while Bert drew up a chair. "You see any dark red marks on the bottom?"

"Yeah, the middle has dark spots, so probably pretty bruised."

"Need to fix her up, and there's things used to be in the barn, but I ain't sure we got 'em anymore. I'll go help you find—"

"You ain't goin' nowhere, old man." Funny how he'd take Buster to task without a thought, but would never say such a thing to Ike. Lingering guilt, he supposed, for what he did to Lorraine. "Just tell me what to look for."

"Ah, leave it be. Ally's a good healer."

Bert shook his head. "Can't. It's Mr. Ike's horse." And he headed for the barn.

When he came back, Bert carried a bucket with a hole in it. "Anything else we can use?"

He was talking to a man asleep. Bert pursed his lips. Had to figure something else out. That gal in town—maybe she knew something about horses, too. Said she wanted to come back out here to check on Buster anyway. That's what he'd do—head back in. Leaving a note for Buster wouldn't make any sense; he probably wouldn't even be able to figure out if it was upside down or not. Besides, the old man would likely be out until he got back anyway.

He motioned to Rowdy to jump up on the bed with Buster, checked on Ally again, and was soon galloping toward Cottonwood.

As town neared, he slowed. Never had felt comfortable around a passel of people. He thought about all those trips he made here to get supplies and those baked goods from Hannah for Lorraine a ways back. Said she made them special for a special friend. Since the family left for Denver, though, Cottonwood had become a stranger.

He passed Sue's boarding house but didn't stop. No time for a social call. Had always admired Ike's sister. She'd owned the boarding house for years, and the few times he'd met her, she always seemed to have a handle on things.

He passed The Sew Pretty and drew up at the Wildfire—the saloon Hannah worked at before taking over The Sew Pretty and then boarding at Sue's for the last several years. So many memories from times past. Mostly bad.

Hannah had held his interest once, but she'd changed ever since her pa died in the streets here years ago. Not that she'd ever had anything nice to say about her father, but the man was her pa nonetheless.

The sign above the entrance hung askew as he stared at the saloon's swinging doors. Ike didn't hold with drinking, so Bert had only been in here a few times since he kidnapped Lorraine.

How had he ever let those outlaws he ran with have sway over him? At the least, he should have hightailed it away from here or been dead. Mr. Ike would have picked the latter, but not Miss Lorraine. Imagine—her taking him in after what he'd done.

Needed to brush those memories away, though. Ally needed help.

He eased the doors open and peered into dim depths that daylight seemed to shy away from.

At the bar, four men leaned on the counter, drinking. Beer and whiskey—what this town lived on. Bert cast a long stare at one of them—Ellison—bent over his glass, nodding at the no-account next to him. A noise to his left caught his attention. A drunk was fooling with Tibbie, who was fighting a losing battle to keep him at arm's length. Before Bert knew it, he was up in the man's face, telling him to leave her alone. A few sloppy jabs, and the man fell face down. Blood mixed with his vomit as he twitched on the wooden floorboards.

"Thank you." Tibbie ran a hand over her mussed hair and motioned for him to come join her. As he bent to sit, a shot zinged by, thudding into the wall behind him. He whirled to see his former boss with a smoking gun leveled at him from the bar.

"Good thing you ducked, you coward. Nothin' worse'n a weasel pretendin' he's a man. Turnin' on your own kind."

Bert's heartbeat raced, and his hand lowered toward his gun. Ellison told him to go ahead and try it. Another choice to make. He'd love to kill Ellison and take some of his goons with him, but no doubt he'd be dead in a shootout, too. Not why he was here, though. He eased off, scanning the smoky room for other threats. Ellison was backed by other riffraff he'd seen before, none worth remembering.

"Shoot me in the back, but I'm sittin' down."

He leaned close to a wide-eyed Tibbie, wondering if these were the last words he'd ever speak. Would a bullet be piercing his back?

"Miss Tibbie, me and Buster need your help with Mr. Ike's horse. Killed one of the raiders the other day by herself, she did. May just be a bruised hoof, but I don't figure it that way—looks worse." He didn't even want to think about that. "Feels plenty warm, too."

"You're Bert, right?"

A nod.

"I don't know much about horses, never done any healin' on 'em, me bein' from back east and all."

"Wish I had more time to talk it over with you, but Ally ain't gettin' any better with us sittin' here. Will you come, please?"

She leaned back, glancing behind him. "You can see I'm workin' now, right? Come back later if you want."

Bert shook his head. "Might be too late then. This is the second time Ally's thumped that hoof recent. May not heal on its own this time, and that'd take the best horse in the Park."

"Sounds like you know more than I do about horses."

"Not so much, but I know people, and that's why I came to see you. Figgered you're the kind that'd help like you done before." He stared at Tibbie, and when she didn't respond, he jammed his hat on. "Sorry to take your time, ma'am." He started to get up.

"Just wait a minute, willya? Wait." She shook her head. "Don't know why I … bah … meet me at the stable."

With a flick of her hand, she waved him out. Bert kept a hand on his gun and an eye on Ellison as he left. The man still had the drop on him, but Bert forced himself to keep walking. Outside, he wondered if he'd make the stable, three buildings down the street. One step in front of the other, and he reached the livery safely. But no doubt he and Ellison would square up sometime down the road, and only one would walk away from that.

He had two horses saddled and ready when Tibbie got there, still dressed in her glittery gown under an old coat. But that didn't matter. Brown hair never looked so pretty before. Her clothes were a far cry from the plain top and pants she wore to the ranch before, but he preferred her simpler look.

They rode south in silence in the early afternoon air until Bert cleared his throat.

Tibbie glanced his way. "You got somethin' to say?"

"Uh … no."

They trotted on, then, "Can we ride a little faster?"

As they broke into a canter, he said, "It's just that I never seen a doctor workin' in a saloon before."

"I ain't a doc."

Silence for a stretch.

He said, "Uh, didn't mean workin' in a saloon was bad, just that—"

He clammed up. His pappy always told him when you're diggin' a hole in the wrong direction, stop diggin'.

As they rode, Tibbie asked, "How's Buster doin'?"

"Old guy seems all right. Sleeps a lot, and when he does get up, walks like a stooped old man."

"Stands to reason after all he's been through. How'd he come to be at the ranch?"

Bert thought back to the first time he saw Buster. Remembered how nervous he was in those days. "Was there when I first came, but I heard some about what he was doin' before. Like when he almost froze in the mountains leading a winter party of settlers, and then some of the times with Ike since that didn't turn out real good for him. They're sure fast pals, though."

Made him wonder if he'd ever have a friend like that.

"Makes sense, considering how beat up his body is."

They rounded the last curve and pulled up at the ranch house's front rail. Bert hurried inside while Tibbie dismounted and followed.

Buster had the good sense to be lying in bed, sleeping. They crept back out of the house and walked to the barn.

Three horses stood in separate stalls, but Tibbie went directly to Ally's. The horse gazed back at her as she opened the door, right rear leg bent slightly on the straw. She eased toward Ally with her hand extended, palm up, speaking softly. Dark brown eyes met hers as she approached.

"Oh … she's such a beauty."

Tibbie rested a hand on Ally's muzzle, then moved her hand along the flank and stopped.

"What's this, Bert?"

She gazed at a long gray scar that Ally's chestnut hair shied away from.

"She's a true warhorse, that one. Was with Ike during the War, and maybe before. Heard she saved his life when she got that. Never seen a horse and rider closer than them."

He didn't even want to think what Ike would do if Ally didn't make it. She'd be fine, wouldn't she?

Chapter Twenty-Two

Sounded like a distant bell ringing. What was that? Something tinkling in the wind? Ike forced an eye open to see darkness surrounding him. Lying on some sort of bed that needed more padding. He rolled to his left side and put a hand to the back of his head. A rough bandage wound over his hair from back to front. The scent of something he couldn't put his finger on drifted throughout the room. He lay back, trying to figure out his surroundings and the throbbing pain that was starting to sharpen his senses. A hand to his gun belt—not there. And what was he wearing? Something flimsy, lighter than cotton, more like a long dress as his hand moved farther down his legs. He bent an ear to pick up any sounds, but there weren't any he could hear except that constant ringing in his head.

There. A rustling came from somewhere off to his left. Soon a small lantern threw light his way. What looked to be a Chinaman held a lamp up and thrust it closer, then uttered some words that were no doubt Chinese. Ike shielded his eyes and tried to get up, but the man put a hand out and eased him back down on the pad. With a finger wag and a shake of his head, he placed the light on a low wooden table next to Ike's pallet. A prayer-like gesture of his hands followed, and he smiled. More gibberish, but his smile grew wider as he checked Ike's bandage. The man turned the lamp up, and Ike surveyed the room. Dingy canvas walls with nothing else except his bed and the table.

"I'm thirsty. Can I have a drink?" Ike still didn't know where he was or why, but the man hadn't threatened him so far. He tried to chase the confusion away as he rubbed his forehead, then eyed the Chinaman closer. Looked to be middle-aged, short, thin—maybe lanky was a better way to put it. Black eyes and black hair braided. A twinkle in his eyes.

The stranger reached to the side of the bed and drew a small jug forth. As he ladled the concoction to Ike, he said, "You are better?"

Could have knocked Ike over with a feather as he eyed this puzzling person. "You speak English?" The words were barely out of his mouth before he belittled himself. Of course, the man did, he just had. What was the matter with his brain? Had the injury taken away all his common sense? A flashback to that war wound years ago.

"Yes. I am happy you are awake." He handed Ike a wet cloth. "Will feel good."

Ike wiped his face and neck. Felt better already. He gazed at the man with the sing-song accent of many railroad workers. "Who are you, and where am I?"

"Later. Now you need food."

He turned to leave as Ike asked, "How long have I been here?"

"Long time." He disappeared.

When Ike woke again, he could tell by the light canvas sides it was daytime. This time he made it to a sitting position on the side of his bed, which was barely thick enough to keep him off the ground. With his bad leg out to the side, it would be difficult to get up. Instead, he dropped to all fours on the floor and pushed to a stand that way. The more he straightened, the more his head pounded. His host appeared out of nowhere again.

"You are better?"

"Y-yes, I'm fine." Ike felt like shaking his head to rid the cobwebs but didn't want the pain of it. And he wasn't fine, the ringing in his ears almost drowning out his voice. How did this man know English, much less speak it as well as he did?

The Chinaman placed a small tray on the table and held a vial of something pungent out to Ike. "Please to drink this."

Ike started to say, "What—" then he paused, took the cup, and downed the liquid.

"It is cinnamon you smell." The man bowed. "I am An Li. You are a guest in my home. We found you two days ago, unconscious in LoDo."

Two days ago? LoDo—what's a LoDo?

"I am pleased to know your name."

Ike pursed his lips, the pounding growing louder. The man was taller than most of the Chinese he'd seen. Maybe thirty years old? Hard to tell. He stared at Li, drifting. But back to his question. "I'm ... um…" His face must have reflected the same uncertainty he saw in Li's. "I … don't know … my name." How could that be? He closed his eyes and wiped at his brow. "Where am I?"

"Chinatown."

"Where's that?"

"Denver."

He knew that but wasn't sure why he would be in Chinatown. He checked his pockets but came up with nothing. "Did I have a hat?"

"Yes, it is here." Li reached into a corner of the room and handed what passed for a hat to Ike.

Bloody, dirty, and torn. He dropped it beside the pallet and gazed at the cloth covering him. "Where are my clothes?"

"They are clean." He bowed. "I will bring. Stay."

Ike shook his head. He wasn't going anywhere—how could he, he didn't even know where *this* was? He had a faint memory of a wife. She must be awfully worried. And what was that smell? A haze of pungent smoke, like burnt cinnamon and maybe orange, hung in the air. Faint sounds from outside—what room was he in? Canvas walls held up by what looked to be scavenged wood weren't doing much to knock back winter's cold. He lifted a hand to the back of his head and lightly rubbed. His thoughts moved in mud.

Li reappeared with a folded bundle he handed to Ike. About time he'd gotten out of his getup; smelled like he'd worn it for too many days. Before Ike could change, though, the man stopped him. "Take bath first." He strode out and led a stumbling Ike down a narrow path between canvas shelters left and right. A pale sun lit the dim passageway. That same strange smell seemed to follow him like a shadow. He passed other canvas tents with lifeless-looking men sprawled on low mats. After a short walk, Li pointed to a canvas opening. Ike stooped through the entrance. In the center of the room was a small metal tub of water—cold, no doubt.

"This?"

His host nodded and left. Ike hesitated, then shucked his loose garment. He dipped a hand in and pursed his lips. Hadn't felt water that cold since Fredericksburg during the War. He swung his bad leg in first, then folded his tall frame the rest of the way in. Wasn't sure what was worse, the freezing water or his pounding head. At least the past two days had given his hip time to calm down. The water wasn't clean but didn't matter; he wasn't either. As his body adjusted to the water, he began to relax despite his shivers. Cold water on his face cut through some of the cobwebs. How'd he come to find himself here with little memory and a knot on the back of his noggin?

After pulling on clean clothes, he followed his caretaker out of the bathhouse. They maneuvered down narrow dirt ways that separated more small, stained canvas-and-wood housing.

At one dwelling, Li held a browned canvas flap up and nodded for Ike to enter. Inside, a woman squatted, stirring a black pot over glowing coals encircled by small stones in the middle of the enclosure. She didn't look up when Li said, "This is my wife, Mei Won. Please sit."

Ike didn't need a second invitation—his stomach was talking to him almost as much as his head. He lowered himself as best he could. Whatever was in the pot sure smelled good, like rich, brown gravy. Did Chinese use garlic in their food? Mei Won ladled several spoonfuls into a round bowl and held it out. She gave him two wooden sticks, but he fumbled with them, one spinning to the floor. Finally, the aroma got the best of him, and he tipped the bowl toward his mouth until it was empty. He started to wipe his beard with his sleeve but stopped. His hosts dropped their gaze to their bowls, trying not to watch him embarrass himself.

Li held out a napkin and stared at him from across the table. "You work for the railroad."

Surprise was all the response Ike could muster.

"Work for the railroad. Yes, you do."

This time his brain found words. "The railroad? How… how do you know that?"

Mei Won gathered the bowls before bowing backward out of the room with a frown. She had never met his gaze. Was she angry with him?

"Do not know where you live." Li poured a steaming liquid.

Ike figured his head was still leading him astray. Nothing since he woke up made sense yet.

"I go to the railroad office and ask."

Ike worked to stand, towering above the man. "I'm goin' with you."

With a small shake of his head, Li said, "No. Still too weak. There is danger. I come back with information."

The food finally hit his stomach, and his eyes grew heavy. "I'll go…" Had his host put something in the food—or the drink?

***

Ike's eyelids felt like weights. When he pried them open, everything was foggy. A pretty young woman with straw-colored hair leaned over his bed.

"Thank heavens you're all right, Ike! We've been so worried about you." She reached down to stroke his cheek. "How did you come to be here?" She staggered slightly.

What was going on? He stared at her until his eyes cleared. His head hurt, and he reached around to the back of his neck, where his fingers trailed over a bandage. Who was she, and who was the slight woman behind her?

"Ain't you gonna say anything, you willful old fool?"

"I … uh … I don't know who you are." Was this his wife?

Before the woman could respond, a Chinese man piped up from behind him. "This is your wife, Lorraine, Ike McAlister."

He heard the words, but they didn't register in his battered brain. "I do have a wife, don't I?"

Lorraine thrust her chin out. "Yes, you do, Ike. You know me well enough to have given me two children!" Panic crossed her face.

He recognized that look well enough. Had to be true, but why couldn't he remember more? The small man said he found him lying in the street.

The Chinaman answered Lorraine's question. "Only reason come here is for opium or Franklin."

He didn't know much, but he knew he didn't smoke opium. But Franklin. The name sounded familiar.

Lorraine raised her eyebrows. "Who's he?"

"Had job before your husband. Died here several months ago."

Lorraine looked as confused as Ike felt. "Why would Ike come lookin' for a dead man?"

"Franklin murdered. Body buried at Como. Perhaps McAlister wanted to know why."

Lorraine turned to the man. "Didn't you tell the sheriff?"

"Who would believe Chinese? If we say anything, they think we killed him. Man who murdered Franklin not worried about what we say."

Ike's head spun. "Wait a minute. How did you know who I was? I didn't even know that 'til now."

The little man sat cross-legged near the bed. "You stop man beating me at railroad. I never forget."

Lorraine spoke up. "Mr. Li told me he went to the railroad office and asked a woman about you. She said you worked there and she told him who you were and where to find your family. Seemed very nervous, accordin' to Mr. Li."

"That's likely the woman down the hall from my office." Ike shook more cobwebs away and stared at Lorraine. "You're my wife." He sat up on the bed.

"Thank you, Ike! 'Bout time you got hold of yourself. Now let's quit this jawin' and get out of here before somethin' else bad happens to you."

Ike put a hand to her cheek. "What are you doin' up and around? You've been near bed-rid since we moved here."

"I'm finally startin' to feel better, and I have Agnes to thank for that. I'm too ornery to just lie in bed all day long anyway. Let's get you back to your children."

Ike leaned on her as she slipped an arm around his waist. Yes, the children.

Agnes broke down and wept. "My dear husband. Always thought he'd been killed. Never knew how or who, though."

Lorraine wrapped an arm around her friend and hugged her close.

Agnes sniffled into her hanky and said, "But whoever did this is still out there—would have done you in too, Ike, if Mr. Li and his friends hadn't seen you getting thrashed."

Li nodded. "They try again. Their way. No loose ends."

Ike pursed his lips. "Who are you talkin' about? Do you know who jumped me?"

His host continued stirring a dark liquid in a small pot without looking up. Ike couldn't figure any of this. Was he beaten on purpose, or just in the wrong place at the wrong time? But his gut told him it wasn't random. Didn't really matter at this point, though.

Lorraine said, "We'll be ready next time."

He put an arm around his wife. "We'll both be ready next time."

Chapter Twenty-Three

Stilwell leaned against the high-backed plush chair and smoked his ever-present cigar. Things were going exceedingly well, all in all. It had taken time, but he'd wound the doddering railroad president around his little finger and now had control of daily operations. It was easy to send cars where he wanted, skim valuables from the cargo they carried, and no one was the wiser.

But the route to Fairplay still wasn't finished. Damn! That would be the most lucrative of his plans if he could ever get through. He had to beat the Denver and Rio Grande there to tie up the area's silver boom. Enormous riches awaited the first train to reach town. He stubbed his half-smoked stogie out in a crystal blue ashtray. Enough of disappointing reports from South Park—he needed to be on-site himself. He glanced at McAlister's empty office as he strolled down the hallway. The man wouldn't ever be there again—the deed no doubt already done. As he walked to the train station, he checked his watch on its golden fob. Just enough time to catch it.

He was a patient man, if anything. Years had passed since he first heard about what happened to his brother in Cottonwood. Now it would be brother for brother. McAlister for his. Meanwhile, he had outfitted the sleeper car with a dining area and claimed the whole car as his. A luxurious way to travel compared to the rugged conditions of his workers, who slept in flimsy tents or unheated boxcars. Workers who needed to hurry track to Fairplay. He could pay them more to lay track faster, but then he had other persuasive methods, too. They'd see his wrath soon enough if need be.

But there was still this other, brother thing. More important in some ways than the railroad. Everything was set up now after years of planning—climbing the railroad's ranks, ingratiating himself with the president, kowtowing to toadies he hated. How stupid they all were. Even his niece hadn't been keen on his plan until he forced her to start helping him.

Unfortunate that little do-gooder woman was helping McAlister's wife. He hadn't counted on anyone else being involved. Maybe he should have, after dispatching her husband. Would be unnecessarily messy to take her out, though. Agnes Franklin could only get in the way; she couldn't stop his revenge. Then again, she was a loose end, and he'd never liked those. He'd have to give some thought to what to do with her, but he'd have to be careful—more so than he'd been with her husband. She was smarter than she looked.

His plan was all he could think about these days. That and getting the railroad rammed through to Fairplay. He imagined both those happening at about the same time. Wouldn't that be the best? He could take credit for the one and long-awaited satisfaction from the other.

"Hello, Mr. Stilwell. You have the train to yourself. Nice to have you with us, sir; we don't get to see you often enough."

Stilwell eyed the conductor. Did he mean that, or was he just kissing up? He glanced back at his newspaper and waved the man away with a "hmmph."

The climb up Kenosha Pass took most of what the locomotive had, huffing and puffing its way to the summit like its out-of-shape passenger. What was that fool engineer doing? Sleeping? Did he have to do everything around here? Ah, forget it. They'd be pulling into Como soon enough, and his foreman better be there to meet him. As the train chugged to a stop at the roundhouse, an attendant stood in the aisle next to Stilwell's seat and bowed. Stilwell rose and brushed off the engine ash that constantly streamed through the drafty windows. Hmmm. They would have to figure out how to fix that if they wanted the gentry riding these rails. That's where the real passenger money was, not from the dirt ranchers who occasioned the station platform with their simple bags and dusty families. Hard to believe his dreams were tied to this brownish, windy land just now getting ready to green up from a grudging winter. And all that silver in Fairplay—and Leadville—just waiting for his cars.

Stepping onto the platform, people scurried about, shouting and pointing. "What's going on?" he yelled to no one in particular.

"Somebody's been shot and killed."

Stilwell instinctively ducked and waddled as well as a corpulent, middle-aged man could to cover in the telegraph office.

That telegrapher he'd tangled with earlier stared at him with a deadpan expression. The man stuffed tobacco into his pipe with a grunt. "Seems like people around you have a funny way of turnin' up dead."

What did he mean by that?

"Got any other puffed-up fools? You're gonna need a new one here by the looks of it. Maybe try findin' one that ain't quite as stupid as your last one." The man spit into a crusted brass spittoon.

Stilwell gazed around. Where was Strothers?

The telegrapher rubbed a finger over his mustache. "Yup, your man just went down. That was who you were lookin' for, wasn't it? The guy with the funny mouth."

Drawing a derringer from his vest pocket, Stilwell pointed it the man's way. "What happened to him?"

"Oh, put that pea shooter away and go find out for yourself— he's the one everyone's fussin' with outside. Man dropped like a stone, he did." He drew on his pipe with a slight smile while smoke drifted Stilwell's way. As the railroader left, the old man said, "You skim any more loads lately?"

Stilwell stopped and turned back to see a very large Colt staring him in the face. Didn't matter; nobody'd pay attention to what some telegraph operator in a backwater town like Como said. Besides, he couldn't kill everybody he didn't like.

Outside, a crowd gathered. Stilwell pushed his way through only to see Strothers lying on his side, a neat hole in the side of his head leaving a messy pool of blood. Damn him. Easily replaced, but still, who would dare … He scanned the crowd. "Who shot him?"

Silence.

"Speak up! A reward to the man who tells me who killed him."

A man's voice from the back. "Don't know, boss. Shot came from over that direction in the distance. Was a real good shooter, too. Musta been hidin' in them trees over there."

"You, you, and you, get after him, now!" A vein in Stilwell's neck pulsed.

Soon, three riders galloped away, headed for who knows where.

Stilwell continued to brush at his clothing and strode toward the only eatery in town. He waited for his food while he drank his coffee with a shaky hand. Who'd have the nerve to shoot one of his men? He finished his eggs and grits, walked out, and mounted a horse that had been brought around the front of the small hotel. The desk clerk stood nearby. "What should we do with him, Mr. Stilwell?"

"Whaddya think? And tell whoever finds the murdering skunk to come get me—I want the coward alive!" He spat a dark circle on the dirt street.

"Where you off to, sir?"

He hesitated. "Cottonwood."

Chapter Twenty-Four

The three of them took a roundabout way back to Agnes's house, bypassing the cesspool known as lower Denver. Halfway there, Lorraine stopped and bent over, hands on her knees. "I gotta sit, Ike. You go on ahead. I'll just be a minute."

"I'm stayin' with you all the way back." They sat by a lone elm, and he patted her hand. "Don't know how you got yourself up and over here today, Lorraine. You been a sight poorly all these months." Agnes continued walking ahead of them.

"That woman there, Ike. I owe her my life. I was gonna surprise you by bein' up when you got home, but you didn't make it, so I came here. And we owe Mr. Li a lot." They held hands on the cool grass until the western sun lost its warmth.

Ike eased her up. "Can you walk?"

"You ever seen a time when I couldn't?"

He raised his eyebrows.

"Don't answer that." She slid a hand around his waist as he draped a long arm across her back. By the time they reached Agnes's home, he'd been carrying her in his arms for the last several blocks, her eyes closed and an arm wrapped around his neck. Brilliant streaks of scattered orange dappled the sky's darkening blue. The day's high temperature was a memory, too.

Agnes sent the children's sitter home and set a perfect table of fine silver, crystal, and china for supper. Ike recognized that smell—steak—and he smiled at Agnes as he helped his wife sit; the children clustered around her. Their host took charge. "Now, Ike, I've run a warm bath for your wife, so you just have a whiskey, and we'll be back down soon."

As they sat together for the evening meal, all eyes fixed on Ike. He bowed his head and fell silent for an awkward spell while the children squirmed, and steaming mashed potatoes threw off a wonderful smell. He cleared his throat. "I c-can't thank you enough for bringing us all together, Lord—and safely." More silence. "Please continue to protect this family and Miss Agnes." Pause. "That's all for now, Lord. Amen."

Morning brought Ike a throbbing reminder of the beating he'd taken. He glanced to his left. Lorraine was still sleeping. She needed it. He crept out of bed and padded down the stairs. The delightful smell of bacon drifted from the kitchen as he walked in on their host. "Can't thank you enough, Mrs. Franklin, for all you've done for us and the kids. Got a second to tell me how you figured out what might be wrong with my wife?"

Agnes glanced at him from the stove and put her spoon down. "Time you started calling me Agnes, Ike. Turns out someone's been poisoning her. Arsenic—hard to detect, but I came across it once before."

"Poison? Do you think back at the ranch, too?"

"Yes, I'd guess there, too. Not quite sure how it was being hidden in her food—probably powder—but small amounts over time will bring a body down. Somebody has been trying to kill your wife, Ike. And a little bit at a time, so it wouldn't be noticed."

Ike sank into one of Agnes's high-back chairs around the kitchen table. All this time, and he hadn't been able to help Lorraine. He'd been nothing more than a frustrated bystander as she slowly slipped away. And who was poisoning her at the ranch? Bert? "Who'd do this—and why?"

"Don't beat yourself up, Ike. I didn't see it either until I sampled food my maid was taking up to Lorraine last week." Agnes ladled potatoes onto plates. "That salad just didn't taste right, so I took some to our doctor. He's the one who recognized it. Guess he's come across it some, as it's released when they process ore. But take in too much of it, and ..." She glanced at Lorraine. "Why the doctor didn't figure it earlier, I can't say, but thank heavens she's getting better. I should have done that sooner. I thought about turning Olivia in to the law, but Stilwell apparently put her up to this by threatening to harm her family unless she went along with him. I pressured her to tell me what Stilwell was up to, but it became clear she didn't know. Just a stupid young girl who didn't figure she had any choice. But if I've learned anything in this life, it's that we always have choices."

Lorraine came into the kitchen. "And sometimes our choices are bad ones."

Ike reddened. That stung a little bit. Arsenic. Almost too much to take in. Ike looked toward the children, and his gaze was met by two small, worried expressions. Lorraine locked eyes with him—a withering look he knew all too well. Now wasn't the time to talk this out, not in front of the children—or Agnes. Was his wife over the worst of it? Please, Lord. Didn't know how he'd carry on without her. Wasn't ready to find out, either. Lorraine looked a little unsteady, so he hurried to help her sit.

"I need to be movin' around, Ike, keep gettin' this poison outta my system, so don't let me sit long, and don't pay me no mind if I start complainin' about things."

Not likely; she'd never complained in her life, and she had more reason to than most. After dinner, the children helped Lorraine back upstairs and snuggled her in bed. Ike sat on the edge, thanking God, who'd done so much for them, even if they had so little.

She grasped his hand. "Last thing I need is a husband moonin' over me, lookin' like a lost puppy. I want you to get started on figurin' out who's behind this poison, and who used your head like a pumpkin. And why."

Agnes said, "Skunks can't hide for long before their smell gives them away. I figure we should start sniffing around and start with what we know—which isn't a lot."

"Maybe you shouldn't get tangled up in this, Agnes. Probably best that you back off. Stilwell's a mean killer."

"I'm already involved, Ike—ever since my husband … since I first met your lovely wife and children."

Lorraine thrust her jaw out. "Well, we haven't figured out why he's been pullin' our strings yet, but we all know who's likely behind this. Never did have a good feelin' about Stilwell from the start, and still not sure what he's up to."

Agnes nodded. "I've always thought he was tied in with my husband's death but never could prove anything." Tears welled in her eyes.

Ike perked up. "Your husband? Who's that?"

"Sam Franklin. He's the one who had the job before Stilwell gave it to you."

"You mean your husband was head of security for the railroad?"

Agnes crumpled the hanky in her hands. "Y-yes. Never did understand how he died all alone there in Chinatown."

Lorraine leaned forward in bed. "What did they tell you?"

"Not much, just that he was found dead in one of the opium dens. Not likely. Not my Sam. As straight a shooter as I ever knew. Never had a chance for a funeral either—the fitting way to honor a fine man. Sam deserved better than that, and I couldn't give him a proper goodbye. That's a wrong I need to right." Tears streaked her cheeks. "They said there was no body for me to claim, but of course there was. And now this An Li fellow tells me about Como."

"I heard somethin' shady about his death, but that's about all." Ike started to pace the room. "Piqued my interest that no one seemed to want to talk about what happened to him. Lately, I been knockin' around askin' questions and gettin' nowhere. Made me more curious, like an itch that needs to be scratched."

Lorraine said, "Is that why you were headin' to Chinatown?"

He nodded. "And appears those fellas that jumped me didn't want me to make it. Like they knew who I was and why I was there. Just waitin' for me. Startin' to add up now."

Agnes put a hand to her mouth. "So you think my husband's murder was just Stilwell's way to get you here for some reason? Kill my man to get him out of the way? That's all he meant to him?"

Ike didn't say anything; didn't want to add to her pain. They'd solved one puzzle about what was wrong with Lorraine, but others still waited for answers he didn't have—yet.

She hugged Agnes, who sobbed into her shoulder. How could she console someone about something that made so little sense? And what *was* going on? She'd been in such a fog for so long that she hadn't realized the lengths to which Ike had gone to get her help. As her head cleared bit by bit, her host's gracious charity became even more touching now that she could fully appreciate it. At least Ike's memory was coming back, and he was recovering. She'd basically ignored him for so many months—unforgivable. There was so much to make up for with the children, too.

And it was past time to take Stilwell down.

Chapter Twenty-Five

Tibbie frowned as she ran her hand down Ally's back leg to the hoof. "I don't like how this feels, Bert. You were right to get me back out here, but I'm not sure what I can do."

"Icin' helps."

They turned to see Buster silhouetted in the light of the open barn door, leaning against the weathered frame.

"Buster, you shouldn't be up—what're you doin', you old fool!" Bert straightened and nearly ran to where his friend stood.

Buster took a halting step. "Lemme take a look at that leg."

Bert helped him over to Ally's stall, where he crumpled rather than knelt next to the big mare. With a hand to the hock, he eyed Tibbie. "Didn't figure a pretty gal like you knew horsin', too."

She reddened a bit and shook her head. "I don't, but a hurt's a hurt, whether man or beast. Don't feel like it's broke, as far as I can tell, but I agree—we gotta get this leg cooled down. Got any ice hereabouts?"

Bert soon returned with a towel wrapped over a lump of snow from the lee side of the barn. "This'll have to do."

Tibbie put an arm around Buster and helped him sit up. She broke the snow apart and gave Buster some in the towel to fasten around Ally's lower leg. Ally eyed him with her large brown eyes. "We're gonna need more snow and gotta keep puttin' this on and takin' it off."

"How long do you think before we know somethin'? I mean, if she's gonna be okay?" Bert kept Buster upright from the other side.

Tibbie ran a hand over the big mare's flank. "How about we stay overnight and see how she's doin' in the morning?"

Bert nodded, then hurried out the barn door, returning with another mound of dirty snow. "Been waitin' for that pile of slush to finish hightailin' it so spring could get off to a runnin' start, but glad we still got some of it. Not ice, but—"

Buster said, "It'll do."

The three spent the rest of the night tending Ally's leg, with snow melting on what almost amounted to a hot plate. Wasn't an evening for sleep anyway. Bert brought food and water, and partway through, they made Buster lie back and sleep against a straw pile.

Toward morning, Bert could tell the leg was settling down. As the sun peeked between stubborn, low clouds, he helped a stooped Buster back to the house while Tibbie stayed with Ally. Later, she came inside with an encouraging update. "I think she'll be all right if we keep coolin' her regular. I'll stay today to help."

Bert shook his head. "Can't let you do that, what with your job in Cottonwood." He avoided naming it.

"Still my choice what I do, ain't it?" She stuck her chin out a tidge and locked eyes with him.

Bert lowered his gaze as a slow blush surged up his neck.

"Well then, that's that." She helped Buster back to bed, then started to make breakfast. "Ever figure out who jumped you?"

Bert shook his head. "Wish I knew. Mr. Ike no sooner leaves, and I mess things up." He cast an eye toward Buster, lying motionless on his back.

"Is that the way you see it?" Tibbie flipped flapjacks on the hot iron stove. "Maybe you ought to take a gander at it from where I stand. You fought off those killers, even dispatched some of them, and kept your friend Buster and Ike's Ally alive."

"I could've done more. Should've done more." What was Ike going to say?

"There's lots of things in this life we can't control, Bert." Tibbie put a hand on his shoulder. "I got a feelin' Ally'll be fine with more ice and rest. And I just learned some horsin', so that can't be all bad."

He looked over at her. She didn't have to come help—she hardly knew him and Buster. Riding into town to fetch her, a woman he'd hardly spoken to, had taken all his gumption. "I… uh, *we* want to thank you for … comin' out here."

"Figured if they hit you once, they could do it again, and you could use an extra gun." She gazed at Bert. "That's right, I can shoot some, too. Besides, Buster still needs more lookin' to." Her grin eased his nervousness.

Was there anything the woman couldn't do?

Bert said, "Why don't you come sit here at the table while I serve stuff up? Time you took a break, got off your feet." He wanted to ask about her salooning, but didn't know how. "Uh …you're lodgin' at Miss Sue's place, aren't you?"

"S'pose I am, since that's where I go when I get off work. How'd you know that?"

His blush deepened. He was treading quicksand. "Musta heard it somewhere." Time to change the subject before he got in any deeper. "You doctorin' the town now, too?" That'd be a safe thing to ask about, he hoped.

"Reckon I am as much as they'll let me since Doc died. There's lots of folks don't hold with me doin' much of anything 'cept saloonin'. Keep me in my place, me bein' a woman and all. Turns out most men won't let a female examine them." She brought a nice stack of pancakes over while he tried not to stare at her.

Bert pulled out a chair. "Please sit, will you?"

"Thank you. Can I have a fork, please?"

His heart raced. Stupid. Get her a fork. And see if there's some syrup around anywhere.

When he'd recovered his senses enough, he sat with eyes fastened on his plate so he wouldn't get more flustered than he already was. First time he'd been knocked off his feet sitting down. He glanced over at Buster, whose soft snoring was distracting yet somehow comforting.

They ate in silence until Tibbie said, "You ever gonna talk to me again?"

A rustle to the side, and Buster said, "Talk to her, young man, and look at her while you're doin' it. She's a sight better lookin' than anything we've had around here in a month of Sundays. And I know you've noticed, because you're all fumbledy. So say something nice to Tibbie—she deserves it, and I know that's what you're feelin'."

"Go back to sleep, old man, or I'll put you back to sleep." Bert's voice echoed in the small ranch house. He snuck a glance at Tibbie.

Tibbie folded her napkin and started up from the table. "You don't hafta say anything, Bert. Lots of folks don't like me bein' around. Not hard to understand why, so I'll just be goin'—"

Bert jumped to a stand. "Hold on, Miss Tibbie, please. I didn't mean no offense, far from it. I-I think… you're swell, and if I said or did anything to make you think otherwise, then I am the fool. We … I … would like you to stay. You're right—Buster and Ally both still need your fixin', Buster most of all." He glared at his injured friend.

Tibbie took her plate back to the kitchen counter. "You don't hafta try to smooth things over by sayin' that. Sue's place is as close to a home as I've had since my father died. He always wanted a son, so he taught me to ride and shoot better'n the boys I grew up with. Drink, too. My ma died young, so I never had anyone to tell me how to be a woman. No matter, I'll just wash these up and head back to town."

Bert took a plate from her soapy hands. "No, please stay. I know what it means to lose your home—how much it hurts. My father, he shot my … it don't matter now, was a long time ago. I was raised by my gramma. She was the only good thing in my life until Miss Lorraine took me in. And that old man over there friended me." He shook his head. "My gramma raised me to be a better person than I been."

Buster raised up on one arm in bed. "You're wrong there, Bert. I seen you the last few years—there's good all over you. You just won't forgive yourself for what you did to Lorraine. That's in the past. She's forgiven you—why can't you forgive yourself?"

Tibbie started washing dishes. "I heard you were sweet on Hannah." She continued scrubbing without looking at him.

Bert almost sputtered. "That's not so … I mean, it used to … uh, we never—" He stopped and drew a breath. "All I'll say is, she ain't near the woman you are."

Buster raised himself to a seated position. "Never thought you were gonna get that out. About time. Now, Miss Tibbie, what can we do to make you more comfortable?"

"I'll tell you what *we* can do, Buster. You can try pryin' yourself up off that bed for starters." Bert helped the old man up. "Miss Tibbie didn't sleep much last night, and it's time we let her get some. You just pick yourself up so's she can lie down. You and me can find lots to do outside if you're up to it."

"I've been up to it for a lot longer than you have, young whippersnapper. Workin' outside for a spell is the best idea you've had in some time. Didya hear that surprise in my voice?"

He chuckled his way off the bed and leaned on Bert as they made their way out of the house. The last thing they heard was the lumpy bed's soft creaks.

Chapter Twenty-Six

The trail ride to Cottonwood put Stilwell in an even worse mood than he'd been in at Como. He didn't care about the man he lost—Strothers was never much for thinking or looking at—but his death threatened to waylay his plans, something he couldn't allow. As he approached the small town from the north, he shook his head. Who would live here? And why? Como was backward enough, but Cottonwood …

A dusty little speck on the Park floor. That's all this was. He eyed The Sew Pretty and started to rein in there but changed his mind. No. Wasn't going to look like he was sneaking into town anymore. The place was small enough that a well-dressed visitor would be noticed anyway. He probably already had been on his previous trips to town. This time he'd make his presence known. He yanked the horse left and continued down what passed for Main Street to the sheriff's office. He tied his horse to the rickety wooden rail, brushed dust off his silk vest, and swiped the bottom of his mustache. That ought to let anyone watching know he was someone to be reckoned with.

Jiggling the worn jail door, he finally gained entrance to a small room with a tired desk and two chairs. Jail cell in back. Behind the desk, a well-dressed man rose. Hugh Walnutt greeted him. They'd met once before after Stilwell offered McAlister a job, then stayed at his sister's boarding house overnight. Stilwell gave a short nod.

"Good day, Sheriff. Perhaps you remember me?" He waited, gauging how sharp the Englishman might be.

"Welcome to Cottonwood, Mr. Stilwell. What brings you back to our little hamlet?"

There it was. The Englishman said 'hamlet' instead of 'town.' Nice touch. Stilwell strolled around the room, especially eyeing the rifles standing tall in a locked case on the wall. He'd try to imitate Walnutt.

"I say, these are some fine firearms you have here, Sheriff. You would think an army of bandits was going to descend on Cottonwood by the look of them. And this Sharps looks well-used." He tucked his thumbs in his vest pockets as he strutted around the room.

"I have heard you Americans say it never hurts to be prepared, Mr. Stilwell. We English have always taken that to heart." He came around from behind the desk. "Is there something in particular that I can be of assistance with?"

"Just a courtesy call to let the local constable know I am in town."

"This local constable appreciates it very much, sir." Walnutt gave his visitor a wan smile. "I must say, I feel more at peace now than before you came in."

Stilwell squinted. He couldn't tell if Walnutt was mocking him or not.

"Yes, well, I am here visiting my niece, Hannah Hawkins. I'm sure you know her." He wanted to say 'as small as this town is,' but let it go. "Owns The Sew Pretty. Ever since her poor father was killed here—a gruesome bit of business—I have taken a special interest in her welfare, helping out wherever I could. Just my way."

"I'm sure you have been a stalwart support for her." The sheriff moved toward the door. "May I be of any other service?"

Stilwell summoned a word intended to impress.

"Indutitally, indutibly … no, thank you, sir." Better leave before he gave himself away as more of an impostor than he already had.

He doffed his hat and exited backward out of the jail. Peering down the street, he dithered between going into The Sew Pretty or mingling with the riffraff of The Wildfire. The rotgut whiskey would still be there when he left Hannah's, so he headed to the dress shop.

He peeked in a front window to see his niece twirling in some of the shop's finery, parading in a green velvet dress with a purple-plumed monstrosity atop her head. All alone. With a shake of his head, he pushed the door open, and the little silver bell tinkled as he strode in. Hannah stared at him as if seeing a ghost. Her frown said everything.

"Come, girl. It hasn't been that long since I've been here."

"You just startled me, that's all. I've been, uh … sorting inventory and didn't see you."

However she wanted to frame it.

"I thought I'd check on my favorite niece. How have you been?"

"Cut the small talk, dear Uncle. You only have one niece. Why are you here? To tell me of the latest problem with your plan?"

Damn her. It's not my fault, and it's *our* plan.

"Yes, things are going a little slower than I had hoped, but everything is still as we planned. Not that you're making any contribution from this dreary little settlement. I'm having to do everything myself."

"Maybe that's why things have run off track, Uncle. And I already did plenty before you even started your part."

The hubris.

"What do you mean by that?" Like she could pull this off by herself.

"Just what I said. You've done nothin' but kill one of your own. And you failed at killin' that repulsive cowboy on McAlister's ranch."

"That boy who threw you over? What was his name?" He'd jab her like she just did him. "Settle down now. We're too close after this many years to have this squabble. Just be ready to do your next part, okay?"

She took the hideous hat off and laid it aside. "I'd have thought that what happened to your brother—excuse me, stepbrother— would have lit more of a fire in you to get this done before now. He took all the whippin's and raised you after you two ran away from home. You owe him—my father!"

A flush surged in Stilwell, and his eyes filled. Yes, his brother Charlie protected him when they were kids. Wouldn't let the wretched old man touch him. Wasn't until Charlie laid the drunk out that the beatings stopped. Never did know if his brother killed him or not. They left their father lying in his own blood on the bleak homestead's dirt floor. He owed Charlie for that, and he owed his killer. He swiped at a cheek.

"Yes, and I plan to pay that debt."

Hannah said, "That's all well and good, but you ain't done nothin' of what you said you'd do. I'm done with this. Just leave my shop and don't come back!"

Stilwell pointed a finger at her.

"No! We're still in this together." Mumbling to himself, he strode out. He'd be back—and soon.

***

Sue met her husband on the boarding house porch with a cool glass of tea. She knew his routine well enough to have his favorite drink ready when he came home. She'd finally broken him of that odd

English habit of tea served hot. Later, a bourbon—an American taste he'd acquired over the years. Better than that horrible port she could never get down.

"Come sit, and I'll have your supper on the table soon."

Sue had two other boarders in the house, so when Hugh came into the dining room, there were four around the table.

He wanted to tell his wife about his encounter with Stilwell but decided to wait until they were alone. Didn't know the boarders well enough, and you couldn't be too careful. As he sat in the parlor after dinner, she brought his drink in.

"So, how was your day, Sheriff?" Sue teased him with his formal title.

"Interesting, that I will say. Usually, my day consists of boredom punctuated by moments of near drama, but today was somewhat different. I had a visitor, a Mr. Stilwell, a rounder who has stayed under this roof before with two questionable associates. You may remember him. I am not entirely sure why he stopped in my office, only that he wanted me to know he was in town. He also divulged that he was here visiting his niece, Hannah Hawkins."

"You mean that ornery man who hired Ike and Lorraine away from here so Ike could work at the railroad doing something he had no idea about?"

"One and the same. And even more interesting, when I went on my rounds this afternoon, I just happened to stroll by The Sew Pretty, and what did I hear?"

Sue knew he was dragging this out just to annoy her, and it was working—she always raised an eyebrow when her temper built.

He continued as if she had answered him. "I am glad you asked that question."

Sue threw a lace doily at him. "Out with it, you foreigner."

"Very well. Indeed. I heard Stilwell and Hannah arguing inside the shop, and, realizing I had something on my boot, I bent down and lingered for a moment."

"You eavesdropped, you conniver, didn't you?"

"I take great umbrage at that description, my dear. I prefer to be referred to as an interested observer; it is so much more civilized-sounding. To continue, they were talking about a plan Stilwell hatched, and it sounded like Hannah had been involved as well. I did not hear what the plan was, but the discussion served to upset Hannah quite a bit."

Sue pursed her lips. "Never did know Hannah's last name 'til now—hopefully, she's not related to that Charlie Hawkins who terrorized this town years ago. But then, I've always enjoyed a good mystery, so perhaps I'll be able to wheedle information out of her unawares when she's here. I'll noodle on that, mister. Gives me something to do besides change sheets and wait on you."

Hugh lifted his drink while he feigned offense. "But you do that so well, my dear, I would hate to deprive—"

She heaved another doily in his direction and stared at him in mock indignation. A slight turn-up of her mouth, followed by a chuckle, and the two of them guffawed themselves silly. Arm in arm, they strolled down the hall and turned in for the night.

Morning would bring new challenges.

Chapter Twenty-Seven

Back at Agnes' house, Lorraine stepped on each rise of the winding staircase twice, her arm on the banister, while she followed her sobbing host up to her bedroom. Agnes threw a bed pillow hard against her headboard. It was as much emotion as Lorraine had seen from her. But then, she had every right to be angry—and miserable.

"What did my Sam ever do to Stilwell that cost him his life and me a husband?"

Lorraine wrapped an arm around her friend, one of the few she had in life. She had only known Agnes a little while, but it didn't take long to build bonds in this harsh frontier.

Agnes stifled her sobs and wiped away tears. "Don't mind me. What will you and Ike do now, dearie? I'd love for you to stay here until you sort things out."

Lorraine didn't know what was next. "Seems like everything's up in the air right now, so I'm not sure about much of anything. Ike and I'll have to talk about that." What she didn't say to her host was that it didn't make much sense to stay with her any longer—or in Denver, for that matter. "Will you be all right while I check on Ike and the children?"

Agnes said, "Yes, of course. Go on now."

Downstairs, Lorraine caught up with her family in the study. They sat in a circle on the brown carpet, playing a game where Jessie and Sonny threw a ball in the air, then swiped beans up off the floor. Ike sat nearby, soaking it in, bad leg out. Lorraine hoped she'd remember this scene forever—all the most important people in her life just enjoying themselves. No drama—at least not right now. She couldn't remember the last time things had been this calm, almost easy. Better lock this away in her memory, as peace wasn't likely to last long. Never had.

Agnes got rid of Olivia, telling her she was lucky not to be in jail and to never return, or she'd drag her to the sheriff. She told Lorraine that the housemaid knew she was adding deadly powder to Lorraine's meals. At least she had enough compassion to leave the children alone.

Lorraine had never been able to figure out why Stilwell would go to all the trouble to recruit Ike and the family to Denver, to a job he wasn't qualified for, and then try to kill her. Ike, too. What had she ever done to him that he hated her so? And how did Ike and the family fit into the monster's plans? None of it made sense. The only thing she truly knew was that they were still in danger in Denver. Only one way to solve that problem, and the sooner they hightailed it back to South Park, the better.

She peeked out a curtained living room window to the west. Daylight was dimming as dusk drifted in to greet it. Unlike the rest of her family, she always looked forward to the winter months, when cool Colorado days grew shorter and shorter until December lengthened them again. A grumbling stomach reminded her she hadn't eaten recently. Lorraine headed for the kitchen when she saw Agnes' new housemaid coming toward her. She wanted to keep her distance—the last maid almost killed her—but natural curiosity overcame her reluctance. She started to say "hello" when the new girl held a hand up.

"I'm leavin'!"

Lorraine shifted in front of her to block the way. She needed to find out more about this new person. "You can't. You just got here, and we need you."

"Can't stay in a house where nobody don't tell me nothin'."

"What do you mean?"

"I been standin' in this kitchen for hours, waitin' to be told what to do."

"The mistress is upstairs, heartbroken, so I won't be callin' her down right now. And didn't you do some housemaidin' before here?"

"Yes, but—"

"No buts about it—please go on about your job and help this household that's grieving. So just turn around, missy, and start makin' dinner. You do know how to cook, don't you?"

"Yes'm, I do."

"Then let's you and me get to work, huh? What's your name?"

"Sally, just Sally."

Lorraine took her by the arm and walked her back into the kitchen. After showing her where everything was and what to make, Lorraine climbed the stairs again, her energy deserting her at the top landing. "Ohhh."

Rushing out of the bedroom, Agnes caught her as she teetered backward. She steadied Lorraine and swiped at her nose. "I have enough worries without worrying about you, too, honey. Come sit with me on the bed and tell me what's going on in that pretty head of yours."

As they sat together, Lorraine stared at the ceiling. "I don't even know what to think, Aggie. Everything's inside out all of a sudden. Somebody's been tryin' to kill me, and Ike's been lured here to a phony job. And we don't know why. Outside of my husband, you're the only person I can count on right now to help me make sense of this. I don't even know where to start, either."

"Don't worry yourself about that, sweetie. We'll figure it all out. No doubt Ike is already putting a plan together. Speaking of Ike, why don't we go down and have dinner with your family?"

"That reminds me, Aggie. Your new housemaid—what do you know about her?"

"More than I knew about the last one. I got references this time; wasn't going to make the same mistake twice. Sorry about Olivia; she hoodwinked me good, and you paid the price. I feel terrible."

"Well, I don't feel terrible anymore, thanks to you. I owe you a lot."

"How about we lean on each other then, here on out? And Ike."

"That sounds like the start of a plan." Lorraine hugged Agnes, and they worked their way down the stairs.

*****

Ike didn't know what to say to Lorraine after the latest turn of events. Didn't even know what to think, much less do. He helped clear dinner, then eased her into the double wicker chair on the cool veranda. He wrapped a blanket around his wife as they sat silently in the darkness. What had he gotten his family into?

"It's gonna be all right, Ike. We've done for each other in the past, and we'll do the same now, the good Lord willin'. I feel it." She patted his hand, then lay hers on his.

"Don't know what to make of this, Lorraine. Stilwell bringin' us here to do—what? Sicken you 'til you die, and have his goons take me out near Chinatown? Don't understand it, but no sense hashin' about 'why' any longer. And he ain't paid me yet, either. Got almost two months comin'; guess I'll never see that. Don't mind not seein' it, though, long as we're both still alive."

"Not sure that made any sense." Lorraine snuggled closer to her husband. "And why all that raidin' at the ranch? Was that him bustin' things up there, too? Must be, but why?"

The front door creaked open, and Agnes walked over to their chair, a shawl wrapped around her small frame. "I don't know much, but I know you two and your children aren't safe here anymore. As it turns out, I'm not sure you ever were."

Ike's stomach knotted. Agnes had just said aloud the same thing that had been rolling around in his head. Got to get the family back to South Park. Now. To either the ranch or Sue's. Probably better at his sister's. Hugh wasn't just the sheriff, he was a damn good shot, probably the best in the Park. He peered into the starry darkness. Were they being watched even now? Maybe a bead being drawn on them as they sat? Couldn't chance being outside anymore tonight. He helped Lorraine to a stand, then put his arms around his wife and their host as he walked them inside. A quick look back, and he locked the door behind him. At a downstairs window, he stopped and pulled the curtains together.

Morning found him on the move. He'd slipped out of bed while Lorraine was still asleep, something she needed a lot more of. A day-old biscuit was his breakfast as he walked to his office, the sun just now waking up. He wasn't sure what he might find in the railroad building, but he didn't know where else to go to start unraveling the mystery surrounding him and his family.

The halls were empty at this time of day, and his footsteps echoed on the wooden floors. He walked into his office and paced the small room, looking for something—anything—out of place. The space seemed foreign to him now. He hadn't spent much time here, and it hadn't grown on him. Stepping back into the hall, he approached Dobbs' office. Never had cottoned to the man from the first time he'd seen him at the ranch. The only other person who'd rubbed him the same way was his boss, Stilwell. Oh, and Hawkins, years ago.

He glanced both ways down the hall, jostled the door open, and eased in. A room he never had been in before. A quick scan revealed nothing out of the ordinary. An empty desk as big as his, with one chair. No pictures on the walls. As empty as he believed Dobbs' heart was. Desk drawers all unlocked except the middle one. Not even a jiggle when he pulled on it. A quick glance around turned up no help. He'd ditched that small Webley Dobbs gave him early on and stood with his Colt strapped to his left side. Would anyone hear a shot this early? Didn't matter—had to find something—anything—out. He pulled his sidearm and blew away the iron desk lock and the oak surrounding it. Wiping away debris, he searched through the drawer's remains. His eyes went to a battered packet that lay on the floor nearby. Inside was money and a note from Stilwell. Ike took what he was owed and flung the rest in the air. No hiding that someone had been in here. Time to visit his boss's lair.

Footsteps came up the hall. He froze behind Dobbs' door. They slowed as they came abreast of the open doorway, then echoed on. Ike waited, then peered left and right down the corridor. No one in sight, so he slipped out and tiptoed to Stilwell's door. Locked. Just then, a woman he recognized came up behind him. Helen something. Morrison. Worked for Stilwell.

"Not sure what you're doing, Ike McAlister. I'm usually the only one here this early, yet here you stand, trying to break into Mr. Stilwell's office."

A flush ran up his neck. "I … uh … just—"

"My sight's not too good anymore, and sometimes my eyes play tricks on me. Hard to tell what I'm seeing most of the time. And I didn't hear a shot a while ago, either." She turned away and disappeared to her desk.

Ike stared after her, heart beating faster than usual. Get a move on. He eyed the large glass insert with the fancy lettering on Stilwell's door. No, busting that still wouldn't get him into the office, so he shot this lock out, too. Even more satisfying than destroying Dobbs' desk. He pushed the door open, stepped over pieces of broken wood, and gazed around the opulent space.

A chandelier! He'd heard of them but had never seen one before. Even with the light off, a circle of hanging crystal dangles glittered in the early daylight. He shot it from the ceiling. Glass burst everywhere as it hit the thinly-carpeted floor. He turned his attention to the desk—sumptuous polished mahogany. His father taught him about good wood in his youth.

The woman came in with a broom. "You don't mind if I tidy up, do you? Never could stand disorder." She set about sweeping the debris into something that resembled a basket.

"Sorry 'bout the mess. Wanted to get in here to see if I could find—" He left the sentence unfinished because she wasn't going to believe him, and he wasn't even sure what he was looking for.

"You might start over there." She pointed the broom handle at a padded hassock that sat innocuously in front of a large, upholstered chair.

He scanned the small piece of furniture and looked back at the woman, but she had resumed sweeping. Walking closer, he couldn't see anything unusual about the ottoman. What was she talking about? He pushed on the top, which gave way slightly. Reaching down to a wooden leg, he lifted. Heavy—too heavy for a footstool. Kneeling, he felt around the sides. He curled a hand underneath and lifted. Would need both hands. Trying again, he tipped the piece over and eyed the black bottom. An outline of something in the middle, almost too faint to see. He pushed on a small depression there, which moved the fabric apart. Feeling in a small hole, his fingers wrapped around a dial, like on a safe.

After half an hour of trying various combinations, Ike turned to the woman, who'd long ago finished cleaning the debris up. She sat reading a book in one of the other chairs, feet resting on another ottoman.

"You have any ideas, Helen?"

"Wasn't sure you even knew my name, and yes."

"Wish you'd—" Ike forced himself to keep the exasperation he felt out of his voice.

"You never asked, young man. But let me ask you a question. Do you have any idea how old Stilwell is? He changes the combination every year." She dropped a small slip of paper on the big desk and started out of the room.

Ike couldn't figure it. He'd been trying to learn anything he could about what was going on around here, and this woman seemed to know everything. And she was helping him.

"How do you know all this?"

"I keep my eyes and ears open. A word to the wise." She turned and left with the broom.

Ike worked the combination. He smiled as he swung the small door wide, then his eyes widened.

The smile disappeared.

Chapter Twenty-Eight

Bert watched Tibbie as she slept. He tried not to stare, but… no luck. Buster labored into the ranch house after checking on Ally. His scuffling gait made enough noise on the wooden floorboards to wake her.

She roused herself with a stretch and rubbed her eyes open.

Bert couldn't look away. Even her sleepy-eyed manner captivated him. He got up from the kitchen chair. "Did you get some rest?" Stupid question—of course she did. What a dumb thing to say. When she nodded, he tried to recover. "Can I get you anything? Water?"

"Yes, there is somethin' you can get me. You can get Buster to change places with me. He still needs a lot of restin' up." She rose from the lumpy mattress.

Bert didn't have to be asked twice. He guided his old friend to the bed and started away.

"Hold on there, young fella. Ain't you gonna tuck me in? Pull the blanket up to my neck, so's I stay nice and snuggly?"

"You keep on talkin' nonsense like that, old man, and I'll pull that blanket over your head for good. Get some rest and leave us alone."

"So it's *us* now, is it? About time. You sure could do a lot worse than Tibbie, but I don't think she could do worse'n you." Buster chuckled.

Bert shook his head and led Tibbie out of the house. He closed the front door behind him. "How's Ally doin'?"

"Why don't we go see?" She had a big smile.

They walked to the pretty mare's stall, where Ally now had almost full weight on that leg. Bert allowed himself a big smile. "Don't know when I've ever been so happy to see a horse lookin' so good. You were just what Ally needed, Miss Tibbie. Thanks for helpin' us out." He tipped his hat.

"I think it's about time you called me Tibbie, Bert. And I was happy to be here, lendin' a hand. But tell me about those raiders. Any idea who they were?"

"Never seen 'em before in my life. Except—" He pursed his lips.

"What?"

"My head's cleared some, and I think I may have seen one of 'em before. Can't be sure, but wasn't anyone from that gang I used to ride with. Tryin' to remember where I mighta come across that fella, 'cause he looked a mite familiar."

"And who would send them—and why?"

"If I could just remember where I saw that hombre before …"

"Whoever they were, they're still out there. You didn't kill them all, did you?"

"Two went down here, and Mr. Ike said he got two more on the Pass, and there was five of 'em—"

"So, someone's still out there. What are you gonna do?"

Bert shrugged. "Never gave it much thought, just been tryin' to keep everything together here."

"I'd say you're doin' a good job of that …"

"There's a 'but' in there, isn't there?"

"Maybe who it was will come to you."

***

Ike grabbed a folded piece of paper, left Stilwell's safe ajar, and strode down the hall to Helen's small desk. "Where's the telegraph office, and what time does it open?" No time to waste after seeing what that safe held.

With a hurried "Thank you," he rushed out of the building, and after several wrong turns, found the right place. The operator was just opening up as Ike hailed him. "Need to send an urgent message, sir. It's going to—"

"Hold your horses there, sonny. Let me get a cup of coffee and limber up my fingers first. I'm a mite old. Then I can—"

"No. No time for that. Need you to send a telegram right now to Sheriff Hugh Walnutt in Cottonwood, over in South Park."

The old man held a hand up. "All right, all right." He sat down with his other hand on the tapper.

"Tell him, 'Get here as soon as possible, and come armed. Hurry! Ike.'" He didn't want to add anything about Hugh taking the family back to Cottonwood. Couldn't be sure who saw these messages. Wasn't sure of much of anything lately.

The operator whistled while he tapped.

When he finished, Ike flipped the man five cents and dashed out for Agnes' place. Lorraine was waiting for him on the front porch with a pinched face. Not a good sign.

"Where the *hell* have you been? I been wearin' out Agnes' floors wonderin' if I was gonna have to deal with the undertaker this time. Tell me true, Ike McAlister, what was so all-fired important that you had to fret us somethin' awful. Huh?"

"I'm sorry about that, Lorraine. Couldn't sleep, so I decided to get an early start lookin' into what's been happening to us. Turns out I came across somethin' I believe you'll be interested in seein'."

"Well, come on in. Don't just stand there with that guilty puppy-dog look on your face." She gave him an irritated hug and led him inside. The children wrapped themselves around him while Agnes smiled off to one side.

Their host said, "Let me fix you a proper breakfast, Ike." Agnes made her way to the kitchen, humming a happy tune.

After eggs, sourdough toast, and black coffee, Ike and Lorraine made their way outside to what had become "their" double wicker chair and sat. Ike draped a wool blanket over his wife.

"So, first I went to the railroad office, figurin' that might be a good place to start searchin' for somethin' or other."

"What were you lookin' for?"

"Anything that might point to why Stilwell's got us in his sights. I went into Dobbs' office first and—"

"Who's Dobbs?"

"One of Stilwell's lackeys who was with him when he came out to the ranch months ago. I blew his desk apart mostly because I wanted to leave a callin' card. Found a bunch of cash inside, so I took what Stilwell owes us. We better make it last, though, 'cause we ain't gettin' any more."

"Did anyone hear the shot?"

"No … well, yes, but the woman who did favored me, 'cause then I shot Stilwell's door apart next. His desk was locked, too, but Helen—the lady I mentioned—pointed out Stilwell's safe to me."

He saw the scowl on her face at the mention of a woman. "By the way, Helen is probably sixty years old. And she gave me the clue I needed to figure out the combination. Can't figure why she did that; must not like the man much."

The glare was gone.

"Then she has good taste. You're livin' right, Ike. The good Lord has been lookin' out for you—and this family."

"I know that when I look at you and the kids; that's enough for me."

"So, tell me what was inside. Anything of interest?"

Ike hesitated. Now he wasn't sure he wanted to show her the drawing and add to her worries.

She must have seen the uncertainty on his face, though, because she said, "What was it?"

"Mostly a bunch of stuff about his thievin' the railroad's loads, which didn't surprise me. The man's made himself rich by skimmin' regular. There was also a stack of papers, and I opened a big, folded one. Had a drawing of *our* ranch on it, with some new buildings in place of the ranch house and barn."

Lorraine gasped. "What? Does that mean what I think it does? That he plans to take over our ranch and destroy it, too?"

"That's the only meanin' I could make of it. He's been plannin' to get rid of us, then take down anything else we have."

"But why? We haven't done anything to him—we don't even know the man."

"There must be somethin' we're overlookin' or don't know about, 'cause a man don't go to all the trouble he's caused us with nothin' behind it."

"We gotta unscramble this, Ike. And we better figure things out sooner than later, or there won't be a later."

"About the only thing I know for sure is things have gotten too dangerous here, Lorraine. We've been through some chancy times before, but nothin' like this. I need to think of you and the children, so I decided—"

"Whoa, hold on there, McAlister. What do you mean you 'decided?' You don't decide anything unless we talked it out together, so just let me in on 'your decision,' and I'll tell you if things are settled."

Ike smoothed his beard and paused. Forget about Stilwell—he was in dangerous territory right here on the porch. Tread carefully.

"Well, since I don't have a job anymore and you're gettin' better, I figured we oughta head back to the ranch and hunker down. No reason to stay here any longer."

"Now you're talkin', husband. Let's leave in the morning."

"Okay … just one more thing. I telegraphed Hugh to come get us."

"And why is that? You've been good at takin' care of us for a long time."

"I figure Hugh will even up the odds." He waited for a protest that never came.

Lorraine smiled and kissed Ike. "Okay, but I'm bettin' on you every time."

Ike hugged her but wondered if her wager would be a winner—or not.

Chapter Twenty-Nine

After leaving The Sew Pretty, Stilwell boarded the train at Como the next morning. He strode into the first coach, the most luxurious of the three passenger cars, and settled into his usual plush seat. A newspaper already lay on the seat next to him. The conductor approached and asked, "Might I bring your cognac, sir?" Stilwell barely nodded while opening the paper. As he turned a page, he glanced for a moment at his surroundings.

A dapper man walked by the windows outside, and Stilwell sat up. That sheriff. Cottonwood. Blasted Englishman. What was he doing here? Riding the train to Denver, too, obviously. A petty lawman going to the big city. As usual, the man was turned out nicely, though. Stilwell's interest was piqued. He motioned the conductor over. "There's a man, well-dressed in black, coming onto the train. Bring him here and seat him across from me." Stilwell stuck a dollar bill in the man's hand and waved the attendant away before he bowed his way out. This was going to be good.

In no time, the conductor ushered Hugh Walnutt into the reserved car. Stilwell rose. "Ah, Sheriff Walnutt, correct? Fancy meeting you here."

"Mr. Stilwell. Seeing you is indeed an unexpected surprise." No smile as he gave a slight bow.

"No need for formalities, Sheriff. Why don't you have a seat right here?" The better to find out what McAlister's brother-in-law was up to. Something was afoot. A small-time lawman doesn't travel to Denver for no reason.

"My pleasure." Hugh swept a hand over the back of his pants and sat across from Stilwell, his holstered Colt just visible under his black great coat.

"You have already made my trip more enjoyable, Sheriff. I look forward to passing the time getting to know you better."

"I do not mean to be rude, sir, but why would you want to do that? I am not very interesting, and our paths are not likely to cross again."

"Come now, Sheriff. A refined Englishman marshalling in remote South Park, Colorado? Who I understand is also a crack shot? Now, that is very interesting indeed. Will you have a drink with me?"

"Very gracious, Mr. Stilwell, I am sure, but I am currently nursing a cold, so I must decline your kind offer." He placed a hand over his mouth and uttered a fake cough.

Stilwell nodded. Turns out the sheriff was evasive as he was. He lifted a cognac to his lips and sipped. A formidable foe, possibly. How to draw him out? He placed his liqueur glass on the silver tray next to him and tried to sound nonchalant. "My guess is you are traveling to Denver to visit your in-laws?" He let his voice rise at the end of his question to make it sound more innocent.

"That is true, sir. It has been several months since we have seen my wife's brother and his family."

A flat-out lie. But why did the man feel the need to? McAlister visited his sister after the raid on the ranch, according to Stilwell's niece. "Ah, absence makes the heart grow fonder, is that it?" He waited for a response, eyes trained on his prey like a hawk. No change of expression on Walnutt's face.

Hugh folded his hands. "Naturally, my wife and I are interested in the McAlisters' welfare—as you are about your family's, I dare say."

So, the sheriff turned Stilwell's question back on him. Deftly done, indeed. How to follow up? "Yes, well, we all value family greatly, don't we?"

Walnutt's pistol showed a little bit more under his coat.

They stared at each other.

The sheriff broke the silence. "Please excuse me; I say, were you waiting for a response from me?" The edges of his mouth turned up.

"It is of no consequence. I fear I have may have somehow offended you with my conversation, Mr. Walnutt." He intentionally used the man's last name instead of his title. Anything to try to throw the sheriff off his feed. By backing off, maybe he could get the lawman to open up more.

"If I have seemed displeased, that is my failure, sir. I would be happy to hear more about your trip to South Park."

Walnutt had done it again—deflected the conversation back. "Quite an unremarkable visit, I assure you. I like to get out of Denver occasionally to check on the railroad's progress to Fairplay." He lit a long cigar, making Walnutt watch while he lazed a ring of smoke into the air between them.

"I trust you found everything satisfactory, sir."

Stilwell paused. How much to share with this stranger? Best to put a polish on it. "Things are coming along, but some coward shot down one of my men today in the performance of his duties." Not that he cared about Strothers; it was just the affront of it all. One of *his* men.

Walnutt swiped a finger over the ends of his mustache. "Most regrettable, indeed. I did hear about the killing when I arrived for the train. The talk of the town, it was. Any idea who might be responsible?"

The way Walnutt said that, almost too offhand, made Stilwell wonder. It had taken an excellent shot from a long way to do the deed, and this man was the best around, if local gossip was to be believed. And he just happened to show up later at the place where Strothers was killed. Stilwell never had believed in coincidences. How to proceed? "No one seems to know anything, except the murderer was an exceptional shot. Was likely a Sharps rifle, or a Winchester even. As I recall, you have one in your office, correct?" He studied Walnutt's face, but the man's expression didn't change. "I see you also use a Colt. Do you find it reliable?"

"It has never let me down, so far. An excellent example of American tradecraft. The weapon never ceases to surprise me with its range."

Sounded like the man was goading him now. "I, myself, have never had occasion to use firearms, so I will take you at your word." How to shut down this conversation? It was treading on dangerous turf, and Walnutt had just maneuvered him into a lie. A lie the sheriff would no doubt never discover, but still, a loose end that made him uneasy. He loathed loose ends.

Stilwell picked the paper back up, snapped the pages, and buried his face behind it. Walnutt would bear watching. Another job for Dobbs.

***

Ike stood on the Denver station platform, watching black coal smoke spew from the approaching train. Had his brother-in-law gotten his telegram, and was he on this one? As the locomotive braked to a screeching stop, the conductor stepped to the platform's wooden planks and helped two female passengers off. Having traveled the train, Ike knew the first car was Stilwell's, with the same, but smaller, ostentatious chandelier that had adorned his office. Couldn't shoot this one down—yet. So, no surprise when Stilwell disembarked from that car, but a big jolt when his brother-in-law stepped off right behind him. What was going on?

Ike greeted Stilwell with a nod and waited for Hugh to reach him before saying anything. Together, they walked toward Agnes' horse-drawn carriage. Ike glanced back at Stilwell on the platform, flicking cigar ashes and sniffing the air while waiting for his coach. Out of hearing, Ike posed the question on his mind. "Why were you travelin' with Stilwell?"

"I was not. I did not know he would be on this train. When I boarded, the conductor summoned me to Stilwell's car for some reason. He thence proceeded to engage me in conversation after I was seated across from him."

"Does he know you're my brother-in-law?"

"Yes, ever since he boarded at your sister's. He also recently paid me a visit at my place of business, alerting me to the fact that he was in town to see his niece."

Ike's brow furrowed. "Who's that?"

"Hannah Hawkins, at The Sew Pretty."

Every time Ike thought of her, he flashed back to that scene on Cottonwood's main street years ago, where her father was shot down after terrorizing Ike's family. "You say she's his niece?"

"That is what he said, yes."

He didn't believe much of anything Stilwell said anymore, but this sounded like it might be true. The man engineered his move to Denver, tried to kill him—and Lorraine—and now shows up in Cottonwood to huddle with his niece. Nothing good could come from those two linking up. "Thanks for comin', Hugh. Didn't want to say anything in the telegram, in case a bad guy read it."

"So, why *am* I here, Ike?"

"Need you to do somethin' for me. The most important thing I've ever asked of anyone." As they stepped into the coach, Ike scanned his surroundings. The footman snapped the leathers, and the horse started away. "Need you to take my family back to Como on the train, Hugh, then on to Cottonwood. They're not safe here anymore."

The sheriff's eyes widened. "I tried to deduce why you wanted me here, and it occurred to me it might involve your family. While I am surprised, I am not totally taken aback. Will you be returning as well?"

"No." Ike left it at that—he had things to square away here. When they arrived at Agnes' house, he introduced Hugh, then laid out the plan. "The next train won't be until tomorrow morning, so we'll have to stay low 'til then. Let's get packed up now so we're ready to go quick." He hadn't told Lorraine yet that he wasn't going with her. He'd wait until they were at the train station so she couldn't back out. She'd give him a tongue-lashing, which she had a right to do, but he'd survived her ire before. Not something he looked forward to, but… as long as they were safe.

Ike saw the questions on Hugh's face and pulled him aside. "You're probably wonderin' what's happened to make us hurry on out of here."

"The question had crossed my mind, so do tell."

Ike took his time bringing Hugh up to date. "Lots been happenin' the last few months. Found out Stilwell lured me and Lorraine here to do us wrong. He's been poisonin' Lorraine and tried to do me in. I stopped tryin' to figure why—that don't matter when someone's after your hide. At least we know who we're up against, and I figure the family'll be safer back in South Park."

"Perhaps so, Ike, but remember they struck the ranch there recently and may do so again."

"Thought on that, so I'm hopin' you and Sue will take them in 'til this is over." Ike had always been able to depend on his sister but never asked her for a favor as important as this. Not even keeping their parents safe in Lawrence during the War was this important.

Hugh smoothed at his starched cuffs. "An extraordinary turn of events. Even though I disliked Stilwell, I did not think he would commit such a dastardly deed. The man deserves a bitter end."

Ike stared into the small fire Agnes laid in the fireplace.

"And I'm ready to give it to him."

Chapter Thirty

Stilwell followed the carriage carrying Ike and Hugh away from the train station. It had to be at a discreet distance since his coach was a flamboyant affair, befitting its owner. Brass knobwork and headlamps, lacquered black paint, and a pale horse with a red tassel on its head.

When he first spied Walnutt back at the Como station, he could have predicted what was happening now—the sheriff was coming to meet up with McAlister. And here they were—conniving in a coach on the dirt road just ahead. He hadn't lost control, had he? Walnutt being here was a development he hadn't counted on and didn't know how to factor into his plan yet. He'd been reduced to a spectator for the moment, forced to react to whatever McAlister and Walnutt did next. That didn't sit well; people had always reacted to him.

The coach pulled up at Agnes' house, and the two passengers stepped inside, seemingly unaware Stilwell was following them. He'd post Dobbs to watch them. Time to head to the telegraph office. When he went inside, he cursed to himself—that cranky Como operator sat at the single desk. Stilwell's heart beat a little faster. No reason that old man should make him nervous; just a ridiculous peon. But Stilwell had always been one to meet a confrontation head-on. The few times in his life he hadn't been in charge, he'd blustered and intimidated to get what he wanted. This old fool was about to see him in action.

All he could see of the man was the top of his white head. He bellowed as he stood in the open door. "What are *you* doing here? You work in Como, don't you?"

"Yup."

When the old man didn't say any more, Stilwell stammered. "Send a telegram for me, you …" He couldn't think of a good bad word. "That *is* what you do, isn't it?"

The operator looked up. "Sorry, young man, what did you say? Don't hear so good as I used to; the wife always said it's 'cause I didn't wanna do what she said, but nah, I don't think that's the—"

"Stop!" Stilwell wasn't going to get into it with him this time. "Either you send it now, or I will." He started for the man's desk where the tapper sat.

White hair pushed it toward him. "Be my guest, sir. Let me know if I can do anything else for you, 'cause we aim to please."

Stilwell reached for the brass apparatus then stopped. "Move, you fossil, you know I need to sit to send anything, so get up out of that chair!"

"Whatever you say, Mr.—uh …"

"Don't pretend you don't know my name, fool. Everybody knows who I am, including you."

"I have a hard time rememberin' things so good these days. My wife always said I have a good memory, it's just short. What were we talkin' about again?"

Stilwell pursed his lips hard. It was all too much. "Gimme a pencil and I'll write it out—but then, maybe you can't read."

"I had a marker around here someplace—lemme see."

Stilwell stared. "What're you talkin' about? There's nothin' in here but that table and no drawers in 'em." Anger always affected his language.

"You know, you're right." The telegrapher eased out of his chair and drew himself up tall. "Look, Mr. Stilwell, why don't we just quit all this foolishness, and I'll pretend you're a decent person. Just tell me what you want to say."

When Stilwell finished, he flipped a penny on the table and walked out to the sound of tapping.

***

After the family went to bed, Ike and Hugh sat around the fire in Agnes' darkened living room. She had hospitably offered whiskeys, which the men were now sipping. Most of their talk centered on how things were in Cottonwood—he wanted to steer away from dwelling on their predicament in Denver. He'd not shared everything that had happened here with his brother-in-law, only enough to get the urgency of their situation across. And Hugh hadn't pressed him about what was going on; it was enough for him to know they were in danger. His brother-in-law wasn't one to talk more than necessary, which is one of the things Ike liked about him. His being a crack shot was another, which made him feel comfortable with Hugh escorting his family.

As the dry wood crackled to coals, Ike set his small glass on the marble table next to him. "By the way, did I mention Stilwell's man got shot the other day at the Como station?" He tried to maintain an offhand tone.

"No, I do not believe you did, Ike."

"Did you hear about it?"

"No one has told me anything about it." Hugh took a sip and balanced the glass on his upholstered chair's arm.

Ike nodded at that non-answer. "Sorta mysterious how it happened, though. Man's name was Strothers and he'd been ramroddin' there for Stilwell. Guess things weren't going fast enough, so Stilwell came to Como to see for himself. Had just got off the train when Strothers stopped a bullet." He took another sip, mirrored by his brother-in-law.

"Any idea who shot him?"

"Nobody knows, but whoever did it was quite the deadeye. Long distance and caught him right in the ear." Ike drummed fingers on the armchair.

"Surely, someone must have seen the killer." Hugh took another sip, followed by Ike.

"That's the thing—no one did. Shooter musta hid in the trees that were some distance away." They both placed empty glasses on the table between them. Ike poured another round and set the crystal decanter down. He eyed Hugh as he raised the glass to his lips. "Had to have been a rifle, probably a Sharps from that far away."

"That is a likely conclusion, Ike. A Winchester fails to match up with a Sharps at longer distances—or so I have been told."

"You have a Sharps, don't you, Hugh?"

"Why yes, I just happen to." He paused for another sip. "I also have a Winchester, and a Remington. All fine weapons."

"Reckon they'll know more when they dig the bullet out." Ike waited for Hugh to respond. In silence, they let their glasses sit while orange, glowing embers warmed the room. Easy to lose yourself in.

Hugh steepled his fingers. "Do I sense a question on your mind, Ike?"

Ike stared at the dying fire and after a long pause said, "Nope."

They lifted their glasses at the same time and with a mutual *clink* finished off the whiskeys.

***

Morning brought a scurrying around as the family gathered the rest of their few possessions. Lorraine didn't want to reflect on it, but there wasn't much left of what they arrived with. Agnes must have read her thoughts, as she had the children fetch more provisions from her storage cabinets.

Lorraine came back to the living room after a sweep around the downstairs. "Agnes, I don't see our valises, do you know where they could be?"

"Yes—they're gone. As much as I didn't want you to, I figured you all might be leaving, so I bought you new luggage. I hope you don't mind. They're in that wardrobe over there, along with more blankets, sheets, and other necessaries. Since your ranch house has so much damage, I thought you could use some new things. Pillows, too. And I packed a picnic for your train trip back." She wiped at her nose as her voice trailed off.

"I can't take all of these things, Agnes. You've already done so much for our family. Don't know what we would have done without you here. I just wish you were comin' with us."

"Thank you, honey. Maybe I will someday. In the meantime, take these gifts, get yourselves settled back in, and let me know when I can come visit." She dabbed at her eyes and whispered to Ike. "Guess there's no need for *us* to say goodbye. Figure you aren't going."

Ike stared at the little woman who was so full of surprises. How did she know that?

The family trundled away in Agnes' coach and arrived just in time to catch the train to South Park. Ike timed it so they wouldn't linger at the station longer than necessary.

Lorraine stepped up into the passenger car and motioned for her husband to get on. "What're you doin', Ike—why're you hangin' back?" A steely stare.

He swiped a hand across his beard and screwed up his courage. "Not goin' with you today. I'll be along directly, though; just have to tie up some loose ends here. You'll be fine with Hugh 'til I get there."

"Ike! You just got beat up here, were stupid for a while afterward, and you want to stay? Bah." She shook her head. "But then I knew you weren't leavin' with me. I know you."

His wife was always full of surprises. "I wouldn't leave you if I didn't have to." No need to get into details.

"So, when should I expect you? Ah, it don't matter. If you ain't back in a week, I'm comin' after you—you keep that in mind, Ike McAlister."

"Yes, ma'am." He reached up, kissed her, and hugged the children.

He started to turn away, but she stopped him with, "Kiss me like you mean it."

Afterward, he walked to the coach, looking back at her again before he mounted up.

Time to right some wrongs.

Chapter Thirty-One

After Tibbie rode off, Bert wiped the kitchen counters down. She'd already cleaned them, but he kept at it—nothing better to do since she left.

Buster raised up on the bed. "What're you doin'? You daydreamin' over there?"

"I'm about ready to put somethin' in your food if you don't knock it off, you old faker." He brought a mug of coffee over to his friend. "Don't bother gettin' up—let me wait on you, so's you can just keep doin' nothin' around here like you been."

"Touched a nerve, did I? So, why'd you let her leave? She wanted to stay, couldn't you see that, young'un?"

Bert set his mug down by the bed and scratched Rowdy's head. "I don't know, Buster, I never been any good with the ladies. Don't know what to say, how to act, don't even know where to put my hands." He pursed his lips and sat down in an old wooden chair.

"That's okay, Bert, she ain't goin' nowhere long as she thinks you're interested in her. You just need to let her know."

Rowdy's low growl stopped their conversation. That dog didn't snarl for nothing.

Buster moved off the bed despite Bert's protests. "Ain't got time for foolin' no more, Bert, just watch Rowdy, he'll let us know what's goin' on." Buster shuffled after the dog to the door, where Rowdy stared as if he could see through it, lips curled and brown fur raised on his back.

Bert grabbed both rifles and handed one to Buster. He kept them cleaned and loaded since the last assault. The two front windows had new wooden shutters he swung shut, leaving a small diamond opening in the middle. Bert peered through that peephole and drew back quickly. "They're out there, Buster; can't see 'em but I know you can feel them—me too."

"I'll keep hold of Rowdy. He's liable to tear on out there if we let him. Need to listen for anybody on the roof, too." Buster stood next to the door, back against the log wall, rifle at the ready, Rowdy at his feet.

A shot slammed through the wooden door, followed by a shout. "Come on out, hands up. I got somebody here you know. Tell 'em your name, sweetheart." Silence. "I said, tell 'em your name!"

Bert snuck another peek out the diamond at the barn. "They're just inside the open door, Buster. It's Tibbie, along with some yellow-dog coward hidin' behind her. Damn!"

The kidnapper sounded off. "Didya get a good look, sodbuster? She your sweetheart? Pretty thing, but I'm gonna kill her if you don't come out in one minute." He fired another round through the door.

Bert gripped the door's sliding wooden lock. "I'm goin' out there."

Buster blocked him. "No, you ain't, leastwise by the front door. Slip on out that side window and I'll lay down some coverin' fire. Go on, git!"

Bert worked his way out the window and eased to the ground where Tibbie and her captor didn't see him. Just then Buster let loose with his Sharps and Bert didn't need an invitation. He crouch-ran to the corral that stood only yards from the barn and flattened behind the lowest rail to size things up. Tibbie and the coward were even with the barn door, which meant Bert's shooting angle was no good. He'd have to move again. They hadn't seen him yet—wait! Tibbie gave a quick glance his way. Her kidnapper kept her close, pistol pressed to her spine and a hand wrapped around her neck. If only Buster would start shooting again, he might have a shot if the outlaw returned fire. Bert scooched to his right to get in better position. Had a clear view now, but couldn't fire yet—the two were too close together.

Tibbie quick-glanced his way again, and with a hand hidden at her side, pointed a finger to the ground.

Bert wasn't sure what she was doing, but the gesture had to mean something. Shoot, Buster, shoot! Come on, old man—fire! You gotta be reloaded by now.

A wild shot from the ranch house zinged over Bert's head and another splatted into a wooden plank on the side of the barn. Buster's eyesight was bad, but he didn't think it was *that* bad. Bert hunkered lower, rifle still pointed at the worthless raider. Two more shots from the house and Tibbie pointed down again. She wrenched herself out of the man's grasp and fell to the ground. Bert sighted in and squeezed the trigger.

Click.

Chapter Thirty-Two

Ike returned Agnes' coach to her house and had started away when she called to him from the front door.

"Ike, come in and let me make you a decent breakfast."

Come to think of it, with all the fuss of the family leaving that morning, it had been a while since he had eaten. A hot meal sounded good right about now. He limped up the front steps and into the dining room, where Agnes had already laid a nice sideboard. Warm eggs, bacon, and jam. Cold milk out of the wooden icebox. He chuckled. "Looks like you were expectin' someone. Am I intrudin'?"

"You're who I was expecting, you know that. I figured you'd be hungry when you got back—noticed you didn't eat anything this morning." She poured cold milk from the tiger oak icebox and sat across the table as Ike finished his plate. "Mind my asking where you were off to right now?"

"Thought I'd do some sniffin' around—no particular plan in mind." Didn't want to drag Agnes into what he was going to do.

"Then do me a favor. Stay in touch with me? Will you? Please?"

"Done." He patted his mouth with a fancy linen napkin. "Agnes, I need to tell you somethin'. Now that the family's gone, Stilwell's gonna be in a fury. Maybe angry enough to come after you, so I'll be around regular. Be careful and lock your doors." He tipped his hat and strode out of the house. After turning right and left down several streets, he passed through lower downtown and stood in the middle of a sea of Chinatown's canvas tents. He called out for An Li. He wasn't sure what Li could do to help him find Stilwell, but he had nowhere else to start.

A tent flap parted and Mei Won appeared in a flowing white robe. She held the flap up like a statue, and Ike ducked as he entered.

These low canvas structures weren't exactly a good fit for him. In the dim light of a small fire, An Li lay on a thin mattress, dressed in a loose white gown with a red blotch at the shoulder. His eyes were closed, but he motioned Ike over with his hand.

Ike knelt by the pad. "What happened?"

"Those who beat you … shot me."

"Damn!" Not what Ike wanted to hear. Helping him got his friend hurt. That wound didn't look good. Mei Won squatted immobile, staring straight ahead. "Have you seen a doctor?"

Li shook his head. "Chinese medicine. No White doctor comes to Chinatown."

"Did they get the bullet out?"

Li said, "Passed through," as his wife lifted a cup to his lips.

"What can I do to help?"

He swallowed and shook his head.

"Why would they do this?"

"I think they watch me … help you." Labored breathing.

Ike's heart rate raced and he put a hand to his forehead. He'd caused this. Stilwell's venom had reached into Chinatown a second time now, like a snake searching for a target to strike. Time to behead him. He'd had it his own way long enough. "Can't tell you how sorry I am. Know where they are?"

"Still in LoDo."

The flap opened. A Chinese man entered the tent and strode straight for Li. He lifted the man's clothing, changed the dressing underneath, and saved a withering glance for Ike as he made his way out.

Ike placed a hand on Li's pad, nodded at Won, and followed the shaman out. He turned away from Chinatown and limped toward LoDo, searching for scraps of clothing to wear. Stepping around bums sprawled on the dirt roads, he focused on grimy bags of belongings holding their owners' meager possessions. Scanning the beggars, he settled on one filthy man lying there who looked about his size. "What've you got in that bag, sir?"

He stared at Ike with bloodshot eyes. "Who's askin'?"

"Name's Murphy, and I'm guessin' you got some clothes in there."

A mumbled, "So?"

"So, I'll give you two dollars for your bag." The man snatched the bills and rolled over as Ike grabbed the sack and strode away. An alley beckoned. He turned that way, shucked his clothes, but hesitated before donning the bum's. Did they have lice? A foul odor to make even derelicts back away. The fit wasn't good, but he wasn't wearing them for how they looked. Frayed sleeves crept up his wrists, and loose buttons struggled to hold the shirt's worn brown fabric together. One dirty pant leg had a long rip, and the shoes were scuffed, holey, and tight. No coat. Perfect.

Now for some mud. He searched the alleyway and grabbed a handful from a putrid puddle that smelled worse than his clothes. His black beard seemed to suck it in as he rubbed it over his face and hair. Bundling his own clothes under an arm, he set out for the mean streets of Denver.

***

Stilwell paced the floor of his sumptuous office. Most of the intruder's damage had been repaired. Had to be McAlister who busted in. He'd get around to having someone look at Dobbs' room sometime. Worse than his torn-up office though, was the theft of his plan. He knew it was gone when he saw the safe lying open.

211

Chandeliers could be replaced, office doors too, but how had the thief gotten the thing open without destroying it? No one else had the combination, but then, someone had to—that's the only way this could have happened. He would have suspected Dobbs, the no-account, if whoever the goon was hadn't ransacked Dobbs' office worse than his.

He drummed fingers on his desk. Where was the answer to his telegram? "Morrison!" His secretary appeared in his newly-repaired doorway, the chandelier still missing from the ceiling. "Any messages yet?"

"Not in the last three minutes, sir." She turned on her heel, and as she walked away, Stilwell yelled, "I'm not through yet." He hated the way she disrespected him. "Come back here!"

Helen Morrison reached her desk just as a messenger handed her a telegram. She brought it in to Stilwell, who then shooed her away as he read the sender's address. Cottonwood.

When he finished, his face purpled. "Damn her!" Imagine, *her* telling him anything. Not hardly—she wasn't getting out of this so easy. He crumpled the telegram and hurled it at a wastebasket. Missed. To an empty room, he said, "We'll see about that. We'll just see about that." His plan was falling apart. And a great time for Dobbs to disappear. He'd need the man for bait for what was coming next. "Morrison! Find that fool Dobbs and get him over here."

She shot him a look as she left her desk and strode out of the building.

A rumpled Dobbs moseyed into Stilwell's office an hour later. "Whatcha need, boss?"

"Don't give me any of your lip and stand up straight. And clean up your office. Can't stand messes, at least any more than you already created. And why didn't you take out McAlister on Kenosha Pass when you had the chance?" Things had only gotten more complicated since then, when he thought they were getting simpler—easier. But the McAlisters were still alive, four or five of his lackeys were dead, and his niece had become a wild card. And that Franklin woman; he'd need to handle her at some point, too. Then there was the railroad delay at Como. Was someone behind that, that he didn't know about? He took a draw on his fat cigar and mumbled like he was talking to his desk.

"So, Boss … you okay?"

"Just do your job—what I pay you for."

Dobbs' face showed his uncertainty. "Uh, what's my job now?"

A flush ran up Stilwell's neck. "See that thing hanging off your belt? That metal thing? Start using it!" He waved the man out.

Dobbs turned for the door, and as he opened it, he looked back at Stilwell. "Now I don't want you should get mad, Boss, but who should I use it on?"

"Get out!" He threw his lit cigar at the retreating form and yelled to his assistant. "Get me the telegraph guy."

She returned later with a white-headed man in tow and left.

Stilwell shook his head. "Hmmmph. You again." The old man he'd had a couple of run-ins with. He silently cursed but needed to send a message. "Thought you were still in Como."

"Sometimes I am, and sometimes I ain't. Right now I ain't."

Stilwell had no answer to that, so he said, "At least you had enough sense to bring your tapper with you." A weak comeback.

The operator said, "That's what I do, so that's why I brought it." He sat at the large table in Stilwell's office and started arranging his equipment. After uncoiling a thin copper wire, he said, "Got anybody who can connect this with the line outside?"

"Morrison! Get Dobbs." His puffing increased and smoke filled the room. "And hurry it up." He daggered the old man with a stare.

"Can't do nothin' 'til your boy hooks this up." He sat back in the large wooden chair, twiddling his fingers.

Dobbs hustled into the room and, after instructions from the telegrapher, hurried out.

Stilwell's tapping on his desk increased. He stubbed his cigar out in the glass ashtray and lit another as the old man stared out the window. He jumped up and strode around the room. What was Dobbs doing? Wasn't he done yet? Something like a small explosion outside caught his attention. "What was that sound?"

"That's the sound of you ain't gonna be able to send your telegram from here." He picked up his equipment and walked out the door.

Stilwell shouted after him, "Don't turn your back on me, you're not done here yet." He started after him as well as an overweight, out-of-shape man could. "I said, come back here!" To no avail. How could that old man walk so fast? Stilwell slowed, then stopped, hands on his hips, huffing. Damn. Now he'd have to go to the telegram office himself and see the old coot again.

When he'd recovered, he grabbed his coat and hat from the office and strode out. At the telegraph office, the first thing he saw was that shock of white hair. Every time he'd been here—same old thing. He'd try a different tack. "Ahem."

Without looking up, "You ready to write that telegram now, Mr. Stilwell?"

"What's your name, sir?"

"Don't bother with my name, I'll still send your message. What do you want to say?"

After Stilwell told him, the operator said, "Who to?" He raised his eyebrows when he heard the name. "Reckon I know where to send it. Ever'body knows where that man's from—and what he does."

Chapter Thirty-Three

A bullet pinged off the split rail above Bert's head. He flattened but took a glancing blow to his cheek. With his Colt jammed, he had to make a move. He spun left to get out of the shooter's view. Another bullet sprayed dirt in his face as the gunman came around the edge of the barn after him. The killer had Bert dead to rights—there was no escape.

Whack! A blow from behind felled the gunman, who toppled to his knees, then dropped flat on his face. He'd let her loose so he could finish Bert off. Tibbie poked the motionless man with the bloodied piece of firewood in her hands. A crimson pool spread around his head.

Buster came out of the house and worked his way down the front steps. "Heard some shots, but you're both still standin', so reckon things must be okay." Rowdy ran loose around them.

Bert forced himself to a stand, a hand to his cheek. He hurried over to his friend and helped him to the barn, where he checked the body for a pulse. Nope.

Tibbie dropped the bludgeon and sank on a pile of split wood. She covered her face with her hands. Soft sobs brought Bert to her side. He put an arm around her, drawing her into a gentle hug where she wept on his shoulder.

"You saved my life, Tibbie. That next shot would have killed me."

Buster said, "Maybe you oughta kiss her for that, Bert. Seems like your life must be worth at least one."

Bert wasn't going to argue that. He held Tibbie's hand as they sat next to each other.

She lifted her head and wiped at her eyes. After a deep breath, she said, "Well, aren't you going to kiss me? Buster and I think you should."

He got lost in her brown eyes as he drew closer. Was he supposed to close his eyes? "I … uh … never done this before."

Buster grinned. "We can tell that, dummy. Quit yer stallin'."

"Well, if you won't kiss me, I'll kiss you." Tibbie leaned forward and kissed Bert on the lips. And smiled as she drew back. Before he could say anything, she said, "Now, let me take a look at your cheek. That bullet was way too close." She took him by the chin and examined the bloody crease. "Let's get you into the house and cleaned up."

Bert stood immobile for a moment. Did that just happen? He let her lead him to the ranch house.

Inside, Tibbie doused a ragged towel with water from a bucket by the sink. "Come here, please." She gently rubbed away dried blood from around the wound, then dabbed along the furrow. As fresh blood seeped, she pressed the cloth against the cut and glanced sideways at him.

"Ain't you gonna say anything?"

"Uh … yes, I am," then he clammed up. Didn't know where to look or what to say or anything else. He finally broke the silence. "Thank you, ma'am."

Tibbie's eyes grew wide.

"Really, Bert?" She looked toward Buster, then back to Bert and shook her head. "That's all you have to say to me?" She tossed the bloodied towel into the sink and started out the door.

Without a word, Buster grabbed the rag and threw it at Bert.

"Sorry, Buster, I'm makin' a mess o' things. I get all tangle-tongued around her."

"Come here, son." He put an arm around the young man's shoulders. "You're a fine kid, Bert. Ain't never seen a better young person. I can tell Tibbie thinks the same thing." He pushed Bert toward the front door as they heard Tibbie's horse trot away. "Now, I want you to do somethin' for me. Will you?"

A nod.

"Go after that young lady—let her know why you're so cotton-mouthed. I know you can do it." Buster started nodding, which drew nods from Bert.

"Good, now load up that buckboard. Can't leave that carcass to moulder—so just stick 'im in the back and be on your way."

"You'll be okay here alone?"

"Lived most of my life alone, young'un. Plus, I got Rowdy to keep me company and he's a heap better companion than you." A small smile appeared on Buster's face. He gave Bert a slight push out the door and eased to a seat on the front porch as the young man wrangled his horse from the corral and hitched the wagon.

With the body aboard, Bert gained the buckboard's bouncy seat, snapped the leathers, and yelled, "Yaaa!" The wagon jumped forward and rolled down the dusty road to Cottonwood. It had been a long time since he looked forward to going to town. Hannah had turned hostile toward him, not that he minded anymore. Hard to believe he once favored her. Without saying much, Tibbie showed him what real character was.

As he neared Cottonwood, light dust still hung in the air from Tibbie's horse. He'd pull up at Sue's boarding house first. Maybe she'd stopped there to clean up before work. No, he couldn't stop yet with that body in back. He kept on to the Sheriff's office and drew up there. Inside, a kid stared wide-eyed at him from behind a desk.

"Where's the sheriff, son?"

The youth got up, still keeping the desk between them. "Uh, gone away, mister."

"I can see that, so where is he?" The kid had a jittery manner about him.

"I'm not supposed to say."

Bert walked toward him.

"Don't hurt me, mister." He backed away.

"I ain't gonna hurt you. What's your name?"

"Benny. Benny Gaston."

"Well, Benny, I understand you're not supposed to tell me, but I got a dead body outside and I need the sheriff to take him off my hands. If you won't tell me, then I'll have to leave him there in the sun. And then he'll be your concern. Now, what do you think the sheriff would want you to do?"

"He's uh, he's over at the boarding house."

"Why didn't you just tell me that in the first place?" Bert left the wagon there and walked to Sue's. As he started up the steps, several sets of eyes in the window stared out at him. He held his arms up. "It's just me. Bert."

From inside, "Come on in."

He squinted to let his eyes adjust to the house's dark interior.

"Bert! What are you doing here?" Sue's familiar voice stopped him short.

"I brought a dead guy in. He's in the wagon in front of the sheriff's office. If you tell me what to do with him, I'll take care of it."

Hugh said, "That is not your task, Bert. I will undertake his final arrangements, so you are free to rendezvous with Miss Tibbie at the Wildfire."

"How'd you know that's who I was lookin' for?"

Sue set another dish on the dining room table. "This is a small town, Bert. Sometimes too small. So get on out of here and find her."

The sheriff gave Sue a rifle and a box of ammo. "I will accompany him to the Wildfire, thence hie me to the corpse."

She pushed a round into the rifle chamber. "Nobody knows what 'hie' even means. Stop using words nobody understands. Just say 'go'."

Bert headed for the door.

Sue yelled after him, "Be careful you two."

Hugh carried his rifle with both hands in front of him. He glanced sideways at Bert. "Unloop your hammer."

"Wh—"

"Please do as I request."

They walked by The Sew Pretty and Bert glanced back.

"There is nothing for you there, son. Never was." As Hugh continued toward the sheriff's office, he looked back. "Mind yourself in the bar."

Bert split off at the saloon. He pushed the swinging doors open and stood for a moment, scanning the dark room. There she was. Tibbie sat at a table on a man's lap. He had a drink in one hand, the other arm around her and held her close. Bert took it all in silently, then turned and left.

Tibbie looked over just then and yelled after him. "Bert!" She rushed out and caught up to him midway across the street. Grabbing his arm, she pulled him to a stop. "Will you wait a minute?"

"I saw all I need to see; what's there to say?"

"Plenty. This is my job, bad as it is, and it means I sit with customers every now and then. And I'll keep doin' that until they fire me or I leave for somethin' better. And you're just gonna have to accept that if we're gonna be together."

Bert's heart raced. "Us? Together? Hope you mean that. Couldn't get my feelin's out at the ranch, but that's what I want, too. And you sittin' on men's laps may be part of your job, but I don't have to like it, and I don't."

Tibbie leaned in and kissed him. "Thanks for bein' jealous; that says more than those words you couldn't get out." She slipped an arm through his. "I'm gonna take the rest of the day off now that you're here."

They walked back to the boarding house as hidden eyes watched from a distance.

Chapter Thirty-Four

Ike pulled a ratty blanket he'd found over his chest and closed his eyes. The dirt ground of LoDo was cold and his hip ached fiercely. A drunk stumbled over his legs and fell face down by his side. Ike pushed his grimy cotton hat back and tried to help the man up.

"Reckon I split my lip in two, but you can just leave me right heah."

Last time Ike heard a southern accent was during the War. "Sorry my legs tangled you up some. Still gettin' the hang of this place. You been here long?" A strong odor of urine surrounded the bum.

"I end up here and there, but this here's my favorite place to flop. Who're you? Ain't seen you around here 'fore."

Ike dodged the question. "I regular sleep a couple blocks over. Got a windbreak there I back into. Thought I'd try here; see if I like it. Any regulars around?"

"Some, there's three or four others here most nights; same ones, but don't see 'em right now." The man pulled his collar tight. "You don't got no food, do ya?"

Ike shook his head. "I been lookin' for some buddies of mine, you seen 'em? There's three of 'em—one's tall, the other two's short. Tall one's got red hair, bushy beard."

"Um, I think I seen 'em, if they's the ones I'm recollectin'. Tall one's name is Dewey somethin'. Keeps company with a bad crowd; they shake fellas down, gives the rest of us a bad name." He squinted and backed up a couple of steps.

Had to be the cowards who beat him. Ike said, "Yeah, them's my friends. Where else do they flop?"

"Why all the questions, stranger? I'm—"

Ike grabbed him by the collar. "Where?" He needed to know.

The vagrant pushed back. "I don't know nothin'."

"Where?" He gave the man two bits and held on.

"Maybe a couple blocks over. Larimer."

Ike let him go and the man ran away in the time it took Ike to struggle to a stand, hand to his hip. Where was Larimer Street? He headed in the general direction the man thumbed toward. When he found the right dirt path, he pulled his worn cap lower over his face. Scanned the tramps on both sides as he limped by. Smoke from small fires couldn't blot the human stink. Hard to see in the evening light, and glare from the fires made it worse.

Spotted them, warming their grimy hands over a faltering flame. He hesitated, then continued to another fire surrounded by several bums. He breathed through his mouth and squeezed in, facing so he could keep an eye on his muggers. Near enough so he caught snatches of conversation, but not close enough to attract their attention. No one else sat with them—they gave off a menacing air. Didn't want to think what they'd do if they knew who he was.

The drifter next to him elbowed him in the ribs. "You're sittin' in my place, mister. Beat it."

A flush ran up Ike's neck. He stared, then leaned close to the derelict's face. "Ain't movin'. I'm tired and hungry and in a real bad mood. Move over or get shot." The man put a hand up, and shifted. Ike settled in, bad leg out. A man across the fire from him held out a piece of stale bread.

"Thanks. Been a while since I et." He finished off the small handout, eyes still on the men who beat him. No way he could take them all on at once, he'd have to waylay them one by one. Wait to see if they split up. As the fire warmed him, he could barely keep his eyes open, but they'd likely be there all night, wouldn't they?

Ike moved away from the fire. He laid down on the dirty alley as weariness overwhelmed him despite the yelling, screaming, and jostling. And even he could tell he stunk. Phew. When he woke, he glanced over at his targets—not there anymore. Damn! Now he'd have to track them down all over again. The man next to him had already rolled his blanket up as the dawn sky came to life. Ike hailed him. "Where's everybody gone to?"

"Breakfast's at the mission church down the road. Closes at eight."

"What time's it now?" This part of town wasn't known for clocks.

"Almost eight."

"How'd you know that?"

"Sun."

Ike nodded. "I'll follow you."

"I'll show ya, but I don't eat that crap."

So his companion had taste. They walked to a rundown brick building where tramps still lined up outside.

"You can wait with them, but best you hurry." He turned and walked away.

Ike waited until the drifter was out of sight. He wasn't here for breakfast. Not when he was on the hunt. When his turn came, he only peered in instead. It just took a second to locate them among the crowd. Sitting together. He backed away and crossed the street, concealing himself among piles of garbage. Vagrants wandered in and out of the mission, hands full of food. Some of the last ones to leave were his assailants. Still together.

He followed at a distance, slumping and stumbling behind to blend in. Getting caught would mean more than a beating this time.

One of them peeled off at a street corner. Ike lingered at that fork, keeping an eye on the two walking away. When they disappeared around another corner, he set off after the third man, his heartbeat quickening. He grabbed a wooden stick lying amid the garbage and used it as a cane. Picked up his pace. The man glanced back and Ike fumbled with some refuse. He looked up and the man still walked away. No more time to lose. A limping walk-run closed the gap and Ike called out to his assailant.

"Hey buddy, you know a good hidin' place around here?"

The man slowed, letting Ike catch up to him. "Whatchoo hidin' from?"

"Don't matter, does it? I been on the run too long. Need a place to hole up for a while."

"You lookin' for work?"

"Might be. These are hard times to get by in."

"Care what you do?"

"Done a lot of stuff in my time I ain't proud of." Flashes of the carnage at Antietam flew through Ike's head. All those lifeless bodies, blue and gray, forever joined in death.

"Come on."

Ike scanned his surroundings then whacked the man across the back of his legs. The coward uttered an oath on his way to his knees. A blow to the back put him face down in the dirt. He raised a hand up against the next blow, which smashed into his arm and sent him curling into a ball, wailing.

"Don't hit me no more!"

"Tell me what I want to know." He held the hard stick high again, his heart pounding.

"Wait! Whaddya want to know?" He radiated raw fear.

Ike leaned close to the wounded mess in front of him. He pulled his thick watch cap off. "Remember me?"

Uncertainty showed in the man's eyes.

"You and your buddies beat the holy crap out of me not far from here. Woulda killed me if my friends hadn't rescued me. Comin' back now?"

Ike's glare was met by a wide-eyed expression. "I dunno you, mister. Never seen you before."

"You ain't real smart—probably why you live in this hellhole." He rapped him hard on the knuckles, which sent the man into another paroxysm of pain. "I got all day. Won't ask again."

The mugger stayed down. "It weren't my idea. Some fella paid us to hurt you."

"To kill me?"

"Yeah, if you put up a fight."

"I heard I did. Don't remember anything after you used my head like a watermelon."

The man cringed even more.

"You got a name?"

"Mine?"

"No, dummy. Name of the coward who set me up." He raised the stick again.

"Wait, wait. Name's … Dobbs."

Big surprise. "You done stuff for him before?"

"Yeah. Some." He held a hand back up.

Ike flung the wooden weapon and turned away. Stilwell. Confirmation for what he already knew. He shed the worst of his clothing—grimy gloves, a tattered watch cap, and the too-small shirt full of holes. He backtracked to where he stashed his clothes, then donned what he had been wearing. He still stunk, but not as bad. Agnes' was the only place he could go now. He zigzagged down different streets to her house and slipped in when she opened the back door.

"Thanks, Agnes, but what are you doin' here? Don't you need to be at your shop?"

"Don't worry about that, I have someone running the store, but you look something terrible. What have you been doing?"

"Searchin' for answers."

"Have you found any?"

"I believe I have." And he didn't like what he'd found out—nor what was liable to come.

"Well, before you do anything rash, come have something to eat, you're a scarecrow. And you sure do stink!" After they'd finished lunch, Agnes kept up her questioning. "I know you well enough by now, Ike, to know you have something planned."

He didn't answer and changed the subject. "How are things here? Seen anybody lurkin' around?"

She shook her head. "There is one thing, though. I've seen a fella ride by here a couple of times. He tries not to look this way, but I can tell he's eyeing the house as he goes by."

"What's he look like? Tan hair, short mustache, smaller fella?"

"That's probably him; I try not to stare out the window."

Dobbs. "I want you to do me a favor, Agnes. Please stay inside and don't go to your shop anymore. Can you do that?" He nodded his head, hoping to get her agreement.

"Don't know what you're so worried about, Ike. Nobody cares about a little old lady."

Ike ignored that. "Will you do that, please? For me—and Lorraine?"

At Lorraine's name, Agnes misted up. "Sure, I will."

"Do you have a rifle or at least a pistol?" Even if she had one, he wasn't sure she was up to using it if need be.

"Got Sam's Remington, and I have an old Colt."

"Can I see them?" She retrieved the weapons, which he cleaned, then loaded. "Do you know how to use these?"

"Sam was always a hand with both. He taught me well." She took both of them, placed them on a dining room table, and mimicked a quick draw, which drew a rare smile from Ike.

"Just be careful. Stilwell hates that you helped us. And you have been such a blessing—one he didn't count on." The man didn't like loose ends.

"Aye, aye, sir."

Ike made a low bow and stole out the back door.

The hunted had become the hunter.

Chapter Thirty-Five

Stilwell drummed his fingers on his new desk, even grander than the old one. He called his assistant in. "Anything yet?"

Helen Morrison said, "No message."

"Go down to the telegraph office and find out—and hurry."

When she didn't come right back, he strode from the building and met her coming out of the telegraph office. "What've you got there?"

She held a piece of paper in her hand. "It's a—"

"Gimme that." He grabbed it from her. After reading it, Stilwell crumpled the message. He started to toss it but then thought better of it. Didn't want to chance anyone besides Morrison seeing what it said. No sense giving his secret away before he needed to. Stuffing the telegram in one of his thick coat pockets, he lit a cigar and turned back for the office. His plan was back on track.

Two days later, he stood on the station platform, rocking back and forth and smoking away. In the distance, the Denver and Rio Grande steamed toward town from Durango. An ear-splitting whistle announced its presence if anyone wasn't already aware of it. The man ought to be on this train. Time he reminded people who was in charge. The locomotive slid on steel wheels to a screeching stop, and passengers started disembarking. Stilwell took a step forward, craning his neck. He'd seen a couple of photos of the man in the newspapers, so he had an idea who he was looking for.

There. A well-dressed man with a striking gold vest under his black coat stepped off. Black hair slicked back and a slim face that sported a salt-and-pepper circle beard. An old scar ran from his cheek to his chin. He wasn't as big as Stilwell pictured him. Surely, he'd be up to the job, based on his well-known exploits. The

229

railroader stepped in front of the stranger and doffed his hat. "Thomas Stilwell at your service, sir."

The newcomer brushed a veneer of black dust off his vest and kept walking. "My hotel."

"Yessir, Mr. Tanner. I have all your accommodations ready, and I trust you will be comfortable."

"My money."

Stilwell hurried to catch up. "Yes, well, here's half now, and the rest after, you know."

"All of it. Now." He held out a calloused hand.

Stilwell stammered. "Uh, that wasn't the deal. How do I know you'll perform, Mr. Tanner?"

"It's Tanner, just Tanner. My money, now."

Stilwell put the cash in Tanner's outstretched hand, fingers pinching the bills as he did.

Tanner tugged once, twice, before Stilwell let go. The money disappeared somewhere inside his coat. "My hotel."

At the Centennial, the desk clerk blanched when he saw who Stilwell walked in with. The railroader was bad enough, but that one… "Welcome to the Centennial Hotel, Mr. uh, Tanner. We have your accommodations all ready. You're in room six, upstairs to the right. Our best room."

Tanner swiped the key from the counter. Without a look back, he told the clerk, "Have a bath prepared. I'll take it before dinner."

"Uh, we don't have a bath here, Mr. Tanner. It's down the street at the mercantile."

"I'll be back in half an hour. Have it ready." He walked up the stairs and disappeared as the clerk dashed out the front door.

Stilwell stood motionless in the lobby, staring up the stairs. Just when he thought he'd regained control, had he lost it again? He shook his head and walked out.

In the morning, he called on his gunman, catching up with Tanner in the hotel dining room. Doffing his hat, he sat across from him.

Tanner looked up from his coffee. He buttered some toast and ate with a decidedly slow pace.

Stilwell said, "Mornin'."

With a dab at his mouth, Tanner put the cotton napkin down and stared at Stilwell. "Now, who?"

Stilwell decided to drag this out. Pay Tanner back for his rudeness yesterday. Show him who was boss. "You don't say much, do you?"

"I never pass up a good chance to shut up. Learned a lot that way."

Stilwell swiped at his mouth and shifted in his chair. "Don't you want to know 'why,' too?"

"Nope. Don't matter much, now does it? Who?"

Stilwell squinted. "Someone I've owed for a long time—too long."

Tanner stared him down with a menacing glare until Stilwell gave a slight cough. He had an overwhelming sense he'd dragged this out as far as it was going to go.

"Man by the name of McAlister—"

Tanner's eyes widened and he interrupted. "Ike McAlister?"

Stilwell leaned forward in his chair. "You *know* him?"

The man nodded and gazed off into the distance. "Served with him during the War. Cavalry raid. Sergeant McAlister saved my life. Never thought I'd get the chance to square things with him."

Stilwell's heart sank and he cursed under his breath. Just when he thought he had things in hand.

Tanner reached into his coat and pulled out a wad of money. He threw the bills on the table and leaned close. "Don't know how you and my sergeant got sideways, but you picked a fight with the wrong man. And hired the wrong gunslinger." He swept his hat up and left Stilwell sitting there, stunned.

***

Ike stopped by his office, but Helen said she hadn't seen Stilwell in a couple of days. He'd just left the building when he came face-to-face with a stranger. Medium build, slick black hair, black suit but also wearing an old forage cap from the War. Odd. The man wouldn't let him by on the sidewalk and breasted his Colt for emphasis. Ike didn't know him but recognized trouble when he saw it. He tried to sidestep, but the stranger blocked him. "Let me by, mister." Ike's hand dropped to his pistol.

The man squinted. "No need for gunplay. I recognize that limp—you and me got business, Sergeant McAlister."

Who was this stranger who knew his name? "Not from where I stand. Don't know you, and don't have any truck with you."

"Look closer, sergeant." He pointed to the scar that rode up his face. "Remember me?"

Ike studied the man. Artillery shells began to explode in his head and his ears rang. Dirt and debris battered his face. Screams of the dying seared his soul as he stared at the man in front of him. Stoneman's raid.

"That's right, sergeant. Cavalry raid on Asheville, 1865."

Ike's voice was raspy. "You got knocked off your horse; wounded in the face."

"And elsewhere. Was on the ground starin' down the barrel of a Confederate rifle 'til you dispatched the reb. Don't nobody forget things like that."

Bullets whined through Ike's head. He pushed his hat back and put a hand to his forehead. "Corporal … Tanner."

The man nodded. His face bore just the hint of a smile. "At your service, sergeant."

"What're you doin' here?"

"Guy named Stilwell hired me to kill you. Don't know what you did to set him against you, but he don't seem the type to let a grudge go. I'd watch your back if I was you."

Ike nodded and reached an arm out. Tanner clasped his with it and the two stared at each other. The corporal touched a finger to his cap brim and walked away. Ike didn't know what he would run into today, but hadn't figured on that. He watched Tanner head for the train station, his heartbeat slowing.

He still had to stop Stilwell—and probably Dobbs. Whichever he ran across first. Where was the last place he'd seen Dobbs? The flunky did his boss's dirty work, so where would he be? Wasn't at the railroad office. He might be tailing Ike right now because of Tanner, but he hadn't seen anyone lurking. That's what the rat was best at.

He'd head back to check on Agnes. He'd told—asked her, you didn't tell Agnes anything—to stay inside, but no telling if she did. A sudden shiver ran up his back that said he needed to get to her house as quickly as he could. He smelled danger. Stilwell had it in for Agnes and he wasn't one to wait around for something he wanted.

Ike hurried with a limp-run, but the fear struck again when he saw the house. Nothing unusual outside, but he could taste trouble. He'd go in the back—knew where that key was. Feeling around an edge in the porch's wooden floorboards, his fingers pinched something metal. In his haste, he broke it off in the lock. Stepping back, he hesitated momentarily, then wrapped an old rag lying on the porch around his fist. A quick punch to the window sent glass flying. Reaching through the broken shards, he grasped the knob and unlocked the door.

He stepped on the scattered glass as he hurried to the living room. "Agnes! Agnes!" No answer. He hurried to the stairs and shouted again. A muffled sound came from above. With a hand on the staircase railing, he propelled himself to the second floor.

"Agnes!"

She came out of the bedroom. "Why, Ike, whatever are you doing here in the middle of the day?"

Relief coursed through his body. "Well, I … uh … just wanted to get a home-cooked lunch."

She smiled at him. "You're a soft-tongued liar, but come on, I'll get Sally to fix you something."

"I called for you downstairs, but you didn't answer."

"Well, I was in my uh, necessary, with the door closed if you must know, and my hearing isn't what it used to be. Don't look so worried, nothing's going to happen here."

"Don't want to alarm you, but I didn't see Sally when I was downstairs. You didn't give her the day off, did you?"

"Well, no, I didn't." She scrunched her mouth but didn't say any more.

"I'm sorry, but I broke the back door window tryin' to get in."

She lifted an eyebrow. "You know there's a key there, don't you?"

"Yeah, well, I broke that, too. Sorry."

"You must have been in a hurry. Did you think something happened to me?"

"No, I'm just a fool." That last part was true. Lorraine always said he did more doing than thinking.

Downstairs, Ike walked through each room. He tried to hide his purpose from Agnes, but no doubt she knew what he was up to. Just then, Sally came in through the back door.

She eyed the scattered glass on the wooden kitchen floor with wide eyes. "W-what's happened here?"

Agnes eased past Ike. "Ike here broke into the house when the key didn't work. I was upstairs and I thought you were down here." Her voice rose at the end of the sentence, making it sound like a question.

Sally hesitated just for a second—long enough for Ike to notice. "I went to the mercantile to pick up some items. I was only gone a little while." Her eyes darted between them as she placed a small sack on the table.

"Mind showing us what you got?" Agnes' voice held a sharp edge.

Sally dashed out the damaged door and disappeared.

Ike started after her, but Agnes stopped him. "What good will that do, Ike? We already know who's behind all this. You'd just end up scaring her silly for no reason."

"Not for no reason. She oughta feel the same fear we been dealin' with."

Agnes stared out the empty door. She undid the sack to find matches and candles and shook her head. "Yes, well, figured as much. And I got what I thought was a good reference, too. What do we do now?"

"No doubt Stilwell bought her off. Man's got a long reach. Gotta get you outta here, Agnes. You're not safe anymore and I can't watch you all the time. Please go put some things together, and I'll take you to the train station. You can stay with Lorraine and the kids at my sister's boarding house. I'll let 'em know you're comin'."

Agnes started to protest, but Ike held a hand up. "I ain't brookin' no argument this time, Mrs. Franklin. You need to listen to me now. Only thing that makes sense. Stilwell's got you in his sights and he's not one to be put off."

"Then you should come with me because it seems like he wants you more than me."

Ike didn't have a good answer to that. Her words had the ring of truth. 'Why' still didn't matter—maybe they'd be able to figure that out after. He diverted the conversation. "So, what can I help you get together?"

Agnes arched an eyebrow at him and started up the stairs. When she'd gathered her belongings, Ike had her stay inside while he hitched the coach, then escorted her to the carriage. Whoever had been coming to kill her was probably watching them right now. Even a wretch like Dobbs wouldn't likely risk shooting two people down in broad daylight, but still …

Ike kept Agnes sheltered in the station until the train to Como was watered and coaled. He hustled her into a passenger car and motioned to the conductor, who nodded and swung his lamp. When the South Park disappeared in the distance, Ike scanned the platform before stepping out of the building, Stilwell in his sights.

Chapter Thirty-Six

Stilwell would have to fall back on who he still had now that Tanner turned on him. No one kept their word anymore. With Strothers dead, that only left Dobbs. He needed to hear from him, see if he'd handled the Franklin woman. Strolling back to his office, he passed his assistant's desk and locked eyes with Helen Morrison. He'd never liked her; knew she didn't like him either. Always did her work well, but he never could tell what she was thinking behind those thick glasses. And that worried him—he suspected she knew about his thievery. But so far, he'd been able to bully her into silence.

She didn't look up as she held something out to him. "There's a message here for you. I didn't see who left it on my desk; it was here when I came in this morning."

The woman didn't get up, which irritated him. Rude person. Stilwell snatched the paper and stormed to his office. Why hadn't he heard from that no-account Dobbs? He picked out a cigar from his canister, lit it, and leaned back in his tooled leather chair. He never liked being at loose ends like he was now. Hmmph. McAlister probably thought he outwitted him by spiriting his family back to South Park, but he didn't know they still weren't out of his reach. Man didn't know who he was up against.

A runner came thumping down the echoey hall. Stilwell heard muffled talking from Morrison's desk. He made out a couple of words—railroad, Como. But that was enough to get him up out of his chair and on his way over to her. This time she looked up as he approached. With a wave of her hand, she dismissed the clerk.

The frown on her face prompted Stilwell. "What's going on?"

She just said, "Here," and handed him a telegram addressed to him.

At least that white-haired old man hadn't come with it. He stared at the words, but they didn't make sense. His eyes ran over the two short lines.

'Track torn up last night both sides of Como. Stop. Please advise. Stationmaster.'

He raced after the youth as well as a portly, middle-aged man could. Out on the street, the kid strolled down the sidewalk. "Hey, you, stop!"

The messenger turned. "You talkin' to me?"

Stilwell huffed himself alongside. "Yeah, is that all you know— what was in the telegram?"

"Yup."

Why didn't that old telegrapher say more? Stupid old goat. He hurried to the station ticket office. "When's the next train west?"

A dim-looking worker stared back at him. "Wahl, would've been in just a few minutes, but trains west is stopped. Track tore up."

The locomotive stood nearby, cars coupled behind. Stilwell yelled, "Get that engineer, and tell him to fire up this train. We're leaving for South Park. Now."

Not half an hour later, they were steaming toward Como. Stilwell held onto a leather grip in the cab as the fireman shoveled more and more coal into the flaming firebox door. The climb up Kenosha Pass took forever. He stared out the locomotive's front window, rising on his toes as if to see over the top into South Park. Once they started down, Como's few buildings lay in the hazy distance. But this side of town was as far as they got.

Workers stood stock-still on both sides of the destroyed track, as if waiting to be told what to do. If Strothers was still here, they'd already be hammering wooden ties back down. Nothing to do but walk the rest of the way. When he got to town, he headed for the telegraph office.

White Hair was back from Denver but didn't look up. "You again? Figured you'd get here; didn't figure so fast."

"Who did this? Who tore up my track?" This could ruin everything. Make his boss look into things, something he hadn't counted on. His smuggling just lay there, waiting to be uncovered.

"Wasn't that man you been doggin', if that's what you're askin'."

McAlister? How did this guy know about that? "Then, who?"

"My memory ain't so good anymore, bein' out here all alone. I'm old and sometimes things get all confusey." He glanced sideways up at Stilwell.

Stilwell threw a silver half dollar on the man's table, but White Hair promptly brushed it off onto the floor. "Don't want your money this time."

"Whaddya want then?"

"I want you to call me by my name."

"What?"

"My name—call me by my name." He spit a chaw into his spittoon.

Consarned fool. Stilwell raised both hands in front of him in mock surrender. "Okay, okay … what's your name?"

"Jim."

"Jim, what?"

"Just Jim."

Stilwell shook his head and took a deep breath. "Okay Jim, who did this?"

"The workers."

"Do you know who?" Had to be the Chinese.

"Nope."

The man was lying, but Stilwell couldn't attack him in broad daylight. Outside, he scanned the laborers. The Chinese were huddled around one man in the middle. When he reached the group, Stilwell parted them like a ball knocking down bowling pins. He strode to the coolie in the center. "You speak English?"

The man nodded.

"Who did this?"

A shrug.

Stilwell grabbed the man's shirt top by the neck and squeezed. "Tell me who." The Chinaman stood his ground. Stilwell slapped him hard, and the man's knees buckled, but he remained standing. A stare, and the bully drew his pistol, touching the man's forehead. He cocked the weapon and pressed harder. The Chinese boss spread his arms. No one moved as Stilwell surveyed the gathering. Hate and crowbars met his gaze, and after an awkward silence, Stilwell lowered the gun while cursing them.

He backed out of the crowd, eyeing them as he did. Other workers had drawn closer to the commotion. They moved away as Stilwell approached. "A twenty-dollar golden eagle to the man who tells me who planned this." Heads lowered to avoid his gaze. One foreigner took a half-step forward before he was stopped by several arms grabbing his. That didn't go unnoticed by Stilwell. "So you understand English." He crooked a finger at the man. "Come here, son." He gripped the worker by the arm and steered him to the station house.

Inside, he pointed to a chair, and the man sat. "What're you? Italian?"

"Si."

"Did you see who's behind this?"

"Chi-nese lead-er."

"Who's that?"

"Chinaman. There."

Stilwell's gaze followed where the man pointed. The same worker he'd braced earlier. When he walked away, the Italian shouted after him. "Where'sa my money?"

The Chinese still circled their leader. This time Stilwell didn't bother moving anyone aside. He drew his Colt and shot the man in the chest, then fired in the air. "Get that body out of here and get this track repaired—now." He pointed to the destroyed track between the train and the station and fired again. Until that section was repaired, they couldn't get the train turned around at the roundhouse and return to Denver. As long as he was stuck here, a side trip to Cottonwood wasn't out of the question.

Workers scattered to grab their picks and hammers. Soon, the sound of metal clanging on metal echoed throughout the Park.

Stilwell took a position inside the station house where he could keep an eye on the workers. Too many windows here, so he moved to the telegraph office where he sat against a wall behind the old man, pistol drawn. "Let me know when they've got that part of the track fixed, Jim."

The old man eased his desk drawer open and drew a small handgun out, his body shielding his movements.

Chapter Thirty-Seven

As dusk fell, Ike kept to side streets on his way back to Agnes'. Both Dobbs and Stilwell were out there somewhere. Her ruined back door still stood open, inviting the worst of Denver's vagrants in. Stepping over the broken glass, he took a quick survey of the downstairs. At least the traitorous housekeeper—a second one!—hadn't returned. He wondered if Stilwell had indeed paid the poor woman whatever he promised her. The man's word was worthless.

Fading daylight dimmed the staircase as he climbed. Ike lit an oil lamp, as that would alert Dobbs to his presence if he was anywhere near. Lure him there. In the guest bedroom, he struck a match, held it to another lantern, and light danced on the walls. Now for his deception. Leaving the lamp on a table, he eased down the stairs. In the kitchen, he closed the back door and cleaned up the glass so it would look like Agnes was still there. He picked out a slim carving knife and opened the pantry door. A large inner room, it held the household's foodstuffs in a cool setting. He settled on a flour barrel as a suitable seat and left the door slightly ajar, waiting.

Darkness reigned when Ike heard the first sounds. Faint enough to be outside but growing louder. As he leaned toward the opening, footsteps padded across the kitchen floor. He couldn't make out who it was in only the dimmest of light from upstairs.

The intruder started up the staircase. Ike followed, keeping his distance. One of the stairs creaked under the man's weight. Ike stood motionless in the dark for a moment. Had to be Dobbs. He'd kill him upstairs. When the man reached the top, he turned for the lit bedroom. Ike avoided the squeaky step, but not by enough. A slight noise seemed to scream throughout the silent house. The shadow of a man fell on the upstairs walls as the stranger came out of the bedroom. Dobbs. Ike backed down, crouched near the bottom of the stairs, and drew his sidearm. When Dobbs reached the last step, Ike thought about pistol-whipping him but held off. The killer could lead him to Stilwell, so he decided not to take his life—yet. The gunmetal felt cold in his hand, as if it held an icy grudge of its own. Ike held back as the killer went past, but oh, he wanted to strike. He followed him out the back door and along a dark dirt path in the backyard but stepped on a branch.

Dobbs turned.

"Who's there?"

Ike froze in the starry night. Strange how a person could disappear in pale moonlight, as long as they didn't move. He stayed still longer than he should have because Dobbs was a ghost when he started after him again. The night had swallowed the killer like he never existed. Ike hurled a rock in the distance and went back to Agnes'. He scattered silverware on the darkened kitchen floor as an alarm in case Dobbs returned.

In the morning, he rose from Lorraine's old bed in the guest room. He'd slept far better than he thought he would. Downstairs, he scavenged a few pieces of bacon from the now-room-temperature wooden icebox. He'd always admired this oaken piece, with its polished brass hinges sitting in the kitchen. Nicer than anything he and Lorraine ever had, and only one of Agnes' many expensive furnishings. Ike put a hand to the flush that ran up his neck. He'd never provided very well for Lorraine and the children, and this fine house was an unwelcome reminder of his shortcomings.

He started the day watching the railroad building to see if Stilwell showed. On the other side of the street, a new two-story building rose out of the ground. There was just enough of a skeleton built to hide him within. He lowered to the floor, bad leg splayed out. The hip pain was getting worse as he aged, not a good sign for what lay ahead. At least his eyesight hadn't turned on him, like Buster's. How was that old coot doing? Thoughts of better days with his friend flashed through his mind as he stared across the street.

Hours passed with a few people in and out, but neither of his targets. He'd shifted his position several times, but now the ache was too great to sit any longer. He worked himself to a throbbing stand and took a moment to let the pain dwindle. Just as he started to sit back down, Helen Morrison emerged from the building. No choice but to limp across the street after her.

When he reached the woman, he put a finger to his lips and steered her into the mercantile.

"Ike, whatever are you doing? I haven't seen you for—"

Ike whispered as he drew her behind a row of canned goods. "Never mind that, I just need to know where Stilwell is, and Dobbs, too."

Her eyes widened. "I wish I knew. There's been a lot of tomfoolery going on since that nice Sam Franklin was killed. I'd see Stilwell come in, head straight for his safe, and stuff paper and envelopes in there. I occasionally took the uh…liberty to see what they were. Saw a map of your ranch."

"Why didn't you say anything?"

"Who was I going to tell? A clerk—female at that—accusing the head of operations of stealing? I'd been the one fired." She looked up and down the aisle. "Now you be careful. He knows you're onto him, and probably already has Dobbs tailing you."

Ike allowed himself a small grin. "Or, I might just be tailin' him. Seen either one this morning?"

Helen shook her head. "They both been mighty scarce of late. Looks like you run a shiver up their backs. Last I saw Stilwell, he said I could reach him in Como."

Ike thanked her and headed to the train station—the track having been fixed. The rocking motion of the railroad rolling to

South Park did nothing to ease his worries. At Como, he walked into the station house and spied the old telegrapher.

White hair didn't look up from his desk. "You again? I declare, we're gettin' to be right friendly."

"What happened to you, Jim?" The man's face was a purple mess, and a bruise had closed one eye.

Without looking up, Jim said, "How'd you know my name?"

"I manage to get around—find out what I need to know. Who did this to you?"

"That snake, Stilwell. Was in here not long ago and I snuck my gun out so's he couldn't see. Was plannin' on takin' him down with it, but I'm clumsier than all get-out, 'cause I dropped it. Stupid!"

Ike nodded. "Droppin' it probably saved your life. You only got a pistol-whippin'. Lettin' you live is his way of sayin' he likes you. How long ago was that?"

"Yesterday afternoon."

"Is he still here?"

"Don't rightly know, I was flat on my back—out for some time."

Now Ike didn't know which way to go. The killer could have gone back to Denver, but he'd gone to Cottonwood from here in the past, too. The man was always on the move. But with most of the McAlister clan in Cottonwood, maybe that's where Stilwell went. Hopefully, Agnes had found her way there by now, too. When Ike got to the small Como livery, three men stood around a hay bale and eyed him as he approached.

"Need a horse for a few days, who should I talk to?"

Grim faces met his question. A man with a full beard said, "Ain't seen you around these parts. Where you headed?" It wasn't said in a friendly way.

"Goin' to Cottonwood. Got family there." No one said anything until Ike broke the silence. "Somethin' goin' on here? You all don't look too neighborly."

"Don't feel very friendly. Man got shot here yesterday. Killed." Beard squinted. "Was murder."

Dying was common these days; murder wasn't. "What happened?"

"Railroad man killed a Chinaman."

Sounded like Stilwell's work. Ike said, "Who was it?"

"Man by the name of Stilwell. Shot a coolie for no reason."

A cold sensation ran down Ike's back. "You know the name?"

"An Li."

Ike's heart sank. His friend, rescuer. Another death at Stilwell's hand. Li had just been recovering from another wound on account of him. A burn rose from his throat up to his ears. "Know where he is?"

"Stilwell?"

"No, An Li."

"They took his body over to the Chinese cemetery, west of the roundhouse."

Ike strode out of the stable.

The stableman called after him. "What about that horse?"

"Don't need it no more. Change of plans." He limp-ran to the separate graveyard where two workers were trying to shovel hard ground. Li's body lay nearby. Red blotches covered most of his pale linen top. His face held a restful appearance, as if he were asleep. The man who saved his life now lay lifeless in front of him. Fury rang in his ears, and his body shook with rage. He wasn't going to let Li be buried in an unmarked grave. "Stop! Go get me a wagon." The workers hesitated until Ike fired a shot above their heads.

Ike wagoned Li to the roundhouse while the train finished the circular change of direction toward Denver. He brought the wagon to a stop at the caboose. The conductor shouted and waved him away over the noise of the locomotive. As the railroad man approached, Ike aimed his Colt at him. "Get me a blanket, I'm puttin' this man in this car." When he'd wrapped Li, he lifted him from the wagon onto the floor, then eased down next to the body and waited for the loading to finish. Several times, men showed at the rear door window but kept going when they spied Ike's gun barrel aimed their way.

At the Denver station, Ike secured a wagon and trundled his friend to Chinatown. He announced himself outside of An Li's tent. Mei Won soon appeared, and Ike removed his hat. Neither spoke as Won lifted the blanket and disappeared back into her home, shoulders slumped. As he walked away, Ike looked back to see two Chinese approaching the wagon.

The railroad building was his next stop. Locked. White anger led him to break a rear window and stride to Stilwell's office. He lit matches that lay beside the ashtray, and flames soon ran up the expensive drapes. After leaving the valuables in the open safe alone, he broke a window, muscled the contraption out, and watched it smash into the courtyard below. City dwellers could have the booty. By the time he left, the new chandelier was a memory, the rest of the window glass broken, paintings and desk destroyed. Fire consumed everything.

Just as it would the railroader.

Chapter Thirty-Eight

Bert stepped with Tibbie onto the boarding house's front porch and stopped, the raid on the ranch still fresh in his mind. He said, "Don't shoot us, please."

Sue's voice came from inside. "Come on in, you two."

In the entry, Tibbie remarked on the crowd. "Didn't know this house could hold that many people. Hope they're all payin' customers." She grinned at Lorraine and the kids as Bert tried to slip into the background. Tibbie grabbed his hand and pulled him forward. "Y'all know my boyfriend, Bert, right?"

Boyfriend? Bert nodded at Lorraine and stood mute, not knowing how to respond. First time he'd ever thought of himself as such. First time he'd ever thought of himself as good enough to attract a woman—that is, a woman worth attracting.

Sue shook his hand and said, "Of course. Please come in, the both of you. Are you hungry?" She bustled to the kitchen while everyone gathered in the dining room. Soon, she returned and started passing plates and glasses. "Everyone, please sit while we sort things out. From what I understand, Lorraine, Ike sent you and the children back here to get away from … Stilwell, was it?"

Lorraine wiped a hand across her eyes. "Yes, he's killed several people already and we were gonna be next. Ike stayed there to—" She didn't finish the thought. "So, I guess we're here for a while, if that's all right, Sue."

Sue nodded. "You and the children are welcome as long as you need to be, sister-in-law. Ike will let us know when the coast is clear."

Tibbie squeezed Bert's hand, but still, a worry nagged him. If Ike stayed back, he must still figure there's a threat.

An alarm about Buster flew through his head. He was alone at the ranch, but they'd just killed the last of the outlaws—hadn't they? He was all right, wasn't he?

Bert turned to the sound of footsteps on the porch. Hannah walked into the house like she owned the place. Her glare said she'd seen him. He tried to keep calm, hoping his face didn't betray his unease. Why should he care if she was here? She didn't mean anything to him anymore. But still, she made him nervous, what with Tibbie right here and all.

Hannah gave Lorraine a withering look. Turning away, she said to Sue, "Do I still have my room?" Without waiting for an answer, she strode down the hallway and disappeared.

As she did, fear about Buster tumbled Bert's stomach again. No reason he wasn't all right, but something told him he needed to check. He pulled Tibbie aside and told her he was going to the ranch. At least she didn't try to talk him out of it, just gave him a quick hug. On his way out of the house, he passed Hannah's room and heard her screaming behind a closed door. He hurried for the livery.

The stable hand said, "You been here a lot lately, mister. Where you off to now?"

"You really want to know?"

"No." He brought a pretty copper-red sorrel out of the last stall and pointed to a saddle.

Bert mounted up and headed down a dirt trail he could ride in his sleep by now. Only this time his head was on a swivel. Rounding the last curve, he eyed the ranch house. He swung off the sorrel and shouted, "Don't shoot me, I'm comin' in!" As he flew up the steps, he reflexively drew his Colt. He pushed the door open and peered in.

Buster sat in the rocking chair smoking and smiled—Rowdy standing at his feet.

Relief surged through Bert. His worry—all for nothing. "I noticed some charrin' on the planks outside. What's that all about?"

"Had to run somebody off last night. Rowdy let me know they were around, and when I came out, there's a little fire creepin' up the corner of the house. Rowdy and me scared 'em away."

As if Rowdy hadn't done all the scaring off.

"Ne'er-do-well got his butt bit. I think I hit him with some buckshot, too."

Not likely. Man couldn't see past his nose. But still, it meant at least one raider was left. His worries hadn't been for naught after all.

"So, whatcha doin' here, young man? Miss me that much?"

"Didn't even know you wasn't around. Got anything to eat around here?" He rummaged through the icebox and found several moldy potatoes. Fortunately, no curdled milk. "What've you been eatin'? And have you even moved out of that chair since I left?"

"What'm I gonna do out of this chair that I can't do right here?"

"That don't even make no sense. Don't know why I even bother with you." Why was Buster holding his one arm funny? "Let me see that."

"What for? I'm fine."

"Lemme see it." He leaned over Buster until his friend fessed up.

"So I got a little scratch—ain't worth botherin' about."

Without another word, Bert took hold of the arm at the wrist. Swollen. Buster sat silently, but his eyes gave away the pain.

"You damn fool! Why didn't you tell me you had a busted arm? How'd you do it?"

"Ah. Got careless chasin' that bandit. Almost caught him, too, but I tripped and fell. Stupid. But Rowdy did his job."

"What were you doin'—just forget it. You ain't got wits enough anymore to use the sense the Good Lord gave you." He unbuttoned the sleeve and rolled it up to see the break better. Buster's eyes filled. "I'm sorry, Buster, but I gotta get a look at that."

A nod.

The break was far up the sleeve, so Bert grabbed a knife from the kitchen and carefully cut the material away. A black-and-blue patch revealed the spot. Bert tore up the only sheet they had and wrapped a strip around Buster's body, anchoring the arm against his chest.

Bert took a deep breath. He'd never *told* Buster anything, all jesting aside, but he had to now. "Buster … uh—"

"You don't gotta say anything, Bert. I think we oughta head to town; you should be with your sweetheart instead of an old coot like me."

The old man had done it again. Managed to take the pressure off him and save face as well. As long as he'd known Buster, he always knew what ought to be done. The man was smarter than he looked. And Bert didn't have a better friend, either. "Well, as long as you think we should go to town, I guess that's what we'll do. We'll take the wagon so Rowdy can come along, too."

As they drove away, Buster glanced back, a faraway look in his eyes.

"What're you thinkin' about?"

"This is the only place that ever felt like home in my life. All I know is there's been a lot of leavin' lately, and not a lot of comin' back."

Bert nodded in agreement. Now if they could only reach town without getting shot.

Chapter Thirty-Nine

Stilwell headed for the Como livery. Going back to Denver now wasn't a choice anymore since he'd just killed that Chinaman, even though the track was fixed. Cottonwood it was, but he didn't look forward to another argument with his niece.

He rode easy in the saddle, not having to bother with the murky clouds of a conscience. He tossed the telegrapher's weapon away in the fragrant early spring sage that bordered the dirt road. A good day so far. As he crested one of the light-brown hills of the Park, the low profile of Cottonwood came into view. Several days had passed since McAlister sent his family back here, but he didn't know exactly where. Maybe at the ranch—or his sister's boarding house.

Stilwell rode his horse at a walk down the dirt main street and scanned left and right. The Sew Pretty was just ahead, and he drew up in front. Might as well get the confrontation with Hannah over so they could get down to business. She was such a child; it was looking like a mistake to bring her in on his plan in the first place. He opened the door—that damn bell tinkling again. Hannah had a customer, and she glanced his way but kept talking. He wandered the store, running his hand over multicolored bolts of material on tables. And those hats hanging off wall hooks; was anything more hideous than them?

She kept talking. Was his niece trying to irritate him? Finally, he walked up and grabbed the hat the customer was considering. Pulling out a wad of bills, he handed a twenty to Hannah. He shoved the hat into the woman's hands and said, "Here, I just bought it for you, now leave us alone." He shooed her out of the store despite her huffing, 'Why I never…I never!' Stilwell closed the door and turned to a furious Hannah.

"You, you, you—"

"Handsome devil? Is that what you were going to say? Charmer? I answer to all of those, thank you."

Hannah was sputtering, she was so mad. "Get out, get out!"

"Now, now, you don't really mean that, because we have things to talk about. Why don't we sit down?" He commandeered a chair near the black cast-iron stove that gave off a weak circle of heat— welcome warmth in this brisk weather. "Come sit with me, Hannah."

"Don't know why I should, we don't have anything to talk about unless you've taken care of things—have you? No need to answer that 'cause I just came from Sue's and she's still there!"

"Who?"

Hannah rolled her eyes. "Lorraine McAlister. And her annoying kids. And their dog."

So that's where they were. "Did you see McAlister?"

She threw a book at him. "You don't even know where he is, do you? Fine partner you are. And why aren't they dead? Are you waitin' for them to shoot themselves?"

Never had gotten anything but grief from her, and he got enough of that from his bosses in Denver. Maybe he should take the wife out here and now. Just one good shot. He could hole up here in the shop and keep an eye on the boarding house. She had to come out sometime. Hannah could set that up. "No, but you can help me end all this."

"You should have ended it long ago."

"I would have if I'd known my brother had been killed. Took me years to track him down and longer to find you here in this backwater town—no thanks to you. You didn't even write me that whole time. You knew he'd been killed and by who, so quit barking at me!" He rubbed his forehead and paused for a second. "Here's what you're going to do now."

When he finished laying out his idea, Hannah broke into a mocking laugh. "So, the big railroad man is going to hide in a dress shop until he can backshoot a woman?" Her laughter seemed to pound his ears.

He'd kill her after this was all over. With pleasure. But her expression looked like she knew what he had in mind.

***

Where was Stilwell? Ike didn't know if he was here in Denver or stayed in Como to rant and rave over the torn rails. And what about Dobbs, who did Stilwell's dirtiest work? He'd be the target now.

Last time he saw Dobbs, the underling was skulking away from Agnes' house in the dark. Ike didn't stand much chance of running him down—the man knew the town a whole lot better than he did. So instead of chasing Dobbs, he'd try to draw him out. But where to do that? The coward's office was destroyed—and wait 'til Stilwell sees *his* office. He'd like to see their faces as the hunters became the hunted. The ambush would have to be at Agnes' house again, since Dobbs had clearly been after her the other night. He couldn't know she was already gone, so Ike would use her house as bait. Lights in different rooms would make it look occupied—he hoped.

Two nights of lights hadn't produced the villain, but nonetheless, Ike sat motionless in the darkened living room on the third. Noises seemed amplified in the empty home. The back door window was still broken, so outside night sounds—and cold— filtered throughout. A charged silence reigned except for the sounds of battle rushing through Ike's head. The same dread that filled him before battles years ago was an unwelcome visitor again now. Sweat beaded his brow as he clenched a fist around his worn Colt. There. A rustling in back. What was it? Something scurried up the stairs.

Ike recognized the scratchings—a raccoon. Didn't do anything to calm him, though.

As the night wore on, stress battered Ike like a stiff wind and he eased into an upholstered chair. That drowsy state between sleep and vigilance soon followed. His Colt slipped from his grasp. A sudden sound startled him awake. So close he could almost touch it, if you could touch a noise. Must be Dobbs. Ike's heartbeat pounded in his ears. An artillery shell exploded in his head.

The man was moving around the pitch-black living room—now, standing still. How had he gotten in this far without being heard? As much as he didn't want to stir, Ike eased his hand back to his holster for his gun—missing. Damn! He let his fingers steal down to the plush carpet, searching in the darkness until they folded around the familiar grip. Whew.

What was the intruder doing? Surely he could 'see' Agnes wasn't in this room—move on so he could get up. His hip shouted it was way past time to. Dobbs finally left and Ike stifled a groan getting up. Footfalls on the stairs. The killer was climbing, apparently having finished searching downstairs. There. Dobbs hit that creaky step, about the fourth one up. Ike followed, vowing to be more careful, gun raised in his left hand. Which bedroom would Dobbs choose to die in?

A bullet ripped through Ike's side and tumbled him down the stairs. The sound screamed through the house and the muzzle flash nearly blinded him. He crawled back into the living room and inched toward the chair he'd just been sitting in. How had he given himself away? Was it a noise in this room or on the stairs? The chair hardly hid his six-foot-two frame with a bad leg sticking out. Worse, he'd dropped his Colt as he careened down the stairs. Maybe Dobbs didn't know that. Maybe. Didn't much matter either way, though. The wound burned as his adrenaline wore off.

Dim light from a match shone as Dobbs came down the steps. Ike figured he had one chance, and not a good one at that. He lifted the glass lamp off the table by the chair. Oil sloshed inside. Dobbs came into the room and lit a second match when the first died. He waved it, and Ike saw the man's face—faintly lit with shadows like a fiend.

Devil Dobbs.

Ike hurled the lamp and the thin glass smashed into smithereens against his enemy's chest, who doused the match before he went up in flames.

Dobbs yelled into the darkness. "You're hit, McAlister, I know it. You ain't got much time left, so come out and meet your end like a man."

The broken lamp bought Ike some time. With a hand to his boot he pulled a knife, peered out from behind the chair, and flung it at Dobbs in one swift motion. The dull *thud* told him he hit his mark. Howls followed while Ike scooted to the adjoining dining room, holding his side and muffling a moan.

Dobbs started firing in Ike's direction. After five more rounds, the shooting stopped. The front door squeaked open, then footsteps sounded on the porch. A few more oaths, and silence reclaimed the night.

Ike sagged to the floor with a hand to his side. His palm was wet—blood no doubt. He wasn't sure how badly hurt Dobbs was, but bad enough to focus on his own skin instead of Ike's. Couldn't stay here, might bleed out. The bullet hit him just above the waist on his left side. Needed help, but a hospital would ask questions he didn't want to answer.

Where to go?

Chapter Forty

Bert peered out the front window as a boy ran up the street toward the boarding house. He leaped up the front steps and rapped on the door. "Miss Sue!"

Sue said, "Bert, keep an eye out," then cracked the door. "What is it, Jeremy?"

"A telegraph, miss. From Mr. Ike in Denver. It says—"

"That's enough, son, I know how to read." The lad handed the piece of paper to Sue, who pressed a penny into his hand. She scanned the rest of the message, and her eyes lit up. "Agnes is coming here, too. She's on her way now." The children grabbed hands and danced around an imaginary maypole in the living room, the dogs scampering with them. Sue handed the message to Lorraine, who studied it silently for a moment and frowned.

"What's wrong?"

"If Ike's sendin' her here, somethin' dangerous must have happened there. And now he has to face whatever it is all alone, which means I'm goin' back to help him."

Sue put her arm on her sister-in-law's. "I understand how you feel, Lorraine, but you know you can't do that. You don't know where he is, and then there's the danger, and also the children to think about."

Lorraine slumped against Sue and tried to stifle tears. When she'd regained her composure, she said, "Well, someone has to go!" She cast pleading eyes on both Hugh and Bert.

Sue piped up immediately. "Whoa, there. Hugh's not going. He just laid himself open to great danger by bringing you all back here, and that's not even his job as sheriff."

Bert didn't hesitate. He flung the front door open and hurried out of the house. Here was a chance to repay Ike for all he'd done for him over the years. The change was slow, for sure, but Ike had warmed up to him eventually.

"Bert, wait!" Tibbie ran after him, catching up at the stable.

"Don't try and stop me, I'm goin'."

"Ain't tryin' to stop you. I know you gotta go, I just wanted a kiss before you get yourself all shot up again." She smiled and leaned into him.

Bert folded her in his arms and kissed her, then held her tight. "I ain't brave enough to get killed; I'll be back before you know it." He saddled a horse, walked him out of the stable, and headed for Como at a gallop.

Pulling in at the train station, Bert tied his horse off and entered the station office to check the train schedules. He'd book passage on the next train to Denver. "Excuse me, sir, but I heard the track to Denver was tore up."

A tired-looking fat man said, "Fixed."

Likely going to be a hard person to have a conversation with. "Can you tell me about Mrs. Agnes Franklin? We got a message sayin' she was comin' here."

"Wouldn't know, I just see people coming and going—don't know their names."

Even though he didn't know how railroads worked, Bert pressed the stationmaster. "Do you at least know who's on a particular train?"

"Yup."

"So, has she gotten here yet?"

The man closed a ledger. "Can't tell you that, sonny."

In the blink of an eye, Bert pressed his Colt up against the clerk's neck. "Maybe you better look those records over again."

The stationmaster adjusted his glasses and fumbled to re-open the ledger. His fingers traced down a page. "N-no, she hasn't arrived yet."

"Stay here." Bert holstered, then walked out onto the wooden platform. She should be on the next train. He scanned his surroundings in the late-morning April sun until a whistle echoed across the flat, heralding the South Park's arrival. When the big locomotive shrieked to a stop, Bert stepped to the back of the platform so he could see who got off without being noticed. More men than women appeared, which made it easier as he scanned the passengers. There. Had to be her. Lorraine said she was small but spirited. He doffed his hat as she neared. "Ma'am, are you Mrs. Agnes Franklin?"

The older lady looked up at him. "Yes, I am, young man. Who are you?"

"A friend of Miss Lorraine's. We got a telegraph sayin' you were comin'."

"Who from?"

"Mr. Ike. Lorraine thinks there's been some big trouble if he wanted you here."

"Ike can handle himself. Did you come to escort me to Lorraine's ranch?"

Bert had a decision to make. Continue to Denver and try to find Ike, or take the woman back to Cottonwood. He thought about what Ike would want him to do—and Lorraine. They'd both want him to take her to safety. "Yes, ma'am." Besides, he'd thought wrong that all the bad guys were disposed of before that last shootout at the ranch. There was still one or two around. No sense having her travel through a strange land alone. Mr. Ike was on his own.

***

"What're you gonna do? Sit at the front window watching for her, then shoot her down in the middle of the street? Is that your great plan?"

Hannah's dismissive words caused Stilwell to reconsider. Maybe he wouldn't hide in the shop—too many customers in and out and he didn't want to switch back and forth between watching and hiding. He looked at the shop's ceiling, a collection of worn, wooden crossbeams, then squinted at his niece. "What's the roof like?"

"You can't be serious." She gave him a dismissive wave with a mocking laugh. "Do you want me to bring you coffee and grits up there, too?" A shake of her head. "How did I ever get hooked up with you and your grand plan? I never shoulda done it. I'm out!"

"You're still part of this! How do I get to the roof?"

Hannah took him to the back of the shop and showed him a rickety, wooden ladder. "But you ain't goin' up it. What with your fancy silk vest and expensive clothes, and that dirty roof, why I'd never hear the end of it. You lay down on that filth and you'll mess up the image you have of yourself."

"Don't be telling me what to do. If I want to get up on that roof, I'll do it."

Hannah swept an arm upward at the ladder. "Be my guest, then." She turned and disappeared into The Sew Pretty.

Stilwell yelled at the closed door. "I'd do it if I felt like it, but I just came up with a better idea." When he came back in, he said, "I've come up with … a foolproof way to kill McAlister."

"If you had a foolproof way, he'd already be dead. The only thing about your 'plan' you got right is the 'fool' part."

He wanted to slap her so bad his fingers itched.

Before he could respond, she said, "You don't even know where he is, do you? The missus is at the boarding house, and the mister is missing." She let out an insulting snicker. "Perfect. You're trying to kill a man who's a hundred miles away. Perhaps, just a guess, maybe you should be there instead of here!" She leaned toward him with her chin stuck out.

The afternoon sun waned as it drew toward the western mountains silhouetting South Park. Stilwell was caught in a dilemma. Stay here and try to kill the wife amid all the other people around her. Likely messy, and uncertain. Or, slink away like a beaten puppy back to Denver and endure his niece's—he didn't even like to say her name anymore—contempt, something he couldn't stomach from anyone. He'd leave, but had to make sure she didn't think he was skulking away. Some bluster would fit the occasion.

He strode toward her wagging a finger. "Don't ever tell me what to do—I tell you what to do. I'll decide when and if I leave here. I've half a mind to march right down to that boarding house and shoot her between the eyes." His chest heaved and sweat beaded his forehead—his finger still pointed at her like a dagger. "And I might just call out that sheriff who thinks he's such a great shootist." His voice rose to a yell. "And you've been no help at all."

Hannah leaned closer. "You're not gonna do that, and besides, you've got something caught in your teeth." She pointed to his mouth.

"Wha—you wretch!" He raised his hand against her, but she stopped him cold when she produced a derringer from under her apron.

"Get out! I never want to see you again. Do you understand?" She motioned to the door with the small barrel. "Out!"

He squinted. "You wouldn't shoot your only family, and that thing wouldn't even hurt anybody."

"Just leave. Now." She turned her back and strode to her room at the rear of the shop while he stood dumbfounded.

When she didn't come back out, he opened the front door and looked back, then closed it behind him. The only thing to do now was return to Denver and try to reclaim whatever pride he had left. Develop a new plan.

But with his deeds discovered, would he be the hunted instead of the hunter?

Chapter Forty-One

Walking the back streets of Denver holding his bloody side wasn't the best idea Ike ever had. He aimed for Chinatown, but LoDo's goons likely loitered on the way. Nighttime offered some haven from prying eyes, but a full moon seemed to hang directly overhead, countering the dark and mocking him.

Where had his Colt gone? The shootout at Agnes' house a few hours ago seemed but a dim memory as he limped along. At least he'd hurt Dobbs, after the rogue got off a lucky shot his way. How much damage the knife did he didn't know, but it was serious enough to have him skedaddle, which no doubt saved Ike's life.

He didn't know Denver well enough to be sure where he was going, and at night these streets all looked alike. Moving from one corner to the next, he hurried in between, then paused at each to catch his breath. Had to get the bleeding stopped.

He lingered at one stop to let his mind clear. A strong sense of direction had always led him, and he'd let it do that now. The night sounds of a bustling, growing city surrounded him as he moved. Bars letting drunks out, people yelling in alleyways, cats yowling. Better than dead silence, which might have given his shuffling gait away to anyone who cared to be listening. He eased around another corner and spied several men lounging ahead. Even in the dark, their menacing air stood out in a warning.

Stop or press ahead? He'd be no match for a kitten right now. Gravel crunched underfoot as he turned to leave. Sounds of footfalls came from behind as he limped away.

"Hey!"

He was in for it now.

"Hey you. Stop!"

Stop or go—either would likely be the last thing he ever did. He turned back around with his hands up, listing to one side.

"Where you headed, man?" They closed on him, one circling behind with a club in his hand.

Might as well tell the truth. Go out on an honest note. "Tryin' to find help. Got shot." There it was, let's see what they did with that. "I got two bucks in my pocket and you're welcome to it."

A voice from behind. "Put your hands down, fella. Where you hit?"

Ike held his side and put a hand on the brick wall next to him. His legs wobbled and he started to drop.

The two in front caught him before he could. "The way you look, you go down you ain't gettin' back up. Let's take him to Soapy's." They picked him up and made an armchair hold to carry him in. Why were they helping?

Zigzagging down streets, the ensemble made good time, arriving at a dingy bar that matched the downtrodden neighborhood. Ike woke up lying on a table inside a small, dimly-lit room.

Faint light struggled his way from a single oil lamp. Shabby men huddled around. "Where am I?"

A husky voice said, "Nowhere. Don't worry about it." A faint sweet aroma wafted as a stranger handed him a glass filled with amber liquid. "Just call me Soapy." His bloodied shirt lay on the floor by the table, and the man named Soapy motioned to drink. As Ike swallowed, a smooth sensation led to a lightheadedness he'd only felt once before—during the War when a surgeon rooted around but failed to locate the bullet in his hip. The last thing he felt was hands pressing on his wound amid mumbled voices.

A slap woke him. Opening his eyes, a fuzzy vision of the same man stood over him. "There ye be, sonny."

Ike rubbed his cheek as his eyes focused. "You pack a punch, mister."

"Had to. Past time for you to get a move on. Didn't know as you was gonna wake up at all. You been out for a day." He waved a hand in the air. "Ah, you'll be all right—bullet went through, and looks like you been in worse scrapes than this."

He didn't know about that. This situation seemed pretty edgy.

"Judgin' by all the scars you carry, past time you stayed away from trouble."

How many times had Lorraine and Buster echoed that same refrain? Never had gone looking for it, but trouble had a way of reaching around the corner and picking his pocket. He felt the bandage that wound around his body just above the waist. But there'd also been many times in his life he'd been lucky—in love, in war, and meeting folks like this.

He said, "Where am I?" again.

"Still right here."

"So you say." Ike was grateful for the man's help but never liked to be in anyone's debt.

"You're in LoDo. I'll be back." The man placed some instruments in a cloth he folded up, then disappeared out a door he forced open.

Ike scratched his head. This place where he'd almost lost his life—LoDo—had also become the place where it had been saved. He scanned the empty room. Where were the drifters who brought him in? Didn't know as he'd recognize them in the light, but they were gone now, too. He couldn't stay here. He struggled to a sitting position and groaned. With a hand to his side, he slid off the table and strained to put on his soiled shirt. Pushing the same door open on the side of the building, he ducked as he went through and limped outside into a dusky sky.

A surprise met him in the alley. A man lounged against a pile of trash, smoking a cigarette in the dim light of late afternoon. Grimy clothes, unkempt dirty beard. About his age, maybe younger. Most folks were these days.

"Figured you might be comin' out soon."

Ike squinted. Did he know him?

"Reckon you was as good as dead if'n we hadn't seen you."

One of his helpers. "Never got a chance to say thanks, so, thanks." They walked down the gritty side street together. Ike struggled for something to say. "Can't figure why you helped me back there. Somebody you didn't know."

"Just returnin' the favor. Got helped myself a while back by somebody who didn't want nothin' for it. And you looked like you was in rough shape. Been shot before?"

"Yup, the War."

"Where'd you serve?"

"Stoneman's cavalry—took a hit on the peninsula. You?"

"Peninsula, too. Was a butternut. Maybe I'm the one shot you. Got knocked out at Mechanicsburg, though. End of the War for me."

Ike stroked his short beard. "Coulda been you. Lots of you rebs let me have it. Stupid War."

"How'd you get shot up here?"

"Got careless, but I returned the favor. Need to run him down now."

"Got a name? I been around here a long time—might know him."

"Dobbs. Works for the railroad."

The man nodded. "Uh, yup, he's a bad 'un all right. Comes through here every now and then on his way to Chinatown for opium. A regular. Heard he killed a guy there."

Ike's lucky night. "Seen him lately?"

"Nah, but if you shot him, and he ain't dead and can still walk, he'll likely be comin' to Chinatown soon to handle the pain. Has a favorite den."

"Can you show me?"

"'Course, but you oughta wait 'til the sun goes full down and check that tent then. Usually comes through here at dusk, then sleeps it off 'til mornin'."

Ike scanned his surroundings. That would be anytime now. Felt drowsy but couldn't afford to fall asleep.

"Come on." They started down another alleyway. The stranger said, "This is the one most everybody comes through."

Ike stopped partway down the passageway. "You should leave now. No sense both of us gettin' shot up."

The man nodded. "Good luck." He held out a pistol. "If you're aimin' to shoot 'im, you probably need somethin' to shoot him with."

"I can't take your gun. Leaves you with nothin'."

"That's one thing I got plenty of. Keep it. Settlin' with Dobbs is worth it." With that, he turned and disappeared into the hazy evening.

Ike was determined to end his sparring with Dobbs, but Stilwell's lackey had shown he was faster than Ike back at Agnes' house. Didn't matter, though.

One of them wasn't going to survive their next meeting.

Chapter Forty-Two

Bert wrangled a wagon in Como to take Agnes to Cottonwood. They were almost there when Bert reined the wagon to a halt. A solitary horse stood by the side of the worn path, saddle in the dirt, and the rider there, too. He lay sprawled on the ground, coughing and groaning.

The young man started to climb off the bouncy seat, but Agnes grabbed his arm and held him back. "Wait. That looks like Stilwell."

Bert didn't reply.

"He runs the South Park railroad. Just about the last person I expected to see all the way out here. He's been poisoning Lorraine and trying to kill Ike. Still don't know why. And here he is lying on the ground in the middle of nowhere, stove up. Not so high and mighty now."

A strong desire to finish the man rose inside of Bert, but he pushed it back. "That may be, but can't just leave him." He got down and extended a hand for Agnes.

"I'll be staying right here. You can tend him if you're a mind to. He killed my husband."

Whoa. A murderer. Bert checked on the downed man, leaning close. "What happened?"

A groan as he turned his bloody head. "Don't know … for sure. Was just riding … along and next I knew … falling off the horse." A deep, racking cough. His saddle lay on the ground next to him, the horse staring at nothing nearby.

"Let's get you on up." Bert helped Stilwell into the wagon bed where he eased the barely conscious man down. Hefting the saddle into the bed, he tied Stilwell's horse off the back of the wagon. He hopped up front and snapped the reins. Turning to Agnes, he said, "Doesn't look like he's got much time left."

Agnes hmmphed. "Wouldn't have any time left if it was up to me."

Back in Cottonwood, Bert pulled the wagon up at The Wildfire and went inside. He hailed the bartender. "Where's Tibbie?"

"Been gone a while. Left early. She might be—" but Bert was already headed for Sue's with Agnes. He stretched a hand out to help her up the front steps, but she shook her head. "I'm old, sonny, but not dead yet." She reached the door first, just as Lorraine opened it.

"Agnes!" She hugged the woman. "I'm so glad you're here! I was so worried about you stayin' in Denver by yourself."

"Ike was there. He saw me to the train and said he'd be along soon." She scanned the room. "Doesn't look like he's here yet."

"Sorry to break in, Miss Lorraine, but I got an injured man in the bed of the wagon 'cross the street. Tibbie!" She hurried down from upstairs and he took her by the hand. "Can you come take a look at him?"

At the wagon, she climbed up into the bed to examine him. Unconscious now. She shook her head. "Let's get him over to Doc Early's office so I can take a better look. Stop by the Wildfire and drag some fellas with strong backs out while I trundle him to the doc's."

When they'd gotten Stilwell into the office, they laid him on an examining table. Tibbie shooed everyone but Bert out. She cut the man's clothes off and listened to his chest. Muffled wheezing. Probably broken ribs from the already-bruised look of his side, likely a concussion too, and definitely a broken arm. Not much she could do except set the arm. She turned to Bert. "Break up that cabinet door and hand me two wooden pieces." When she'd wrapped the arm with them, she said, "He'll sleep for a while now. I gave him enough laudanum to put him out for the night."

Bert went out to the wagon and drove it to the stable. He climbed into the bed, grabbed Stilwell's saddle and eyed the saddle strap. Sliced partway through and ripped the rest of the way. Caused the fall. Man sure deserved it.

At the boarding house, he didn't mention the strap.

Tibbie came in a little later. Lorraine introduced her to Agnes, who said with a slight smile, "I've heard a lot about all of you."

Buster bowed slightly. "Well, you probably know all about me, owin' as how I handle most everything at the ranch." He squinted at Bert.

"Don't pay him no mind, Miss Agnes." Bert smacked Buster with his hat. "He ain't been right for some time. Keeps gettin' shot up and don't have the sense to die."

"Somebody's gotta keep you company, son. Can't leave you all alone out there; no tellin' what trouble you'd get into."

They shared small grins.

The sheriff came in and doffed his hat. He shook Agnes' outstretched hand. "I had the distinct pleasure of making your acquaintance in Denver."

Bert took pains not to be too obvious that he was studying everyone as they all moved to the dining room. He'd always fidgeted when nervous, so he scanned the room for the same unease. Everyone was here now, except Ike. Hannah came in a while ago, but hardly said a thing. Was it discomfort from being around him or was it all the people?

***

Ike watched his ally walk away in that darkening alley of LoDo. Man saved his life after Dobbs shot him. He checked the Colt's action and spun the cylinder. Two bullets. He eased behind some refuse and lowered to the cold ground. Drowsiness had almost overcome him when he heard crunches coming his way. Two fellas were heading for the promised land of Chinatown. One held the other up as they passed by. Dobbs. When they were far enough away, Ike struggled to a stand and came out from behind the pile of trash.

His stumbling gait on the uneven alley threatened to give him away. He kept just close enough to keep the two in sight. Didn't know the other man. Killing made no sense in the first place, so he'd let that man live if he didn't interfere. When they reached Chinatown, the two disappeared for a moment among the maze of dimly-lit hovels. Ike's heart raced as he stumbled from one path to another, searching between the huts. A nearby groan gave Dobbs away.

Man must be lying down in that shelter. Ike lingered outside to give Dobbs' companion time to go. Half an hour later, they still talked inside the tent, although the opium was making mumbling fools of them.

Wasn't going to wait any longer for the other man to leave. Ike burst into the tent, gun drawn. Dobbs eyed him dully, confusion reflected in vacant eyes. Ike waved the other man out with the barrel of his gun. He knelt by Dobbs' low bed, but there was no recognition to be had. Pausing, he holstered the Colt. Wasn't going to shoot a man who didn't know he was gonna be shot—or why. He scanned the small room and found what he was looking for. A pot half-full of brownish powder.

Dobbs lay there, a pipe hanging from his mouth, barely conscious. Ike filled the pipe full and lit a small fire under the glass bulb at the bottom. A faint smell of vinegar filled the room as the killer inhaled the lethal mixture. Ike waited. When the man's head lolled for the last time, he turned and left.

With Dobbs out of the way, Ike limped back to LoDo. He kept a hand to his side and sagged against a sticky, dark alley wall, his get-up-and-go gone. Stilwell was all that was left to square with, but would he live that long? His mind fogged from the exhaustion his wound brought on. He'd hole up in Agnes' house now. That's what he'd do. With her at Sue's, Stilwell wouldn't look for him there. But… then again, maybe Stilwell didn't know she was gone yet. Either way, as his body cramped, he wasn't sure he could make it that far.

He scraped along the wall, using it as a crutch until he reached the end of the building and stopped. An Li's, that's where he'd go instead, if Mei Won would have him. Didn't know why she would, since it was because of him that Li was killed. Never had gotten a warm welcome from her, and not likely to get one now, but no choice. Agnes's was too far.

Low music wakened him. A man played a strange-looking instrument in the corner of the tent. Ike turned his head toward a voice.

"Ike Mc… Alister. Good you wake up."

Mei Won speaking to him? Red eyes showed her grief.

"You are shot, but shooter will never shoot again."

Ike rose on an elbow. "How did I get here?"

"Came last night. Not making sense."

"Thank you for takin' me in."

She brought a foul-smelling liquid in a small pot. "Drink, please."

When he'd finished, he thanked her again and lay back down on his mat. As he drifted, he wondered if he'd ever be able to take Stilwell down, the shape he was in.

Chapter Forty-Three

Sue's boarding house had never held this many people. Bert let everyone know about Stilwell's injuries, but left the part about the cut leather out. Now that the rogue had been captured, everyone breathed a sigh of relief. Bert helped Lorraine and the kids get ready to go back to the ranch—Buster, too.

Hugh relaxed some as well; not on the lookout for Stilwell anymore.

Tibbie continued to tend Stilwell in Doc Early's office. That night after dinner, she pulled Bert aside and whispered, "He's dead. Stilwell's dead."

Bert nodded, then leaned close. "Let's don't tell anyone about this. At least not until I've had time to do some figurin'."

"Figurin'? Whaddya mean by that?"

He said, "Guess Hugh's gonna try to piece together who might have cut that saddle now."

Tibbie protested. "Well, anybody coulda done that. And why do you even care?"

"I don't, but… maybe it's one of us ten 'cause nobody else held him a grudge."

"Not ten," she said. "The kids didn't have anything to do with it."

"Okay, eight, then." He shook his head. "Nope. Only six, 'cause I was in Como pickin' up Agnes. That's Hugh and Sue, Buster, Lorraine, and Hannah. Only five."

"Six countin' me." Tibbie locked eyes with him.

"Okay, six with you."

"Seven with you."

Bert scowled. "I weren't nowhere near here when he went down."

"Yeah, but no one knows when those straps were cut."

"Yeah, okay. Hugh's probably gonna ask where everybody was when the skunk was gettin' his horse."

"Not when he was gettin' his horse—likely happened before that. And everybody has knives. I have them for cuttin' skin, I've seen one the sheriff keeps handy for lawin', I guess. Sue has her kitchen, and Lorraine, well, I don't think she has any except at the ranch."

Bert frowned. "But she could've gotten one from Sue's kitchen. And Hannah has cuttin' shears for cloth. That leaves Buster out, I think, plus he doesn't have the strength anymore to cut much of anything."

Tibbie shook her head. "You must not be payin' attention. When we were in the barn at the ranch fixin' Ally up, Buster was pretty handy slicin' up that towel we wound around her leg. As for strength, you don't live as long as he has, and go through what he has, without bein' real strong."

Bert had to admit she made sense. He'd been attracted to Tibbie because of her looks, but as he'd gotten to know her better, her common sense stood out as well. Never thought he'd wonder how he stacked up against a saloon gal—one who was more than she seemed.

He and Tibbie parted ways and he headed for the stable, where the saddle still lay outside a stall on a rail. Inside, he lit a hanging oil lamp. Bringing the light close, he swung it over the saddle's riggings, then bent down for a closer look at the cinch strap on the right side. Anyone who saw it would know it'd been cut because the leather was too thick to tear. Too many things rolling around in his head. But they couldn't keep the secret much longer. Dead was dead. He blew the lamp out and headed for the boarding house.

On the way, Bert walked past Doc Early's. A light shone in the front window, but it was so late, why would Tibbie be there now? He stepped up to the wooden sidewalk outside and peered in. Tibbie and Lorraine were talking over Stilwell's corpse. Why did she tell Lorraine? And did the others know now, too? Sleep came hard that night.

***

Nothing was keeping him in Denver anymore, except if Stilwell was here, but then again Ike didn't actually know where the man was. Hard choice coming. Stay here and search for a ghost, or return to his family and give Stilwell a free hand? He left Chinatown and Mei Won's in much better shape than when he staggered in there. His side still hurt, but it was the kind of pain that was on the edge of tolerable, so it was almost welcome, if pain ever could be.

He stopped by the railroad office to pick up the few things of his still there. As he took down the painting of his ranch that Stilwell commissioned, footsteps sounded on the wooden hall floorboards. A familiar face peeked in. Helen Morrison. "I just wanted to say goodbye, Ike. I'm sorry you're leaving. You're the most fun I've had in years, and you're the best thing that's happened around here in a long time. Things used to be better ..." her voice trailed off.

"Thank you. I feel the same way about you. I'm still tryin' to find out where your boss is. Any ideas?"

"Haven't seen him for a couple of days now, but I'll let you know if I find out more. If I can find you."

Ike put a finger to his hat brim, then his heart seized as he stood there. He'd never had a panic attack before, but like lots of things in life, panic is something you don't have to have experienced to know what it is. Turning away, he hurried off, his heart thumping and cold sweat beading his brow. Needed to get back home and now. Didn't know exactly why but he had to. A vision of Lorraine flew through his head. Was she all right? And Stilwell, is that where he was? He stumbled a few blocks to the train station and broke into a lurching run after the train as it started to pull out. Grabbing onto the metal bar outside the last car, he pulled himself up and onto a steel platform. A sharp pain in his side made him bend over and a hand to his bandage showed new blood. As he caught his breath, he wondered where his youth had gone. He wasn't that old he kept telling himself, but his body said different.

A quick scan inside the last car but no Stilwell. Ike settled into one of the empty bench seats, and soon the sway of the car lulled him to sleep. A tap on the shoulder and he stared up into the face of the conductor. "We're here, son, last stop, Como. You need—"

But Ike was already up and soon striding along the platform to the stable. He wanted to send Lorraine a telegram, but didn't want to take any more time than he had to. Then he changed his mind and headed for the telegraph office. The white-haired man there barely looked up when he came in.

"I ain't seen him, sonny, if that's your question."

How did this old man always seem to know what was going on? "Figured he mighta come through here recent."

A shake of the head. "Still in Cottonwood from what I can tell."

That was good and bad news. Good that he finally knew where Stilwell was, and bad that he was in Cottonwood. Ike headed for the stable and saddled a bay. Swinging up, he jerked the horse toward town and his ranch. What was he going to say to Lorraine about what he'd been doing? And about Dobbs.

As he neared Cottonwood, Ike noticed a roughed-up spot just off the path. Probably a horse spooked by a coyote. Hurry. He galloped past and slowed when he reached Sue's place, tying the horse off on the front rail.

Lorraine hurried out the front door and wrapped her arms around him. "I knew you were comin', I had a feelin'."

He tried to hide his pain but she could tell he was hurt. "I'm okay now that I'm with you." She snuck an arm around him and they walked into the house. Greetings all around, then he pulled Lorraine to the side. "How're things here? I had this awful feelin' somethin' was wrong."

"Well, you had a right notion. Stilwell's dead."

"What?" The news hit him strange. He'd wanted to kill the railroader for some time, but now that he was gone, Ike wasn't as relieved as he thought he'd be. More that he didn't feel much of anything. Like during the War after a battle. There was little left except exhaustion.

"Fell off his horse on the way to Como, and Bert found him when he was wagonin' Agnes here from the train station. Might not have been an accident. Died after they got him here. Tibbie was tendin' him at Doc's. Said his body was just too beat up and too fat to live."

"Can't say as I'm sorry to hear that." Ike pursed his lips as he thought about the last of his enemies. The move to Denver had brought nothing but trouble and near-death for both him and Lorraine. The sooner they could put all that behind them, the better.

His brother-in-law corralled him into the parlor. "Care for a whiskey, Ike?" Hugh poured two tumblers and handed him one. "Here is to proceeding with our lives."

They clinked glasses, and Hugh leaned close. "You have not had time to process Stilwell's death, but I would like to advise you of a new dilemma."

"What's that, Hugh?"

"With Stilwell gone, it seems we have a killer on our hands." He raised his glass in emphasis and locked eyes with his brother-in-law. He took a sip.

Ike sat in an upholstered chair, silent for a time. "How so?"

"Stilwell's leathers were sliced through, which led to his fall from the horse."

"Who cut 'em? I'd like to shake their hand." Then, he shook his head. "Didn't mean that, only some of it."

"Yes, well, that is indeed the question."

Ike's moment of peace had been brief. "What do you know about how it played out?"

"I do not know much, but it seems someone stole into the stable at night and accomplished the nefarious deed, unbeknownst to anyone else. Whoever did it was clever, too, as the cut was on the inside of the right saddle strap, which is not typically seen or noticed."

Ike considered. "Anybody you suspect yet?"

"No, but I will be inquiring about whereabouts and times, and cross-checking what people are saying against other statements."

"Speak plain, Hugh—there's times I don't pick up on your meanin', and this is one of them."

"Sorry, Ike. It involves seeing if there are any discrepancies in what people are saying about where they were and when and what they saw."

"Come up with any peculiarities yet?"

"I have yet to discuss particulars with everyone at this juncture. I plan to conduct interviews tomorrow."

Ike finished his drink, nodded an exit, and sought out Lorraine. His sister pointed upstairs, where he found his wife sitting in a chair in their bedroom.

"Have a good chat with Hugh?"

He recognized that look—a little preoccupied. "Just catchin' up and thankin' him for bringin' you back here safe. As sheriff, he's interviewin' everybody. Talk to you yet?"

"Nope. Why's he doin' that? Whoever killed Stilwell oughta get a medal."

"Guess he figures murder is murder." Ike splashed his face in the water basin and dried himself with a towel.

"As far as I'm concerned, that's the end of it. And Agnes won't have to worry no more, either. I'll talk to her tomorrow and see when she wants to go back to Denver." She yawned, and Ike patted a spot on the bed beside him. "I'm for that." She got up, snuggled into bed against him, and Ike blew the lamp out.

He lay in the dark, staring at the shadowy ceiling, wondering if they would ever find out now why Stilwell targeted them in the first place.

Chapter Forty-Four

The next morning, Sue enticed her guests to the dining room table with the irresistible smell of bacon frying. After Agnes' short prayer, they dove into scrambled eggs, honey biscuits, bacon, and steaming coffee. All but Hannah, who, upon coming downstairs, screamed, "He was my uncle!" before rushing out without a single look back.

Sue held court. "Now that Stilwell's been dispatched, does anyone have anything to say?"

No one moved for a minute, then Ike struggled up. He gazed around the table. "Uh, I never was any—" Silence filled the room as they stared at the man none of them really knew, except for Lorraine and maybe Buster. A slight clearing of the throat. He stared at his wife. "Don't know how I would have survived out here without this woman. She knows how stupid I can be but never says anything, knows how bullheaded I get and ignores it, but when it comes down to it, she's always in my corner, and me in hers. And I thank the good Lord for her." He locked eyes with his wife, staring into those comforting brown eyes he knew so well. Like they could see into his very soul.

After breakfast, the adults retired to the smallish parlor at Hugh's request. When everyone had snugged into seats, Agnes stood in the middle of the gathering. She produced a bottle and asked Ike to do the honors. He handed out small glasses and poured the liquor.

Sue took a sip and sputtered. "L-Lordy, what is this, Agnes?" A shake of the head.

"It's my own special concoction. A blend of several spirits—do you like it?"

"Um, yes."

Agnes raised her glass in a toast. "To whoever disposed of Stilwell."

Followed by a "hear, hear," from Ike.

Hugh raised his glass and sipped while he watched for reactions. Everyone toasted except Lorraine. He wasn't sure why, but maybe it didn't mean anything. He put his tumbler down and stood. "Be advised, I will be making inquiries today. Standard procedure, not to worry."

Bert called out. "Why? Why do we even care who cut that strap?"

Hugh rocked forward on his boots. "I confess I am not familiar with all American practices, but I did not realize it is your custom to overlook a murder if the victim is despised." Silence reigned as he scanned the room. "As I said, please make yourselves available after the midday meal."

The rest of the morning passed with Hugh in his office. Never figured he'd take to the job like he had, an Englishman out here in the Wild West. So different from what he'd grown up with back home—bobbies who twirled batons and tipped their hats to ladies. But England didn't feel like home anymore. As rough as conditions were here, he'd come to appreciate them.

Preparing for the questioning was a new experience. One he wasn't too sure how to do. He'd always been the one to be questioned. A soft approach for the ladies, firm for the men? No, better to play it straight down the middle. He wrote out some notes and called the young kid who hung around his office, wanting to be a lawman when he grew up. "James, go get Miss Tibbie and bring her here. She is either at the boarding house or the Wildfire."

James took off like a shot and soon corralled Tibbie. When she came in, Hugh rose with a slight bow, motioned to the single chair on the other side of his desk, and shooed James off with a penny.

Hugh asked if she wanted a cup of coffee, and when she shook her head, he sat behind his desk. "First, is there anything you would like to say, Tibbie?"

She crossed her arms. "Nope."

Not a good start. "Then please tell me what you remember doing on the day Stilwell died."

"You mean the day he was murdered, don'tcha?"

"Yes, rather. Please continue." He tried to look nonchalant.

"I'd just said goodbye to Bert who was headed for Denver to help Ike."

"Where was that?"

"I was by the livery 'cause that's the only place you can saddle up around here."

Hugh ignored her sarcasm. "Did you see Stilwell that day?"

"Came out of The Sew Pretty late in the afternoon."

"Right. His niece Hannah's shop. Where was he going?"

"Don't know, didn't pay him no mind. I was late for work."

Hugh made a note. "About what time was that?"

"Sun was dimmin' to the west, so guess around five."

"What time did you get off work?"

"Later than that."

"Did you head straight for the boarding house then?"

"Nope, took my time leavin'. Had a few shots with the men— that's how I make most of my money."

"So what time did you get back to Sue's?"

"Ain't too sure—was sad Bert headed off."

"Did you see Stilwell after that?"

Another, "Nope. Well, I mean yes, I was tendin' him."

"Thank you, Miss Tibbie. Please do not leave Cottonwood until I have had a chance to talk with everyone, all right?"

A nod. "I ain't got nowhere else to go anyway," and she was out the door.

After she left, Hugh thought of another question. Did she see Bert leave before or after she saw Stilwell? He scribbled on a piece of paper.

"James!"

The boy soon had Bert in hand and after another penny, scooted back out the door.

"Please sit, Bert. Would you like some coffee?"

"If it ain't better'n Sue's, no thanks."

Hugh scratched his neck. "It is not, to my chagrin." They sat across from each other, Bert clenching and unclenching his hands. "There is no need to be concerned, Bert, I am only attempting to construct an accurate sequence of events. Now then, when did you see Stilwell last?"

"When I picked him up off the ground just north of town."

"Ah yes, I meant before that, when he was still alive."

Bert pursed his lips. "Well, I was walkin' across the street with Tibbie, goin' for the Wildfire, and he was comin' out of The Sew Pretty. Looked pretty mad, too."

"Mad? How so?"

"Was stridin' like he was punchin' holes in the ground, and never looked at us."

Hugh tapped his fingers. "Was he heading for the stable?"

"Don't think so, but I couldn't tell. I was tryin' to stay out of his way."

"Do I understand that you found him on the road between Cottonwood and Como?"

A nod. "He was lyin' on the ground, not movin' and his horse stood nearby, saddle off."

"How long would you say he had been there?"

"Wasn't there on my way to Como, so probably between fifteen minutes to nigh onto an hour. But didn't see no vulture circlin', so probably less'n an hour."

"Thank you very much for your cooperation, Bert. I think those are all the questions I have for you at the moment." He thought about adding not to leave town, but didn't think it was necessary.

James appeared at the door when Bert left. "Who's next, Sheriff?"

Hugh smoothed a hand over his impeccable mustache. "I believe that is all I will ask to come here today, James. Thank you for your invaluable assistance." The boy's wide grin said it all as he scampered out. The sheriff leaned back in his chair and stared at a painting of a spreading field of yellow rapeseed back home. Not much to go on yet. He made some final notes, then locked the office on his way to Sue's.

Dinner was strained. No one made eye contact with him, and conversation was halting. He tried not to look up very often so they might be more comfortable.

Lorraine made an early exit from the table. "I'm goin' to check on the children." Agnes rose and said, "I'll help."

That left him, Ike, Sue, Bert, Buster, and Tibbie. Hannah hadn't joined them; in fact, he had not seen her all day. With a napkin pat-

pat to his mouth, Hugh said, "I have not had occasion to encounter Hannah today. Have any of you?"

Shakes of the head all around. The rest of the meal passed in edgy silence. "That was a fine repast, Sue. I—"

She held a palm up and shook her head. A wintry coolness seemed to surround the table. With a slow rise, he said, "Thank you, regardless," and left for the front porch, where he sank into a wicker chair and pulled his pipe out. A match and he was soon puffing rapidly, like a train working hard to climb Kenosha Pass. He hadn't counted on the thinly veiled hostility his questioning had provoked—even from his wife.

A creak of the front door, and Buster joined him. With only a nod, he took the other chair on the porch and rocked back and forth.

Hugh laid his pipe down. Should he start a conversation? And what would he say? Better to sit tight and see if Buster had anything on his mind. He didn't even want to shift in his chair, as any sound in the quiet evening would be loud and only add to his unease.

The two sat in gathering darkness as stars twinkled under stringy clouds that drifted in a light wind, like they owned the heavens.

When his pipe went out, he made no move to refill it. A slight turn of the head toward Buster. The man sat with his hands in his lap, folded, looking straight down the town's shrouded main street.

Out of the silence, Buster said, "Sometimes you gotta do what you gotta do."

What did he mean by that? Was he talking about what he was doing as sheriff, or what someone else had done?

The moon hung a quarter of the way in the sky by the time Buster went inside. A cool breeze ruffled Hugh's longish black hair, and he pulled his collar tighter. When there was no more thinking—or avoiding—to do, he rose and called it a night.

What surprises would morning bring?

Chapter Forty-Five

A gray, overcast day matched the mood at the morning table. Hannah was still missing, and everyone else hurried through their meal. No one even pretended to try to start a conversation. Even Sue, eternally upbeat, seemed dour as she portioned food onto plates.

Ike lingered so he'd be the last to leave, giving him time to watch everyone. Nothing was adding up about this. Buster, Bert, and Tibbie made eye contact with him, but Lorraine and Agnes seemed in a world of their own, whispering to each other like grade-school children. Even Hugh seemed withdrawn, as if the weight of what he was doing—questioning everyone—had darkened his manner. When the table was empty, Ike cleared dishes away to the kitchen, where Sue leaned over the sink, washing plates.

"Guess you and me are up today."

She looked at him with fear or scorn; he couldn't tell which. "Doesn't much matter. I doubt we'll ever find out who killed that man."

An odd comment from his black-and-white sister. She usually parceled problems out the best of the three siblings, so he puzzled over where that was coming from. "Not sure what you mean." He dried dishes with an old towel, waiting for her response.

"I don't mean anything by it, brother. Just seems like everyone wanted him dead, and that's how he turned up."

Ike had to agree with that. When he found out Stilwell was poisoning Lorraine and trying to kill him, he'd wanted revenge in the worst way. The rogue took his reason to the grave with him, though. He kissed Sue on the forehead and went in search of his wife. Not in the house. Stepping out onto the porch, a kid hurried up to him from the street.

"Your wife's in with the marshal, mister."

Hugh wasn't a marshal, but correcting the boy didn't seem important right now. The sheriff was getting an early start. Ike idled around the lawman's office, trying to look like he was doing something that needed doing. Hard to blend in when you're as tall and conspicuous as him. Walking back and forth, then sitting in a solitary chair out front, should have brought him within hearing, but no such luck. He was just about to give up when the door opened and Lorraine emerged.

She gazed at him with surprise in her eyes. "Ike, what're you doin'? Spyin' on us?" She cocked her head and waited.

"Uh, no, I was just goin' to… uh, yeah, I was tryin' to hear what you were talkin' about."

Hugh broke in. "I am gratified you are so interested in this case, Ike. As long as you are here, please come in, and we can chat." He swept an arm toward the open door.

As Ike limped in, Hugh turned to Lorraine and doffed his hat. "I thank you again for coming down here when I know you would have been more comfortable at the boarding house. Your information has been most helpful." A slight bow.

Ike berated himself as he stood by Hugh's desk. Stupid to be 'caught' eavesdropping when there was no good reason for it. But still, he couldn't shake a sense of unease about the manner of Stilwell's death.

"Please sit, Ike. I would like you to be comfortable. Would you care for a whiskey?"

A drink might indeed help him focus.

Hugh poured two glasses. "Here is to a swift and satisfying resolution to this intriguing crime. With your help, I am sure that is what will happen. Thank you for spending a few minutes with me." He raised his glass toward Ike, who returned the gesture, and they both drank. "Now then, what can you tell me about this nasty business?"

That put a harsh tone on things, calling it a crime, even though that's what it was. Retribution was more like it. "Don't know nothin', Hugh. Was still in Denver when he was killed. You know that."

"I thought perchance you would have overheard something while here that might be helpful."

"Overhearin' can get you in trouble out here, Hugh. You should know that by now."

"Ah yes, The Code of the West, correct?"

A shrug of Ike's shoulders.

"So, you know nothing about the circumstances?"

"Only what you and Lorraine have told me. Sorry I can't be of help." A lie.

The two men stared at each other for a moment, then Hugh finished his drink. "I do appreciate your time, Ike, and I would also ask you to please let me know of any new information you may be privy to."

Knowing his brother-in-law, though, that request was hardly necessary—Ike being who he was.

They shook hands, and Ike walked out into the overcast day. He considered the little he knew and how much he didn't. The stable beckoned. Once inside, he scanned the surroundings. A small tack room lay to the rear, straw strewn about everywhere; four stalls, one empty. Two dusty saddles hung on wooden rails, along with a clean third one.

The stabler called out from the back. "Anything I can do for you, Ike? Don't usually see you in these parts."

Old George. Had likely been here since the town was founded. "Good to see you, George. Just tryin' to figure out what happened to Stilwell. How he fell off his horse. That his saddle over there?"

"Yup. Not hard to parse out. Got his saddle cut out from under him. I'd guess it was sliced partway, then his ridin' pulled the strap apart the rest of the way."

"You sleep here, George?"

"Sometimes I do. Didn't that night, though. Got a little sloppy at the Wildfire and found myself lyin' in the alley next morning. Not real proud of it, but …"

Ike nodded. "Bedded down in a few spots like that myself in my younger years. What time did you get here that day?"

"Around sunup. I remember because it was the first pink dawn in a while. Horse and saddle was still here. Stilwell didn't leave until late mornin'. Seemed upset about somethin'. Don't think we had a word 'tween us before he left. Saddled the gelding himself; reckon he didn't pay no attention to the strap."

"Mind if I take a look?"

He walked to the rail and studied the saddle. Had to step into the stall to see the right side, where the broken strap was. One ragged cut. He already knew how hard it was to slice through leather, but he ran a finger along the slash nevertheless. Had to have been made by a knife—or knives. Someone strong.

"You ever see anything like this, George?"

"Can't say as I have. It's a mystery. Could be the cutter tried with one knife, then switched to a sharper one."

Ike nodded. "Possible. Thanks, be seein' you."

Outside, he stopped at Doc Early's office and peeked in the front window. Tibbie wasn't there, but the front door was unlocked, so he made himself at home inside. He'd studied most of the pill bottles neatly arranged on a bureau when she came in.

"Why … hello, Ike. What can I do for you?"

"Well, first of all, you can let me apologize for bargin' in when you weren't here." She nodded. "I'd like to know a little more about Stilwell's death. Would that be all right?" Another nod. "Can you tell me what he died of?"

"Far's I can tell, his ribs were busted up bad, and he was bleedin' inside. I could see that because his chest was purplin' up even before he passed. And the concussion alone might've killed him."

"Any knife wounds?"

"No, but I'd be interested in knowin' why you asked that."

"Well, his strap was sliced by a knife, or knives. I was just wonderin' if the killer got a head start on Stilwell before he even left town."

"No, no other cuts. Is that all?"

"Just one more thing. I noticed you have an arsenic bottle over there." He pointed. "What do you use that for?"

A pause. She said, "Haven't had occasion to use any since Doc died."

Ike nodded. Hmmm. With a finger to his hat brim, he said, "Thanks" and left. As he walked down the street toward Sue's, he wished he'd gotten a better look at that bottle—with only a glance at it, hard to tell if it had been used recently.

Chapter Forty-Six

Hugh crossed the street toward The Sew Pretty as the sun lowered toward the horizon. No one had seen Hannah for a while, and he needed to talk with her. He opened the front door, and the little bell atop it tinkled at his entrance. He scanned the empty shop. Moving around tables laden with multicolored bolts of cloth, he walked to the rear of the room, where a door stood open to a small space that looked like it served as a bedroom. Hannah slept here off and on, according to his wife. She said there were times when Hannah got into a tiff with Tibbie, her, or one of the other boarders, and she'd stay away for a day or two.

No one was in there, although rumpled sheets lay on a low mattress. Not much of a refuge. He headed for the street. Where could the young woman be? There were only so many places in this town to hide. Was that what she was doing? He crossed the street and pushed through the Wildfire's swinging doors. The bartender was pouring drinks for two locals who frequented the place. He walked up beside them and motioned to Pete.

"Howdy, Sheriff, what can I do for you?"

"I am wondering if you have seen Hannah recently."

A shake of the head.

"I would appreciate it if you would let me know if you see her, Pete."

"Righto."

"Thank you." He walked out but couldn't shake the feeling he was being watched.

Back in his office, he went over several notes and called the young boy over. "Would you please bring Miss Agnes to this office, James?"

"Sure, Sheriff. You're the only one who calls me 'James.' I like that." He hurried out the door and soon ushered the older woman in. Hugh flipped him a coin.

"Would you like a cup of coffee, ma'am?"

"No, thank you."

"May I call you Agnes?"

"That's my name."

Had it gotten cold in here? "Please be seated, then. What can you tell me about that day?"

"As you no doubt already know, I didn't arrive until Bert brought me in the wagon with Stilwell in the back. We found him lying on the road when we were coming here. I'm afraid I don't know any more. I'm sure there are others you could spend time with who would be more helpful."

"Indeed, madam. Did you happen to notice anyone else on the road where you spied Stilwell?"

"Just his horse, if that's anyone."

Another cold gust. "Did you have occasion to know Stilwell in Denver?"

"Yes, he killed my husband."

"I am sorry. I did not mean to intrude on your grief."

"Too late."

"Yes, well, is there anything else you can tell me?"

Agnes shook her head.

"May I ask that you advise me if you do learn of something new?"

A silent nod.

Hugh rose. "Then thank you for seeing me, ma'am." He opened the door, and Agnes left with a look but not a goodbye.

He sat down, brooding. Not only was he being shunned, but he hadn't learned anything new. Was it worth continuing to chase the killer? Pouring another cup of coffee, he fortified it with a shot of whiskey. He still had to talk with Buster—and, what was worse, his wife. And there was still Hannah.

He'd been slighted enough today. Time to get out of the office and intensify his search for the shopkeeper—take his mind off other things. Where else could she be? This town wasn't that big. No hotel, only the boarding house. The stable? Worth a look.

When he walked in, the white-haired stabler locked eyes with him and nodded upwards. Hugh gazed at the barn's hayloft filled mostly with straw. The two of them whispered for a moment, then the sheriff said in a loud voice, "Hannah, please come down from there. Now."

A soft rustling from above, and she poked her head out at the edge of the loft. "I can't, Sheriff. I just can't face everyone. Now that my uncle's dead, they're all happy, and I'm sorrowful."

"Please come down, Hannah. I would like to speak with you. We can do it right here. It will not take long, and afterward, if you want to return to the loft, you may. I will steady the ladder for you." Hugh glanced at the stabler and motioned him outside. The old man nodded and ambled out the open double doors while Hannah backed down the ladder, sobbing.

"Why are you crying, my dear?" He held out a hand for the last couple of rungs. "You are not in any trouble. I only want to ask you a few questions. Standard procedure, really, as I am asking questions of everyone."

Hannah wiped at her eyes with an embroidered hanky.

"Please sit here on this hay bale and tell me why you are upset."

A few sniffles, and she calmed down. "I didn't want to do it, but he kept after me and after me until I said I would help. He was going to kill them, and I think he was comin' for me, too."

"To whom are you referring, my good lass? Who is 'he'?" As if Hugh hadn't already guessed.

"My uncle, Thomas Stilwell."

Hugh's mind raced. "For what reason would your uncle want to kill Ike and Lorraine?"

"Happened years ago, right here on this street. My father was killed when he drew down on Ike. Stilwell was my father's younger half-brother. He always idolized my father, so when he found out what happened, he went sort of crazy. He's been working for years to get revenge."

The sheriff sat back against a wooden post.

"You were here then, Sheriff. You know what happened."

"So your uncle—he came to Denver—"

Hannah took a breath. "Joined the railroad and killed Agnes' husband so he could draw Ike near. Put him in that job to kill him."

Hugh wiped at his brow. "But why Lorraine? Why poison her?"

"Because she was the one who shot my father. Stilwell wanted her to suffer a slow, painful death. But first, he wanted to take everything and everyone away from them so they'd suffer mightily before he killed them." She broke out in sobbing again. "And at first, I helped him by giving Bert arsenic I put in special baked goods for Lorraine." She hung her head. "But then I couldn't anymore. I'm so sorry I hurt her!" She wept into cupped hands. "Will you tell Ike and Lorraine? I don't think I could bear to."

Hugh laid a hand on her shoulder and let her cry until her breath came in short gasps. "I still need to ask you some questions, Hannah.

We can accomplish that here or at my office another day, as you wish."

She wiped her eyes again. "Guess I'd rather do that here in the stable, where no one can see me."

Hugh sat on a bale across from her. "Where were you on the day your uncle died?"

"In my shop. He came in yellin' at me because Ike and Lorraine were still alive. I said I wanted nothin' more to do with his vicious plan and told him to get out. I thought he was going to hit me—or worse. He stormed away and headed across the street."

"Did you see where?"

"No, I was upset and wanted nothin' more to do with him."

"Did you see him after that?"

"No, just his crumpled body the next day."

"How did you feel when you saw him?"

"Didn't feel much of anything—mixed, I guess. He was a killer, but he was family, too."

"Did you happen to notice anyone at the stables that night?"

"The stables? Why would you ask about that?"

Hugh dodged the question. "I'm still trying to determine where everyone was that evening and the next morning."

She said, "I saw no one at the stables that night."

A non-answer if he'd ever heard one.

"I think those are all the questions I have for you right now, Hannah. Thank you for your time, and may I make a suggestion? I advise you to resume your position at The Sew Pretty and to take up lodging again at the boarding house. Hiding in here makes you appear guilty of something."

"Yes, I will, thank you."

"Shall I head over with you?"

She nodded and walked out into an uncertain reception.

Chapter Forty-Seven

Hugh sought Ike out when he got to Sue's. The place was so crowded they went outside for a walk. Ike lit a cigarette and offered one to the sheriff.

"Normally, I prefer a pipe, but I am afraid your Wild West has rubbed off on me." He took the handmade one Ike held out. They smoked their way down the street until Hugh said, "I am somewhat at a loss, Ike."

"Why's that?"

"I only have my wife and Buster left to interview, and thus far, I have not been able to determine even one likely suspect."

Ike took a long drag and exhaled. "Sure you're askin' the right questions?"

"No, I am not."

"You ever asked them directly?"

"You mean, have I inquired as to whether they killed him?"

Ike said, "Why not? When you're done with your questions, and if you still don't know, why not look 'em in the eye and ask 'em direct?"

"A simple but sensible plan, brother-in-law. When did you get so smart?"

"Been hangin' around Buster for years, and some of his tomfool notions sunk in. Don't ever tell him that."

Hugh smoothed his mustache. "There is something else I must tell you, though."

When Hugh filled him in on Stilwell's plan, Ike picked up a rock and hurled it with a fury he hadn't felt in years. "Damn him for bringin' all that misery down on our family! Damn him! The man's brother was a murderer and a thief—deserved what he got." Telling Lorraine why Stilwell preyed on them wouldn't be easy.

"In your vernacular, Ike, I reckon we oughta be headin' back."

"Not too eager to do that, Hugh. Gotta tell Lorraine." Ike snuffed his smoke out, and they turned for the boarding house. "Late spring evenings still got some 'brrrr' in 'em, don't they?" He braced his collar against the constant wind, which was nothing compared to the passion he was about to see from Lorraine.

Inside, they both warmed up with short whiskeys. Lorraine grasped her husband by the arm and led him upstairs. Their bedroom served as her sounding board. "What are you hearin' from Hugh, husband?" She leaned forward.

"He's stumped right now, but hasn't talked with Sue or Buster yet. Don't know what they're gonna be able to add—we'll just have to wait and see if anything new pops up."

She locked eyes with him. "That's all you got from him?"

"Not exactly." When he'd filled her in on Stilwell's purpose, she surprised him by breaking down instead of raging at the wickedness of it all. He went over to her and knelt on the floor. "I'm sorry for this, Lorraine, you bein' in the middle of it. And I'm sorry for what I put the family through all these months. I shoulda been smarter, shoulda known he wasn't on the up and up, givin' me a job I didn't know anything about."

She sniffled her way into his arms. "But you did it for me and my health—I knew that all along. You didn't know I knew, did you?"

He shook his head. "Nope. Thanks for not tellin' me 'til now."

Lorraine wiped at her eyes with her dress. "We made it through, and that's all that matters. Besides, I have a great new friend in Agnes."

"What about her? How long's she gonna be here?"

"I think she wants to stay; at least, that's what she told me. Looks like she's taken a shine to Buster too, so she may stick around."

"What? Now I know you're crazy, woman."

"If you missed that, you ain't been payin' attention."

Ike kissed her softly and shrugged. "Didn't realize I was supposed to be. No matter, no one can keep a secret around here."

"And Bert and Tibbie are hittin' it off. Never can tell about love. Pops up in the strangest places sometimes." She squeezed his hand.

"Guess you and me should be retirin' to our ranch now that things are set right again. No more messes to fix. Then you just have to put up with me."

Lorraine returned his smile. "Oh, Ike, I'd love that."

Ike drew her close. "Sounds pretty good, huh?"

"Think it's time to put your hug to bed. I have a feelin' mornin' will bring new surprises."

***

The sheriff was up and out before sunrise, headed for the stable. Old George lay curled on dirty straw in one of the stalls. Hugh shook his head. How did anyone live like that? He scanned the livery for Stilwell's saddle, but it was nowhere to be found. He yelled, "George, get up! Get up!"

The old man rose unsteadily, nearly toppling on his wooden leg.

"Where is that saddle? Stilwell's saddle."

The stabler shrugged. "Can't say as I know. Was here when I drifted off last night."

"Were you drunk?"

"Now that's a libe, a liber … a dang nasty thing to accuse me of."

"So were you a patron of the Wildfire last evening?"

"I seem to recall somethin' like that."

Hugh shook his head. "I will take that as a 'yes.'" Who could have taken it, and where? The work of the guilty person, surely. He strode out of the stable, headed for the boarding house. Inside, he stood in the entryway and said in an uncharacteristically loud tone, "I want everyone here, now!" When that produced no results, he banged on closed doors until he got everyone's attention. "Into the dining room, please." When they had all gathered, he walked in.

His forehead was furrowed as he stood with feet apart. "I would like to know who departed this house last evening." His eyes daggered the groggy group one by one. Silence.

Ike piped up. "What's this about, Hugh?"

"Someone stole Stilwell's saddle from the stable, and I surmise the guilty party is right here." No one moved. Strange. He would have thought they would be glancing at each other. "No confession? Then I would like to see Sue now, followed by Buster." He turned on his heel and pushed out the front door, striding to the jail.

When Sue came in, Hugh was deferential to his wife. His questions were general in nature—like when did you last see him, where were you during that night, how did you feel about his death? Thankfully, she was forthcoming when he had expected subtle resistance. Nothing new came from their discussion, and he hugged her after his last question.

Buster was different. He was of an older generation than today's settlers. Having spent all those years as a mountain man, he parsed his responses carefully, with a skeptical attitude about what the law was trying to do—solve a murder.

"Man got what's comin' to him, is my take." Buster sat in an old chair, bent but not addled. "Ain't nothin' to it. I seen bad hombres like Stilwell get theirs all my life. This ain't anything out of the ordinary. A year from now, no one will even remember his name."

Hugh leaned back, fingers resting on the arms of his chair. Where to take the questioning? Buster's declaration surprised him, although he knew The Code required Stilwell's death. The two men stared at each other, each waiting for the other to speak.

The sheriff gave a slight cough. "Thank you for enlightening me about your opinion. Do you have anything else you would like to say about what happened?"

"Nope."

The two rose, and Hugh walked Buster back to the boarding house. With a tip of his bowler, he returned to the livery and hailed Old George. "I have several loose ends I would like to tie up if you do not mind."

"What's on your mind, Sheriff?"

"You said you didn't see anyone else in here that night, is that correct?"

The stabler paused, then said, "That's right."

Why did he hesitate? Something didn't feel right. "Tell me what really happened, George."

The stabler scanned the shed and put a hand to his forehead. "Uh, there *was* somebody here. That's all I'm gonna say."

"At least tell me who it was."

"You're the sheriff, you figure that out. I already said more'n I should've." He turned and walked toward the tack area.

Who would have been here then? Who could have cut the strap? As he sat, he rummaged through the interviews he conducted. None stood out, which was frustrating. If one of them offered even a slightly conflicting scenario, he would have something to go on. But no, he would have to rely on his intuition as a next step. Time to talk with Ike again, perhaps the only member of the household who could not have killed Stilwell.

This time, he'd sit with Ike in the parlor within earshot of the others instead of talking in secret. Who knew what effect overhearing them might have on someone in the house? When they had gotten drinks and settled in, Hugh opened with an observation in a louder-than-normal voice. "I have whittled the number of prospects down to two, and I have an idea which one is guilty." A lie.

Ike nodded. "That's good sleuthin'. How'd you get there?"

"I have been a student of people all my life, and I noticed some nervous mannerisms during my questioning."

Ike took a sip. "Like what?"

"Some did not maintain eye contact with me."

"Didn't or couldn't?"

"I believe that is a distinction without a difference."

"Not sure what that means, Hugh, but to my way of thinkin', you're on the right track."

Sounds of people coming and going echoed in the entryway. Hopefully, they overheard what he and Ike were talking about. "I think it is time to call everyone together again."

Ike took a last swig and put his glass down. "What for this time?"

"To reveal my findings." In a lower voice, he said, "And see who reacts to the news." Scurrying noises came from the hall as the two rose to leave. "I have to return to my office for a short time, Ike. Please ask everyone to gather for dinner." He shook Ike's hand and left.

He hadn't been at the jail long when there came a knock on the door. "Come in, please." Lorraine stepped in and stood wringing her hands. "Lorraine. What can I do for you?" Hugh ushered her to a seat. "Coffee?"

"No, thank you, Hugh. I just came to … um …"

"What brings you here, sister-in-law?"

"I killed Stilwell. There, I've said it. Heard you say you know who the killer was, so I decided I'd come and confess in person. In private."

"What do you mean you killed him?"

"I did him in. I had Old George put somethin' in his coffee that mornin' to knock him out so when he was ridin', he'd fall off and…"

Hugh paused a second. "Why would you do that?"

"The scoundrel tried to waylay my Ike—me too. And almost did. I couldn't let that stand."

"Poisoning him sounds like what he was doing to you."

She nodded, a tear trailing down her cheek. "You need to lock me up or somethin'?"

Hugh raised a hand. "That can wait until I have this all figured out." He escorted her out of the office, then plopped in his chair. Cold coffee, but he finished it anyway and drummed his fingers on the desk. When he left, he tracked George down at the stable.

The old man looked up. "By the look in your eye, guess I can figure why you're here, Sheriff. Save your breath, there'll be no confessin', and you can't prove nothin'." He kept forking dirty straw from a stall.

Hugh turned to leave for the boarding house when Bert came in.

"Saw you come in here, Sheriff; you got a second?"

Hugh took his hat off and nodded. "I am involved in a serious matter, Bert, but what is it?" He said that a little too sharply, still reeling from Lorraine's admission.

The young man stood in front of him, face flushed and eyes red.

"What do you want, Bert?"

"Wanted to let you know I killed Stilwell. Heard you talkin' to Mr. Ike in the parlor, and I knew I had to tell you."

"What?" Almost as big a surprise as Lorraine's. He could not make sense of two people confessing. "How are you supposed to have done that?"

"You seen that cut on the saddle's strap? I did that. Sliced it partway through, and I knew the rest would give way when he'd been ridin' a while. I killed him." He put his wrists together and held them out.

"Did you steal his saddle?"

"Yup, buried it where it'll never be found. Hard work, though— ground's still pretty froze."

Hugh shook his head. "Lower your arms, Bert. I do not have any handcuffs, if that is why you made that gesture."

"Then I'll walk with you to the jail, Sheriff."

"There is no need for that at this time, but please remain in town. I will accompany you back to Sue's."

At the boarding house, word about Lorraine's confession had already spread, and everyone was seated around the dining room table. Hugh came in and rested both hands on the table.

Buster pushed a whiskey his way with a cryptic, "Think you're gonna need this."

Hugh rubbed his eyes. "Do not tell me you killed him, too."

The old man nodded. "Yup."

Hard to believe—a third murder confession. "I hesitate to ask, but how?"

"I was waitin' for him just outside town on the way to Como—hidin' so I could waylay him. When he came ridin' by, I fired a round just over his horse. The gelding reared and threw Stilwell off. Man was nearly done in after he hit the ground. I checked. Right about then, Bert came along with Mrs. Franklin, and I hurried out of there."

"Why would you kill him, Buster?"

"A man like me don't ever have many friends, but Ike and me is pals. Made me feel like I was worth bein' chums with. When I found out what Stilwell'd been doin' to him and Lorraine, that cut it for me. Man deserved to die, and I'd do it again."

Lorraine put a hand on his shoulder and wiped her eyes with a worn hanky.

Bert stood nearby. "You old liar. I killed him, not you."

Buster shook his head. "You know I said right. Truth don't even know there's such a thing as a lie."

Silence reclaimed the crowded room. No one made eye contact with anyone else. Ike pursed his lips. "What happens now, Sheriff?"

Tibbie leaned forward. "Um ..."

"Not you, too?"

She nodded.

Hugh swigged his drink, then choked out a, "How?"

"With a pillow in Doc's office."

"But why?"

"Murderer sent raiders to kill Bert and Buster and almost succeeded. Killed Agnes's husband. I seen a lot of worthless men in my day, but he stood out. Decided he wasn't gonna do any more killin'. I think poor Hannah decided the same thing when she put that arsenic in his coffee at her shop."

Hugh stared at Hannah, who wouldn't meet his gaze. He sat, almost dropping into the chair. Shaking his head, he pulled a pipe from his vest pocket, followed by a cotton bag of tobacco. After he stuffed the bowl full, he struck a match and lit it. Several draws later, he scanned the wide-eyed faces watching him. For a long time. The pipe went out, and he tapped ashes into a small ashtray on the table.

Glancing around the silent room, he packed tobacco in the bowl again and struck another match. Bringing the lit pipe to his mouth, he inhaled, then exhaled a long smoky ring.

As the lazy O floated in the air above, the sheriff eyed them and said, "I do not believe we are ever going to be able to solve this crime."

The End

Inspiration for *The Return*

I've had a lifelong fascination with the Old West. Back in the fifth grade in Ohio, I had a teacher who made us read a book a week and write a report. Imagine that! Someone was going to give their report in front of the whole class, so you had to be ready. That first week she took us down to the little grade school library and told us to pick something out. The library was actually just a single shelf of books at one end of the cafeteria.

I scanned the various books' spines until I came across one that said 'Zane Grey'. I was so taken with this unusual name I pulled it off the shelf. I wish I could remember which of his 85 books it was, but alas. When I read his wonderful descriptions of the good guys chasing bad guys across the base of red sandstone bluffs in the Painted Desert, I was hooked. I read every book of his I could put my hands on and that fanned my interest in the American West into a lifelong flame.

The Return is the third in my South Park series, all set in South Park (not the TV show ☺), Colorado in the 1870s. The first book, *The Reckoning*, started me researching the history of the area, which turns out is as big as Delaware! I was also amazed to find that the Park's basin was 10,000 feet high, an elevation higher than in most states. The West is a such a vast place with a fascinating history.

Ike and Lorraine face the severe trial of Lorraine's mystery illness, at a time when medicine hadn't advanced much beyond taking opium or laudanum for almost every pain. Hannah secretly administered arsenic in baked goods she sent to the ranch with Bert. When the family moved to Denver, she threw Bert over, having no more use for him. Ike and Lorraine's move to Denver allowed Stilwell to continue poisoning Lorraine through Agnes' housemaids, another part of his elaborate plan.

As for characters, Ike continues his rugged nature. He's a decent, flawed, but honorable man who has to make several hard choices. He doesn't trust Stilwell, the secret murderer who offered him a job he wasn't qualified for in Denver—but Lorraine needs better medical attention than she has in the fictional South Park town of Cottonwood. Perhaps we can all see ourselves in some of Ike's missteps and uncertainties. At least I can.

Does he take a man who he doesn't trust up on his job offer, or try to figure a different way to help Lorraine with her sickness? Arsenic, the mystery element in Lorraine's illness, was readily available in those days, as it was released in the smelting of various ores.

Much of the story revolves around the coming of the railroad from Denver to South Park. Railroads played an outsized role in opening and settling the West. They brought an end to iconic undertakings like cattle drives, the Pony Express, and many stagecoach lines. The proliferation of barbed wire further altered this land. But railroads were also magnets for industrial barons and shady political shenanigans that involved huge sums of money and graft.

In *The Return*, I also wanted to include a glimpse into the workers' world who laid track for the railroads. Not a shining moment for America as foreign workers like the Chinese and other nationalities suffered significant abuse where they worked and lived. The deadly Chinese riot in Denver in 1880 was set off by white racial animosity, which I wanted to showcase in the story.

Another focus of *The Return* was highlighting the unintended consequences that often result from mindless revenge. A familiar saying is 'revenge is a dish best served cold.' But passion drove the action in this story—there was no cold vengeance to be had here. And that's the way it was in much of the Old West, especially where there was no law, which was the case in the majority of towns.

Larger western cities, like Denver, did have perhaps a lawman, but not a lot of laws.

Stilwell—and Hannah initially—wanted revenge, and in the process of their scheming, they lured Ike and Lorraine into their dark web. He wanted nothing more than to slowly take everything away from the McAlisters, then kill them. His nefarious plan also extended to Buster, Bert, Agnes, Hugh, Sue, and Tibbie, all of whom got caught up in their own emotions and reasoning.

History is replete with the consequences of murder and revenge, from when Cain slew Abel all the way to present-day society. *The Return's* subtitle is 'The Grass Isn't Always Greener,' a nod to Ike's hope that Denver would be the answer to the family's woes, both medical and financial—but it wasn't. As William Kent Krueger said in *This Tender Land*, "In every good tale there is a seed of truth, and from that seed a lovely story grows."

The Return bookends two of my favorite characters, Ike and Lorraine. I hope Lorraine's wonderful feistiness and clear-headedness came through in this last instalment. Frontier women were as hardy as the men—they had to be. They played the hands they were dealt. I've enjoyed creating strong women characters like Lorraine, Agnes, Tibbie and Sue in all my books.

The Old West attracted certain types of Americans—people who were willing to leave everything behind to start a new life with a promising, but uncertain future, much like the immigrants who fled Europe for America during this same time period. The untamed nature of the land transformed settlers, who in turn transformed it. But tales of the Old West still have a fascinating grip on many of us today, and I hope this tale, *The Return*, has given you an enjoyable glimpse into a storied past.

About the Author

Mike Torreano is a multiple award-winning author of traditional western mysteries and historical fiction. In the fifth grade in Ohio, he read his first Zane Grey novel and has been hooked on the Old West ever since.

Mike's debut western mystery, *The Reckoning*, was released in 2016 by The Wild Rose Press and the sequel, *The Renewal*, another mystery, was released in 2018. Both are set in South Park Colorado, circa 1870. *The Return,* which was released in 2025, is the third in the South Park series, also set in the 1870s and completes the South Park mysteries. The series features Ike and Lorraine McAlister and their fight to keep their family and ranch together amid dramatic changes coming to the Old West.

The legendary Goodnight-Loving cattle trail inspired his first stand-alone western mystery, *A Score to Settle*, (2020) set on that New Mexico Territory trail in 1870.

Mike's second stand-alone western mystery, *White Sands Gold,* (2022) is also set in New Mexico Territory in 1890. It follows a fantastic legend of untold gold bars mysteriously hidden centuries ago and has received five literary awards.

A lifelong interest in American history led to his first historical novel, *Fireflies at Dusk*, released in 2023. *Fireflies* is a coming-of-age tale about a young man torn between his pacifist family and his urge to fight the injustice of slavery as the Civil War breaks out. *Fireflies* has received three literary awards and was long-listed for the Historical Fiction Company's Book of the Year competition.

Mike is a member of many western organizations, and is a trustee of the Western Museum of Mining and Industry. He also speaks at clubs and organizations about the timeless values of the

Old West and The Code of the West, and how those values are still relevant today.

He can be found on Amazon, Facebook, Barnes and Noble, X, LinkedIn, Instagram, and Goodreads, and lives in Colorado Springs with his wife, Anne.

www.ingramcontent.com/pod-product-compliance
Lightning Source LLC
Chambersburg PA
CBHW061055100726
47911CB00012B/233